I0670464

Living Twice

The 2023 University of Sydney Anthology

Foreword by Shankari Chandran

The University of Sydney

First published in 2024 by the University of Sydney.

Funded by the University of Sydney, Faculty of Arts and Social Sciences, School of Art, Communication and English.

Sydney University Press
Fisher Library F03
University of Sydney
NSW 2006 AUSTRALIA

Email: sup.info@sydney.edu.au
sydneyuniversitypress.com.au

A catalogue record for this book is available from the National Library of Australia

ISBN: 978-1-74210-569-7 (paperback)
ISBN: 978-1-74210-570-3 (epub)

Cover image: Michaela Robinson
Cover design: Michaela Robinson, Sophie Belotti and Michaela Gall
Text layout: Hanna Holford

Contents

Contents

Contents

Acknowlegments

As humans, we exist in a constant cycle of beginnings and endings. We ricochet between hope and grief and come out the other side a little more ... textured. Change can be hard to cope with, but literature reminds us that new chapters often hold a lot of good.

Within this anthology you will find stories of relief, renewal, closure and connection. We are amazed by the University of Sydney's talented writers. Thank you for sharing your insights with us.

We are indebted to Agata Mrva-Montoya, whose vision and dedication is the foundation of this anthology. Thank you to the brilliant Shankari Chandran for contributing the foreword.

We also want to thank Linda Funnell who provided invaluable advice and the students in MECO6944, who workshopped some of the pieces in this anthology.

To the volunteer editors – Aries, Eeshita, Eva, Hank, Hanna, Holly, Jessamine, Linxiao, Michaela, Sophie and Sumi – thank you for your passion. It is an act of public service to put words into the hands of readers. We also want to thank Neha John, Rose Cousins, and Yiyi Chen for their help.

We are grateful to the team at Sydney University Press for making publication a smooth process.

Readers: how could we forget to thank you? May you find as much comfort and delight in these pieces as we did.

Foreword

Shankari Chandran

All human beings have multiple lives. The one we live, the one we try to leave behind, the one(s) we want to live. A million universes experienced, edited, and re-lived in one mind. Memory and imagination colliding into each other. No life more important, but some more painful, and some more wondrous than others.

The difference between the Writer and other human beings, is that the Writer sits down at a blank page and tries to give words to these lives.

The Writer – formerly known as the Storyteller – is now called the Content Creator, a title that sadly lacks poetry and gravitas.

The content human beings consume – through books, film, TV and the permanent appendage that is our phone – gives us access to the lives of others. To me, the storytelling of the written word still reigns supreme. It helps us experience these lives within our minds, better than any other content, artform or technology.

I obviously have a natural bias towards the written Word. Words are my friends, and writing is my therapy, meditation and prayer.

Writers lie when they say they are passionate about writing. We're not passionate about writing, we are obsessed with and enslaved by it. We are energised *and* agonised by the process. We love writing. We hate writing. We love it more than we hate it. We can't *not* do it.

Once I start writing a novel, I don't know how to stop until it's done. I feel sorry for my husband, as he must live with that. It is hard to love the Writer, their mind is so often turned inwards. It is hard to be the Writer, in a world that values other forms of capital so much more than the Words created by the Writer.

Writing is often (incorrectly) described as a lonely career path – accompanied only by lifelong office-mates, Anxiety and Insecurity, who bellow loudly from the cubicles. Occasionally the Writer's team is expanded to include the Agent and the Publisher. As elusive as they are powerful, the Agent and the Publisher illuminate the pathway to publication the Writer desperately desires. And yet, before we gave Anxiety and Insecurity a microphone, there were Words. Before we sent unsolicited manuscripts to an impersonal email address, furiously refreshed our inboxes awaiting replies, cried over standard rejection responses, and eagerly signed contracts we didn't fully understand, there were Words.

There are always Words.

Words penned by Writers who observe their own lives and the lives of others. Writers who are attentive to the details; respectful of people; curious about their motivations and concerned about the consequences of their actions. Writers who are courageous enough to be honest and vulnerable by placing all of the above on the blank page for publishers to reject, and for readers to enjoy or critique.

How is it possible then, for the Writer to be lonely, when there are so many lives inside our minds? Let's be honest.

The Writer is *never* lonely. Non-Writers propagate this myth to explain career "choices" they don't understand. Writers perpetuate this myth because we prefer the company of our Words to the company of people. We are immersed in characters, surrounded by Words and exploring the million universes in our one mind.

The Writers in this anthology embody this. They have drawn many lives, with attentiveness, respect, curiosity, concern, courage – and with the skill that comes from hard work. Talking about writing, thinking about writing and imagining writing are for daydreamers. Writing is for Writers.

This anthology and these Writers remind me of a realisation I had recently. I was at a "content market", surrounded by content creators. Writers. Storytellers even. The collective body of work in the room – published and unpublished – was exceptional. The collective resilience in the face of rejection was inspiring. The collective respect for the value of what we do, despite the constant pressure to publish, sell and comply with market analytics, was affirming. I was reminded then and I am reminded now, that I am part of a profession. A profession that is ancient and speaks in many languages and even more Words. A profession that records the old and new plagues and passions of human beings. A profession conducted by Writers who live, imagine and honour an infinite number of lives. I am proud to be a part of this profession. After reading this anthology, I am even prouder.

The Writer gives the reader access to a diversity of lives that history, the media, and political discourse sometimes deny. The Writer gives the reader access to the challenges and richness of these lives, that our indifference, privilege and laziness often prevent us from seeing. The Writers in this brilliant anthology have accomplished all this – through poetry, prose, memoir, essay and myth. They challenge us to experience the vastness of both their memories and their imaginations. They invite us into these lives and in doing so, they deeply enrich our own.

Living Twice

Living Twice

Ray Zhou

Once

The body wakes, groping for the phone to turn off the alarm clock, finding its feet on the ground, boiling the water and pouring a bag of Nescafe Hazelnut Latte into the AC/DC mug. The body washes the face and eases into a shirt, trousers and leather shoes. It puts on a pair of black-rimmed glasses. In this clearer world, it becomes *he*.

A handmade sandwich is his usual breakfast. He straddles his bicycle, rushing off to the University of Sydney to teach his first postgraduate seminar, Professional Editing. He has been an academic editor for six years and will obtain his PhD degree in English Literature in the next couple of years. It is March 2023. He will not turn twenty-six until next Wednesday.

The students will see a boyish face smiling kindly behind the lectern and a left hand pulling the longest strand of hair, hanging lonely on the downy chin, when he is thinking.

Thank you, sir. He hears what students say to him, one by one, waving goodbye.

He remembers a little girl learning to skip rope at his grandpa's old residence. Aged seven or eight. Her lovely braids are dancing on the back of her uniform. He hears her talking

1

happily while holding Grandpa's hands (she gets full marks in multiplication and division that day). She stumbles at two or three skips at first, throwing away the rope and sitting there crying. As a grown-up he always wants to help her, but he does not move. He sees the girl practising every day and witnesses her becoming proficient in skipping as time passes.

Time passes. He is no longer the young man who could not find the right word to start a self-introduction at his academic referee's office, when doing a master's in Hong Kong. Nor is he simply repeating "I love literature" as the main reason for transferring to the English Department when being interviewed in Shanghai during his second undergraduate year.

He finishes his first seminar, hopefully a success. He rushes off again along Eastern Avenue, among a sea of students, heading to his next class on the other side of campus.

This is not his first time teaching; in Shanghai, he privately tutored more than fifteen university and secondary-school students, and most of them achieved excellent scores. In Hong Kong, he lived in a manufacturing mogul's house where he taught their second son in exchange for his board, meals and most of the tuition fees.

In his remote memory, the little girl disappears after she masters skipping. He wants to meet her again and write a story about her. He walks along the bridge near Grandpa's old residence where the four rising statues suggest ancient Chinese myths. Grandpa tells the kid about the myths, teaches the kid to read, to write, to use a dictionary, and sends the kid to learn English, which the kid is too young to learn at school. He desperately wants to find the girl, hoping to ask whether she knows what Grandpa has taught her, but she has disappeared.

In his birthplace, an industrial city always shrouded in grey in northeast China, kids only learn basic English words from Grade 3: ruler, eraser, book ... Most people remain in this city all their lives. Grandpa, who was well educated during the early and destitute days of New China (the 1950s), notices the kid's voracious appetite for reading. He takes the kid to an English educational office and convinces the teacher that the eight-year-old kid will have no problem in catching up with the class. The kid outperforms the middle-schoolers in a writing contest and wins an abridged version of *Gulliver's Travels*.

That is the first English novel he has ever read, and he wants to read more. When his classmates are mechanically memorising English words and cramming for multiple-choice grammar tests, he indulges himself in the worlds of *The Great Gatsby* and *The Catcher in the Rye*. When his classmates are struggling with a one-hundred-word English composition, he writes his first little poem in English. In that gloomy and self-enclosed hometown, those English novels, often abridged and annotated by Chinese publishers, have opened his eyes to a remote world full of rhythmic and humanistic beauty.

At nineteen, he comes home from Shanghai and announces his decision to transfer to the English Department. No one supports him but Grandpa. His father advises him to continue learning mathematics since it will guarantee a good job. His mother dismisses literature as a useless pursuit, urging him to study finance instead. Only Grandpa says, "You are talented, go ahead and learn whatever you want." He refuses to go home again. Grandpa comes to Shanghai to support him, and they take a photo at the university gate. The hair he kept cutting grows longer, making him look feminine. He destroys the photo as he did with many others.

The only family photo he keeps was taken in 2007 in Changchun during the only family trip he and his parents ever took. They went there to watch the first 4-D film in the world. The kid in the photo is about ten years old, wearing his favourite blue T-shirt, white shorts and red sneakers. He looks small under Dad's masculine figure and Mum's hands are resting on his skinny shoulders. Both Mum and Dad are smiling, but it is hard to tell whether the kid, head tilting and a hand clutching clumsily onto shorts, is smiling or not, just as it is hard to tell whether it is a boy or a girl under the cropped short hair.

The little girl is *disappearing*.

He successfully transfers to the English Department and becomes financially independent in Shanghai. He takes up various part-time jobs, being a waiter, housekeeper, promoter, private tutor, translator, editor, teaching assistant ... and commutes between districts.

He also commutes between universities, two hours each way to audit a class that lasts for an hour and a half, taught by some brilliant scholars he admires. As an academic editor, he has read their work on Comparative Literature or Chinese Literature. He always sits in the front row.

In China, the word "transgender" was unheard of. He has long abandoned the attempt to perform as a good girl or connect with those around him, except in the literature classes where he lives in worlds constructed by words, getting close to the glow of human hearts.

The moments of reading and writing make me feel alive.

In 2019, I start hormone replacement therapy (HRT). Feeling the right hormone permeate my body, I close my eyes to become one with testosterone. "Remember, the surgery is irreversible," the surgeon tells me as I lie on the operating table. "I know," I say. I become he.

The little girl has *disappeared*. I have lived twice.

Once as an excellent girl whose parents had high expectations of her; the second time as a young man who spares no effort to find his place in this world through literature.

On a hospital bench in the dermatological department, I try to tell my grandpa that I was the little girl. I had started HRT half a year ago by then. Worried about my pimpled skin, Grandpa took me to a doctor. While waiting for the result of the hormone examination, I summoned the courage to tell him that the changes were caused by HRT. He listened and nodded in silence. After we arrived home, he crossed out the "male" on the doctor's report and replaced it with "female." He had forgotten what I'd told him. Perhaps he was too old.

Twice

I have few memories of my father. I remember the little wooden gun he made for me. I enjoyed putting a row of empty tins on the windowsill and shooting them one by one with rubber bands. One day, when I was six, I woke up finding no trace of him but a note: *Dear daughter, I am leaving for a remote city to work. Take care of yourself and Mum.* My father returned home once or twice a year. We seldom talked.

I didn't feel different from others until I was sixteen. The English essays I wrote won me an admission to a high school students' summit held by Harvard in 2013. Most attendees received international education from a very young age, while I learnt English by reading books with a dictionary. I was dwarfed by my provinciality. Meanwhile, I was attracted to a young seminar leader and her profile always lingered in my mind. I got an A+ in her seminar and the farewell seemed more saddening than it should be. I soon experienced such a feeling again for my best female friend. The image of my friend reading a book by the window in a white dress is the most beautiful memory from my teens. My unspoken emotion was sensed and the friendship ended with her withdrawal. The night I knew she had a boyfriend I lost sleep, and that was just the start of my losing sleep every night.

My mother tried her best to cultivate me into a decent girl. She sometimes, looking at me, expressed her expectation for a *jin-gui-xu* (good son-in-law). Since my kindergarten years, she would warn me about staying too close to boys. In high school, she advised me to keep my hair long, insisting that it was the pathway to womanhood. When she was happily selecting underwear for me in a supermarket, I sneakily waited afar. I had a vague feeling that I did not want them and would never want them. Having no information about gender diversity in my hometown, I could not understand or explain my feelings, so I had to wear them under the silly pink uniform.

Most nights during high school, I stayed awake and doubted my gender: why I was attracted to girls and disliked the physical female attributes that were forced on me. My classmates did not seem to have these troubles. They had the sole aim of succeeding in *gaokao* (the university entrance examination). In those endless hours of the night, I became familiar with how the moon moved by recognising the shadows of the lattice window on the white wall. Sometimes I gave up trying to sleep and picked up a book or wrote a diary entry instead.

My excellent grades dropped sharply and my parents blamed it on my artistic indulgence in drawing and photography. On my eighteenth birthday, my outraged father smashed my camera on the ground because I had spent a long time making a video of my birthday photos. The fawn Canon digital camera fell into an eternal sleep. Its broken glass eye cast a silent gaze at me, as if it could understand my misery.

In 2015, I enrolled in a university and started living in a female dormitory. I felt uncomfortable changing clothes openly or joining my three roommates' night talks about ex-boyfriends or cosmetics or fashion. I feigned sleep to avoid joining their talks but was awake the whole night. During the military training, all the girls rushed to the bathroom as soon as each long day came to an end. I waited until midnight to take a shower alone.

In the second year, I came across the word "transgender" on some overseas websites and finally understood the reason for all that happened to me. I cut off the hair that I had reluctantly kept long and threw away the girlish clothes my mother had bought. I started buying gender-neutral or boyish clothes and contacted home less frequently.

I knew I would never live up to my parents' expectations, so I rejected their financial aid and avoided returning home for vacations, using the excuse of having part-time jobs. That year I was reading Albert Camus's *The Outsider* and W. Somerset Maugham's *The Moon and Sixpence* and empathised wholeheartedly with the marginalised heroes. I stood alone on a rooftop, listening to Eagles' "Desperado", thinking about ending my life. Interestingly, no matter how hard I wanted to erase my bodily existence I still had a passion for the literary world. I quit my mathematics classes and wandered around the campus during class time. I read the timetable outside every classroom and sneaked in if the class interested me. One day I audited a Chinese-English translation class by Doctor Gu, my soon-to-be supervisor, and was infected by his genteel demeanour and erudite scholarship. I decided to change my major – I wanted to "live deep and suck out all the marrow of life" like Thoreau and let my heart dance with the daffodils in Wordsworth's poems. I made up my mind to publish something before the age of twenty-five and then kill myself. I made a list of songs to be played at my funeral, including Radiohead's "Creep" and Nirvana's "Something in The Way". I bought a used typewriter and typed an epitaph for myself: *He lived, loved and left.*

During a summer vacation, I went to the United States to work as a housekeeper at a camping site near Glacier National Park in Montana. I shared a cabin with three Chinese girls who ended up despising my nerdy character and refusing to talk to me. In early July 2017, an anti-LGBT tide was surging on Chinese social media platforms which drove me into despair. I cried until midnight. Two weeks later, a notification popped up on my phone: Chester Bennington, the vocalist of Linkin Park, had hanged himself in his own house. Grieved at the news, I repeatedly played "One More Light" on my iPod. What was worse, my roommates threw my chair out of the cabin and I had to have my meals on the porch. I took a day off and tried to write my farewell letter to the world, apologising for the shouldn't-exist me. The door suddenly flung open and my roommates' girlish gossips flew in. I put away my unfinished letter and again put on the mask of a normal girl.

Returning to university, Doctor Gu accepted me in his Advanced English class. Discovering my passion for literary translation and comparative literature, he paid special attention to me, taking me for lunch every Tuesday after his class and recommending books he had recently read. Doctor Gu was culturally inclusive and referred to me as "he/him" in the class. His understanding and encouragement gradually saved me from the suicidal thoughts.

My knowledge of literature steadily grew. Doctor Gu, who supervised my Bachelor thesis in my final year, became my supervisor and invited me to his house for the first time on 2 July 2018. In his tearoom, amid the fragrance of sandalwood and the freshness of tea, he signed his name and the date on his recently published book with a brush pen and entreated me to keep it.

He said, "I have nothing to teach you anymore. I'll recommend you to a master's program in Hong Kong. There you can read both Chinese and English literature."

I completed my thesis in 2019 and took a gap year for my official female-to-male transition. I moved out of the university and started to live cautiously with male roommates in an apartment. I lived near the best Chinese Department in Shanghai, audited literature classes during the day and tutored my students in their home at night, often commuting for hours by train. Sometimes I missed the last train at 10:30 pm and had to wait for an overnight bus home. My Kindle became my loyal companion during those dark and long commutes. On weekends, I worked at an educational office thirteen hours a day, teaching Chinese and English to secondary-school students. There were only "male" and "female" restrooms in my workplace. To avoid the discomfort of choosing one restroom, I drank very little water and would run to the nearest train station to use an accessible toilet if I could not hold off anymore.

Every time I had to show my ID card, its authenticity was questioned before I was able to officially change the gender marker. I was stopped many times – at a train station, at an airport, at a hospital, at a hostel – and sometimes the information on the ID card was read out: *Are you a female?* I nodded bashfully and those around would gaze at me with a curious look. Being a tutor did not require identity documents, but my gender was constantly put into question. Once, a parent of my one-on-one student refused to shake my hand because of my androgynous appearance when she met me for the first time. She dismissed my services several weeks later. Another time, a class of twelve-year-old students encircled me at the corner of the classroom, throwing arrows of difficult questions: *Teacher, why don't you have a beard? Teacher, why are you so short? Teacher, are you a man or a woman?*

I remember those nights when I lay alone and naked, eagerly hoping for changes to my body. When my hair grew and my voice became low and my face and body reshaped, I felt unfamiliar with the vessel I had lived in for twenty years. I was becoming an impostor of my parents' only daughter who had disappeared from family reunions when she went to uni. (In fact, I was at home during the 2022 Lunar New Year when I had to register a new ID card. I was lying on my small bed, turning off the light, avoiding joining the merry family reunions.) My initial months of HRT coincided with my commencing anti-depressant medication and my memory became blunted and blurred. Who was I? What would I become?

I remember those vivid moments of staying alive. I remember the first time my birth name appeared in a green-covered American journal in Chinese literary studies as a copyeditor, and on the cover of the Chinese edition of a young adults' detective novel as the translator. I remember I picked "Ray" as my new name during the entrance interview of the English Department at the Chinese University of Hong Kong and was recognised as a man for the whole master's year. I remember how I cherished being a part of the intellectual community among the mountains and seas in Hong Kong and how I infused these emotions into a memoir-essay that was published in the university literary journal under my new name.

I am still involved in a lawsuit appeal to change the gender on my bachelor's degree. My appeal was rejected and my lawyers could do nothing with it.

I am still afraid of exposing my scars in public. I got my first testosterone from the black market without a doctor's guidance, limited to the scarce HRT resources in China. The overdosed testosterone left dotted scars over my skin and the top surgery left cuts on my now flat but asymmetrical chests.

I need to read and write like a drowning man needs to swim. Literature is what ties me to this world, my reason to live. It enables me to live a thousand times, not just twice.

I departed from Shanghai for a PhD program at the University of Sydney on 3 January 2023. Doctor Gu saw me off at the airport, giving me some tea as a farewell gift; three years ago, he had given me a Parker pen before I headed to Hong Kong.

In some ways, my supervisor is my spiritual father. I chose my clothes following his style. I followed his path to be a comparative literature scholar. He didn't know how much he meant to me until the day before my departure when I told him about the hardest years, about my distanced relationship with family and how I survived.

I said, "I will try my best not to let you down." He answered, "You have never let me down."

We were drinking beer in the tearoom. Sunlight poured in. It was winter in Shanghai. The wind was rolling fallen leaves around. Neighbours chattered, recuperating from the pandemic lockdown. So were we. Outside, buds were preparing to blossom again in his garden. I could not tell their names but remembered their best season every year.

That is the force of life. No matter how ruined it becomes, a city will rise again. No matter how down I am, I will stand again. The boy who was concentrating on writing his last words to the world has survived. I marvel at the simple fact that he survived.

Before I left China, I sealed all my diaries in a carton as a farewell ceremony of my first life. I had a brief read of them and found some lines from before my transition in 2019:

> Crawling, twisting and trembling
> at the feet of the known principle,
> I tried to tell you, in my weakening voice,
> "do not cry at my funeral."
> See, my darling, see
> the stone is falling,
> the sword is swaying,
> and the world is crumbling.
> But there I'll stand, bone ignited,
> soul lifted and eyes burning fiercely
> at the unfathomable fate.
> I'll smile like a newborn and
> murmur to you
> "I have already lived."

I have lived the most of my life, a life of artwork, intertwined with pain and passion.

Now I'm in Sydney writing about it.

The lovely braids dance on the back of the uniform. The little girl is skipping rope. Eighty. Eighty-one. Eighty-two ... She counts in a childlike voice. I see the familiar figure in the Life Writing Workshop. The figure I have intentionally buried in the dusted past.

In the afternoon sun, I will walk to greet her and examine her face which looks so much like mine. I will tell her: *You have amazing perseverance. You have practised skipping very well.* I will not ask where her grandpa is, nor mention the tortured adolescence awaiting. I will encourage her with my constant smile: *Go ahead to become whoever you might be.*

She will smile back, much brighter and braver. There is a deep, black gap in her front teeth, a passage that connects everything I have suffered and achieved.

I am because she has been.

2 October 2023

The Tower

Kelsey Goldsbro

A day,
reborn,   afresh with spring.
There are the Rabbits,   and there are their myths.

      Their stories of misery, loss, and grace.
      How to look upon the sky, sea, and earth –

           There is a ritual.   There is a sunlit kitchen.
      Flows of lace curtains   dancing with the motes,
      only visible in the light's blessing.

           There is yellow wallpaper.

    The Rabbits   make tea here.
    The Rabbits   who stand on their hind legs. Wear
           Aprons. Hold   Knives. Hold
           Knives! Hold   Spoons.

for scooping sugar,
and shaking the hands of   Mice.
    Mice   who sleep in teacups and shortcake tins.
      who wear sleeping caps and gowns.

            there is a   Human Baby.
            sunburnt.
                a sweetness in the oranges.

fitted in envy,
the sun is too harsh for them.

    wear Rabbit ears,   Baby.
    wear an Apron!
      you can cut berries
      and cakes better that way.

    follow the Rabbits and
    sip their tea –
            the taste of pomegranates and
            daffodils from early Spring.

Charlotte

Alex Ma

The subtle light of dawn trailed across Charlotte Fitzroy's bedchamber walls. Naught but the merry chirping of early rising birds could disturb her sweet slumber. She awoke, though slowly, her eyes still tinged with the saccharine afterimage of dreams. All was placid – she preferred to rise in the early hours when the sun was making its sojourn to the skies, and the rest of her family were asleep. It was an hour whose pleasures were lost to many. Charlotte parted the heavy curtains and gazed without. The scenery was akin to a pastoral painting: clouds rolled past the endlessly clear sky, and the greenery below flourished with unearthly vitality. She lingered and mused about the possibilities she could encounter beyond the gates. Today, she will dare to defy her lot. Too long had she waited by the constrains of the window, merely hoping for a difference. Now was the chance to act on her resolve; she was willing to risk losing her honour in pursuit of a new life.

Soon Charlotte's maidservant, Nell, wholly innocent to her designs, came to dress her. Nell brought in her mistress's usual garb; but Charlotte protested. A robe was unfit for her needs, for travelling garb was required. Without further inquiries, Nell submitted to her request. A travelling ensemble was procured, and Charlotte got dressed. She was wont to make conversation during her dressing, for Charlotte was of an amiable character, and Nell too was eager to speak with her mistress. However, on this quiet dawn, not a word was exchanged. Charlotte suppressed her temptation to confess her devious machinations and repent. There was no tolerance for temperamental changes of heart in such expeditions. She bowed her head and let Nell pin her hair. The reflection in the mirror betrayed a mellow face and unusual pallor. Nell caught a glimpse of this uncharacteristic countenance.

"Will you not take breakfast, madam?"

"No. I have not the time. Once I finish dressing, I shall leave."

"Yes, madam," Nell could but comply.

The dressing was complete, and Charlotte rose. Before dismissing Nell, however, she beckoned her to come and receive a gift. Nell, who was Charlotte's domestic confidant, had never been privy to such an extent of confidence. She assented; her hands clasped modestly on her apron.

"Please, Nell, do give me your hand." She held out her palm, which trembled a little. A silver chain with a cross was placed there.

"But – madam! How could I receive this prized possession of yours, and without having done you a deserving service?"

"You have indeed done me a very laudable service, Nell. I am eternally grateful for your work, hence my gift." Charlotte could not help but regret her true sentiments as she gave her reasoning. "I believe that not even this chain can recompense you. Why, you have been so accommodating as to rise every day at dawn just for me! You have toiled beyond expectations for my sake. You must have this, as testament to your service. I insist."

"I'll remember your kindness, madam," Nell curtsied.

"You may go down now and stow the chain in a safe place. Pray, do not tell anyone of this gift. I require no more of your service today. Do retreat to your quarters and rest."

As Charlotte dismissed her maid, she felt a flush rise to her cheeks and tears welling up in her eyes. She sharply threw a hood over her face to obscure those last tumultuous emotions. Nell could do nothing more than to bow and exit the bedchamber. Now Charlotte was left wholly alone – the condition she wished to remain in for the duration of her expedition. Yet, as she had nearly betrayed to Nell, she felt a great trepidation on this affair. She was leaving in pursuit of freedom – and as she spoke her final words with Nell, she had realised that she was merely exchanging one kind of freedom for another. While she remained as a loyal daughter, she had the freedom of comfort; living without cost, or fear of losing all that was vital. Then, once she embarked on this pursuit, she would have the freedom of character; she would never be constrained by the expectations of her sex. It seemed to her an inequality. One may endure to live in decided comfort but give up their desires, and not perish. However, one who endeavours to give up all comforts in favour of indulging their utmost passions will surely fall victim to a serious malady, whether mental or physical. That Charlotte considered deeply. Should she commit herself to such a dangerous pursuit for the rare chance of achieving both freedoms? She clasped her hands to her bosom and thought – but she must decide in haste. The entire course of her future happiness depended on one fleeting choice. She was not fain to make such a conclusion, yet the true answer had stirred in her mind for eons, so that she secretly knew her penultimate decision.

"I must depart now!" she declared and padded through the corridor with naught but a faint tremor. The house was quiet still, and Charlotte successfully stole across the winding paths inside and reached the stables. A stable boy was fast asleep on a pile of hay. Charlotte precipitately awoke the boy and bade him to prepare the horses for a carriage. He obliged, though in ill humour, and Charlotte had but to wait for the preparation. She watched the sun crown the open sky and the men slowly beginning to undertake their days' work. The world was rising from its deep slumber, ready to face all its mortal toils – and at this very moment Charlotte was embarking to escape this configuration. She knew that she sought a sweet and lucid slumber, for being awake was more injurious to her body and mind alike.

"Madam, the carriage is ready," the stable boy announced. Charlotte gave the boy a penny for his troubles and set off resolutely. The time was nigh; the life she once knew was dissipating. Upon boarding she called out, "Out! Towards London!" and the carriage began to move swiftly. Such speeds put her heart at ease, for she would soon be far, far, away from the clutches of vindicative pursuit. The cultivated greenery would morph into wild meadows, then into primitive forests, and there, along the solitary paths, she would find repose. Charlotte passed through the village largely unrecognised, for there were few awake at the hour. Some stray village people stared and pointed at the peculiarity of a noble carriage driving so early, but it did not capture their attentions for long. The want of curiosity relieved Charlotte's trepidation; she had feared that she would be found out through petty gossip.

Erelong the carriage had passed the village, and thus began Charlotte's solitary journey. In her alacrity of departure, she had not carried a volume or needlework to pass the time. Thus, she had to content herself with contemplation and admiring the verdant scenery – both of which were very agreeable. She longed to alight and frolic among the ancient trees and hear the quaint whispers of zephyrs rustling the leaves. But she could not delay her journey any further. Every minute was precious, and each passed so quickly that an hour was but a trifle.

Noontide arrived, though for Charlotte, the bright rays were shielded by the dense growth of the old forest. All was untouched; she mused that the forest had not altered for a century, and that it would remain so for another century. Humans are but ephemeral creatures who leave imperceptible marks upon Nature. Then, she considered, her sudden flight was naught but a comma in the grand transcript of history.

The carriage drove through the lonesome path with such placidity that Charlotte was put into a gentle daze. She rested herself upon the cushions and closed her eyes. A short slumber may be advantageous, for sleep erases all of her doubts – though little, she had some scruples on the coachman's ability to find the way, and that her journey could be delayed. Sleep, she deemed, was indeed a worthy occupation, especially on long travels. Thus she let herself succumb. Dreams did not visit her; it was those empty dreams which appear in a brief darkness but are infinite in their duration. When she awoke, Charlotte could not divine how many hours had passed in her undisturbed sleep. The forest was still subtly illuminated, thus night-time was not nigh. Charlotte rapt on the carriage roof and called out to the coachman.

"Pray do tell me, how long have we been travelling?"

"Most of the light'd day has elapsed, madam, and dusk shall come soon. But, madam, this forest bears arcane pow'rs, for I cannot behold of any clearing."

"Then continue! Find a way out! We shall not drive in the darkness."

"Yes, very good, madam," the coachman replied, as he brought down his whip, putting the steeds into a furious gallop.

The dirt path was as isolated as ever, and the rumble of the carriage echoed ceaselessly through the forest. A translucent brume began to rise over the undergrowth, its wispy tendrils floating like phantoms, seeking a place to reside. Charlotte felt that she had been transported into a supernatural dimension where all mortal laws were void. She quivered, for the pleasant sun gave way to a chill. Being wholly alone in an unknown forest – 'twas the stuff of nightmares, ghost stories and tragic ballads. She hoped that none would dare ambush her, a solitary and vulnerable traveller. Between a chance vacuity in a cluster of ancient trees, Charlotte spied the setting sun. It had sunken nearly to the horizon, spilling hellish rubescent hues upon the sky. The sight struck a terror in her breast, for she thought it an omen. If she was in possession of a match and candle, she would have been more at ease, for light warded off even the most persistent evil spirits. The impending darkness harboured violence she dared not contemplate.

Betimes her scruples were answered by a sudden halt of the carriage. Charlotte's breath faltered. A demon had come to claim her life! The vivid crimson hues of the sunset indeed foretold of a malicious visitor.

"Whoever be inside, come forth! Stand and deliver, your money or your life!"

The click of a pistol sounded. A weakness overcame Charlotte; she could not comprehend the speech, nor move a finger. The words of reprimand she intended to speak were lost.

"Come forth now, or I shall force you out!" His voice was unyielding, yet its firmness softened once Charlotte listened closely.

"Sir, I do yield to your request." She stepped into the dusk and revealed herself to the assailant with her arms up in surrender. "But spare me, for I am but a humble traveller with naught but my clothes and a purse."

"Hand me your purse and you shall be spared."

Charlotte assented, handing over her purse with complaisance. She did not dare to look up and behold the malignant visage of the assailant.

"Prithee, lady, will you take off your hood?"

"Why do you make this request?"

"If you obey, both of us shall be answered."

"Then I shall, sir," Charlotte pulled off the wide hood which had obscured her pallid face. At once the assailant dropped his pistol.

"'Tis most astonishing to find you once again, Charlotte Fitzroy! What power of Fate has led us to this reunion?"

"Who are you to speak of me in such familiar terms?" But as Charlotte raised her watery eyes to meet his, her fright was relinquished.

"George Walton!" She gasped. Indeed, it was the boy she once knew – the boy who lived beyond the lake. His features had matured, but she could still behold traces of effulgent naivete. "How ever did you fall into this unfortunate profession! It is surely cruel that you have been dragged into the basest pits of desperation."

"I admire your amiability, dear Miss Fitzroy, for even at a robbery you exhibit compassion."

"Oh, how could I not express pity towards a cherished friend of former years? After a long decade you still remember my name – your heart stays true."

"I could not bear to strip my dearest Miss Fitzroy of her money and her honour." He held out his hand clad in a tough leather glove. "Prithee, let us reconcile anon. I shall be more than honoured to aid you on your journey."

"Mr Walton – George – I cannot express the contentment, nay, overflowing mirth at this encounter. Let us travel together. I cannot dispense of your kindness. You see, I have embarked on a journey far away into London, but I doubt of its success. These arcane woods have inhibited my carriage, for there seems to be no clearing."

"London indeed! It must be divine intervention. I alike was travelling to London."

"You were indeed? What brings you on such a treacherous journey?"

"This life of vagrancy does not bring satisfaction. Though I earn my keep, it is an undependable profession. I wish to travel to London to establish myself in an honest living. Indeed, I never intended to become a highwayman."

"What had thwarted you, then?"

"'Twas a grave predicament which sent my family into an irredeemably impoverished state. My father had lost all our money – to this day I know not how – and thus we were forced into poverty. Do you recall when seemingly without reason I ceased to go to the village green?"

"Indeed, I do! I thought you had vanished forever. For five and twenty days I sat out on the eminence awaiting your return."

"I could never return. That day my mother and I were turned out of our home. We lived in a deserted stable in utter poverty. I resorted to petty crimes to bring us meagre portions of victuals. Then my mama perished from an ailment, and I was left to fend for myself. Thenceforth I travelled across sequestered roads and robbed any carriage that came upon my path. Many a time did I feel sorry for my unsuspecting victims. It was after countless days of wandering and thieving that I finally came upon a resolution: that I could abandon this profession forever. Thus, a sennight ago, I set off towards the city along this secluded path. I knew that I would not be welcome along the more frequented roads. But indeed, I never did except another traveller on this path, hence my return to old habits. I had heard the sound of a speedy carriage and thought that it was a magistrate in pursuit of me. Thereupon I broke into a gallop, but it was too late. When you stopped, I adopted a guise of intimidation, thinking that arrest was imminent. All of my scruples were proved wrong. Such is my tale."

The relation of George's history produced a manifest difference in Charlotte's countenance. It was not that of sorrow or pity, though she certainly did feel so; it was that of determined strength. On leaving, she had been under the strong influence of obstinate independence. Her journey was decided to be wholly unaccompanied, and indeed devoid of society – she could not risk being found out through a slip of the tongue. But this fault was greatly suppressed, as Charlotte had nearly betrayed on her parting with Nell. At that very moment, she much regretted the necessity of leaving behind a close confidant. Charlotte believed, perchance too firmly, in the abandonment of a former life. However much she could deny it, she still cherished familiarity. Beginning anew presented an array of difficulties which she had not acknowledged out of uncertainty. Now, with the return of a cherished friend,

Charlotte need not worry about lonesome prospects. There was courage to be found in a trusty accomplice.

"Come, George, let's make way out of this old forest. We shall embark on the journey to London together, in a companionship which surpasses convention. I wish to abandon my cheerless existence here in the country. Oh, the only advantage is the appearance of a pastoral! I cannot live here and be content; I shall grow to resent my very being. A life bound by duty will suffocate me." Charlotte hesitated a while. "We bear the same motivations for our escape indeed! It must be the work of Fate to reunite us so pertinently. Fate was watching us from the vault above and listening to our wishes."

"Aye, verily spoken, dear Charlotte! To the horse and carriage!"

George gallantly helped his accomplice into her seat, then mounted his steed in one swift motion.

"Hark, coachman, I know the way out of this dreary forest. Follow behind me and you shall travel with ease. Onwards!" He pulled the reins and his steed reared under the fresh moonlight.

"Onwards we shall go, and not a fear to cloud our hearts!"

Museum Logistics

Kate Leckie

If you were to hang my skeleton
from the ceiling of a museum –
like a blue whale, or a dinosaur,
or *some other*, once-great creature –
what would you do
with all the other parts of me?

Amputate my usefulness
and light a fire for the scraps of me –
those red fleshy parts,
(all the messy parts)
scrubbed from my ivory.
Exhibit me, picture perfect at last -
the only parts to last of me
now unfamiliar.

Holes, space and emptiness where
you could never see them before.
Caverns and nakedness, with not-quite-invisible string
looped around my fragments,
holding there a purgatory conference.

You are a bishop moving across white squares.
I am a puzzle, made entirely of diagonal pieces.

Dream Girl

Kelsey Goldsbro

If I were to die beautiful,   what a happy being I would be.

      With beauty comes brevity.

Emergence as an empress of whispers, Cinnabar
and pine needles.
      Tattoo
      my skin –
                  imprint   the fresco plaster –
                              pictures of lovely
                                    nights, fruits and wine.

      Sculpt the bones   under my tender Flesh.
      Make them grow,   flush red,   and shriek!
                                    With frightening Age.

      I would   hold the concern of many,
                        terrify with my consideration,
                        be the patient Machiavelli.

I am not to myself,
therefore onto others:
               Roses –   For a chore.
                         For the service.

               Vain –   To impress.
                         To nurture.

butterfly weed and Hibiscus ink – myrtle, make me smooth.
                              Drape me in veils and furs,

       – Love –   The quiet riots,
their buried softness.   Violet love,   immortalise my image.

   The Adorned –
Hated –
Beauty in youth.

XVII RX

Kelsey Goldsbro

In the garden,
        I AM FEMININE...

A Star   that shows herself only to Her–
                  The Earth.

To fall down,
down between midday   and sunset,
Where birds hide away,
and snapdragons   close their petal eyelids.

To dream:
        escape in the reaper's form.

        I am the Star   fallen to Earth,
                  finding no friends.
                  Everything hidden away and broken.

I am the Shooting Star that yearns for dawn to hide them;
for buds to open again.

To release their sweet scent:
escape in resurrection.

Three layers and nine fairy rings.
That fine mycelium journey
down, down–

I am *feminine*!

and The World arises,
present for my arrival.

Missive from Medusa

Kate Leckie

To / Dear mortal men mislabelling me a monster:

When you look at me, I do not
"turn you to stone".
Your actions are completely your own.
Maybe, you're a little reaction prone,
have a traction bone in your no-action zone?
Are you bitter re a lack of attraction shown
on my end?
Now you've promised *my* end;
"A monster of the gods" penned.
Think *you're* such a godsend?
Please! The gods send
protectors for the Greek
and champions of the weak;
definitely not *you*, threatening to behead me as I sleep;
my soul to reap. Head: yours to keep.
(One more ego-threatened creep.)
Threatened I have some "power" over you?
As if I'm waging witchcraft! – the "woe" I'll do.
Still want us to rendezvous? (I know you do)

Well, just let me show to you,
what I fucking *owe* to you:

Once Upon a Time on a Red-Light Street

Sharmila Jayasinghe

Hair curled and face painted, Snow White sits inside her glass box, a storefront mannequin.

Neon lights stream in, projecting a red halo around her.

Snow: a princess for sale.

Seven men, dwarfs and not, circle outside, uniformed – keeping Snow safe.

Charming arrives late, intoxicated, and chooses Snow for the night.

Payment made for services rendered, Charming returns to his life, to his wife, in a far, far away land.

Hair curled and face fixed, Snow White takes her place inside her glass box again.

A storefront mannequin, a princess for sale.

Six Yards of Expectation

Janika Fernando

I: Her

Knock, knock.

"Eromi, *nægitinna*! The sun has risen!" Eromi rubbed her weary eyelids while hearing

Saumya's brusque, abrasive voice. Saumya, that is, her Amma-in-law.

Eromi's grip tightened around the coarse cover of her wooden bed. She moaned silently at the thought of rising yet again to another day in the heaving heat of their home. It was only a matter of time before her husband, Hirosh, would emerge from slumber and cast a spell on her that she would not be able to escape. In the eyes of Hirosh and his mother, domesticity and marriage were everything – a sense of magic, as if Eromi was destined for nothing more than sprinkling seasoned curry and sweeping the dust off their tiled floors.

She wished Saumya Aunty hadn't roused her so early so that she could return to her gracious dreams, which were far more captivating than the day that was laid out before her. Travel was one of her greatest dreams. Her list of dream destinations went on and on: the United States, France, Japan. She imagined smelling rich new foods, turning new pages in library books and absorbing every word until she had carved a story out of them.

It would be a story that she could tell the –

Knock, knock.

As Eromi rolled out of bed, she breathed a sigh of remorse. She pulled aside the curtains to find small rays of light travelling through the prison-bar like windows. After slowly darting across the cold tiles, which sent piercing shivers through her body, she opened the wooden wardrobe. Within were piles of the finest silk and cotton in vibrant shades of pink, purple, blue, orange and yellow, neatly folded. Nothing identifies a Sri Lankan woman as unequivocally as her saree – the quintessential article of clothing. Saumya Aunty insisted that it was "quinessential".

Trying to clip her turquoise hatte together at the back, Eromi assessed herself in the tall, wooden framed mirror. Saumya Aunty barged into her room and tightly clipped the blouse, resolving the problem much to Eromi's chagrin. There was no sign that Saumya Aunty even cared that Eromi wanted this time to herself; to look in the mirror at herself for herself, without others changing her own reflection for her. Almost like a doll, she was stitched tight and poked with a needle so she could fit into her saree and stand out from the sea of Sri Lankan women who, in the past, desperately wanted to charm her now husband. That was at least what she heard the aunties gossip about in their village shops. It seemed to be that way all the time, people being downright nosy. After marriage, the gossip still didn't stop, even today. Saumya Aunty poked a needle and tightened her blouse once more.

"Ah, *eka ridenava!*" Eromi gasped. While ignoring her remarks of pain, the older women carried on as though clothing her was her proudest accomplishment. Her saree's six-yard tail was neatly pleated down, rather than left to flow freely. Like a darling, the saree tempted the faculties and exuded the most extreme elegance, providing satisfaction. In spite of Saumya Aunty's instructions to clip, pleat and tuck the saree every morning before the mirror, Eromi's thoughts frequently floated: What did she need to hide about her skin? Under the whine of coarse cotton, what could she not uncover about her glimmering pride? Only for a moment did she dare unravel her saree pota, revealing her flat pecan midriff.

"Eromi, *oyā mokada karannē? dœn kussiyaṭa enna!*"

Once again, she covered it and followed her Amma-in-law's cries to the kitchen.

II: Him

"*Ah, Mokakda mē saddē?*" Hirosh sighed, clutching his pillow around his ears to muffle the yells and cries he heard. His sarong and white tank singlet were soaked in sweat as he tossed and turned in bed, the fan above his head insufficient to cool him down. Amma and Eromi were at it again. Bickering over everything, as if being married wasn't already hard enough. Marriage. He'd once dreamed of it, but now it had become something else entirely. Hell.

Again, Hirosh sighed as the pillow failed to muffle the misery of life. Having discarded the pillow, he tumbled to the tiles where the coldness soothed his dark, brown skin. After getting up, he went to the bathroom to wash his face. In the midst of rubbing his face with his small, flowered towel, he smiled. This was the towel Eromi had given him for his birthday three years ago when they'd first started dating. *The moment you rub it on your face, you will think of me*, she'd said. Looking into the mirror, he laughed, thinking about the woman he loved as he gazed into his twenty-seven-year-old face.

The kind of dating he'd had experienced was not quite American or white but the Sri Lankan way. He'd just known she was the one for him. When his Amma had sifted through proposal advertisements and eventually their families had met, that was what he first thought. What had started as a simple meeting between two families over curry and dhal had turned into a series of adventures between two beautiful figures – from riding his motorcycle around his city to visiting jungles and all sorts of places where they had grown up together. It was more than just a proposal. It made him wonder if Eromi still remembered it.

As he retied his sarong around his waist, he put on the blue checkered shirt that he had worn when he met Eromi at that first family dinner. In spite of their miserable cries, he exited the bedroom with bare feet, eager for another scene with the two people he loved most in the world and to eat some dhal and curry.

III: Her

Once again, Eromi slipped the pota over her shoulder and tucked it into the tail of her saree. "Quinessential," she mocked. Distancing herself from her mirror, the saree danced around her, revealing just a glimpse of her shapely brown legs for a split-second. In the kitchen, she joined Saumya Aunty.

During Eromi's stirring of the curry, aromas of spices floated in the air, along with the frying of pappadams, elevating her status in the eyes of the older woman. The kitchen was laden with the familiar fumes of turmeric, chilli powder and cloves. She was feeling sick as beads of sweat adhered to her saree from the sun's blazing rays. Sick, as if there was no difference between her bedroom and kitchen. The feeling remained the same. In a bind.

Eromi remembered the adventures she'd had with Hirosh once overseas in Australia, when they were both young. What a release it had been for her soul to wear that rose-coloured short dress. Her light layers of dress had glistened in the sunlight, reflecting the beauty of her uncovered skin. Oh, how the short rose-coloured dress had freed her soul. Through the open window of the holiday house, the brilliant sun's light had reflected her essence. After tying the knot with Hirosh, moving in with Saumya Aunty and marrying into his family, she shook at the mere thought of wearing anything other than a traditional saree. The expectation was that.

As far as Hirosh was concerned, he seemed to agree. His presence continued to linger around her. He would always wander around her each morning, inhaling her cooking and waiting for breakfast to be served. Chicken curry, rice and dhal. The equivalent of what they had for lunch and dinner as well. Nevertheless, this time, rather than lingering around and wandering away from her, he curled his hands around her waist and drew her in for a sensual embrace, an experience that Eromi felt she had not had in a long time, something she needed, something that brought back memories she wished to keep hidden so that no one could see or gossip about them. Seeing his eyes and their chocolate hue, she felt warm. Home.

Hirosh whispered, *"ēka ættaṭama hoňda suvaňdak."* Eromi kissed his cheek.

"And you know what else smells good?"

"mō?ayek!"

Idiot.

Eromi sighed and pulled him closer, their lips pressing together. In between, a chuckle escaped his lips during which he mouthed the words. You.

But the lips of the two soon parted once the figure of an older woman entered, her beady eyes shining with discord, reminding her that she needed to finish the curry. Hirosh's eyes were fixated on the ground as he walked away. In a bind. Once again.

IV: Him

In the soothing embrace their lips collided, and Hirosh's heart beat like a drum. The softness of her lips made him not want the moment to end. More was what he wanted. He was scared, though. Increasingly heavy footsteps echoed through the tiles as someone edged closer to the kitchen. Amma.

After letting go of her lips abruptly, he backed away as if he hadn't ever touched her before. There was pain in it. Nevertheless, it had to be done. Anymore making out would have resulted in his Amma sending them to their respective rooms and his plans to make love to Eromi would have failed. A dazed, confused and look filled Eromi's eyes and Hirosh felt awful. There was nothing he could do but walk away.

"Good morning Amma."

"Ah, my *putha*!"

Double kissing Amma, he left the kitchen without looking back at Eromi and waited for breakfast at the table. Other than that, what else could he do? It seemed like the best course of action. His women will come to him as he sits and waits. The dolls.

V: Her

She wanted to be free of those six yards of oppression. Having her skin move carelessly to the rhythm of the beat, roaming freely. In that pretty little dress, she had been so profanely woman that everyone had looked at her – not because of her entrapment in the saree, but because of the way she had looked in her little dress. In the end, it didn't matter. She was duty-bound to satisfy Hirosh with her artful curry cooking, her saree complementing the stereotype. Saumya Aunty smiled as he nodded thank you. The sinking feeling in her heart told her that she had been moulded into someone she was not.

After untucking, unclipping and unplaiting her saree that night, Eromi climbed under the coarse covers and let her mind drift until –

Knock, knock.

Family Packed

Anna Liang

It began every night at five o'clock. The front door was unlocked, the dining room lights were switched on and the kitchen stirred, readying itself for a busy night ahead. As the exhaust fans began to purr, Ba lit the burners under the woks, and the kitchen hands finished arranging the tubs of marinated meats and sliced vegetables into neat rows on the bench. Customers started calling for takeaways, and my two older sisters frantically jotted their orders down at the front counter. The dockets were ferried to Ma in the kitchen, who called out what needed to be cooked over the sizzle of the stir-fries as they were tossed into the woks. Soon, the wait staff would start bringing in the orders from tables they had seated as the restaurant came to life.

Tucked away among boxes of spare containers and shelves of clean crockery in the back corner, I sat at a small wooden desk, listening for when I was needed. Not yet it seemed, so I turned back to my homework. It was usually maths. That was all I could manage with half a mind while keeping an ear out over the chatter that filled the dining room and the bustle in the kitchen. The phone rang. Could I finish one more question? The kitchen bell dinged as the first orders were ready, staff dashing to retrieve the bags of meals. But when the phone continued to ring, I raced out to grab the receiver. I sighed. The rest of the algebra would have to wait.

* * *

Since 1992, our family's lives have revolved around a Chinese restaurant. During the day, my sisters and I would go to school, classes or our day jobs, but most of our nights were spent helping at the restaurant. Instead of resting, weekends were when we worked the hardest and public holidays were a full family effort. My friends called it my "permanent part-time job". Sometimes, it felt more like a repetitive, gruelling existence.

However hard and long our nights were, I don't regret growing up in a Chinese restaurant. I'm only sorry it took the end for me to appreciate our time there.

* * *

After migrating to Australia, my parents settled in Goondiwindi, a rural town on the Queensland and New South Wales border. Just like in almost every country town, there was a local Chinese restaurant when my parents arrived, and soon they became its new owners. This was the restaurant my sisters grew up in. When I turned seven and my sisters finished high school, we moved to Brisbane. We found another restaurant to run in the bayside suburb of Manly and we stayed there until we sold the business in 2021.

Our restaurant was on the upper floor of a complex along the Manly Harbour, its presence marked by a white metal sign on the street that read "CHINESE FOOD" painted in big red letters. The only way to get in was up two flights of stairs.

It was not the most popular feature of our restaurant. But it was certainly easier carrying takeaways down than bringing up a week's worth of stock. The climb was usually worth it for the views from our dining room of the vivid sunsets and red moonrises over the bay.

The dining room was a modest space that preserved all its original décor, dated by the stack of worn *Women's Weekly* magazines at the front counter. Vases of brightly coloured fake flowers decorated the countertops and ink brush paintings hung on the walls. The statues of Fu Lu Shou – the gods embodying fortune, prosperity and longevity – overlooked the rows of tables from a shelf at one end of the room, and a large bronze Laughing Buddha sat at the other. And towards the back of the restaurant stood a dividing wall, about a metre and a half tall, that carved out a storage corner between the kitchen and the dining room. Here was where I spent most of my nights when I was younger, out of everyone's way.

Behind this wall, I was hidden but helpful. But I couldn't make these nights pass any faster no matter how hard I tried. As I folded box after box of napkins or packed enough bags of prawn chips to last a week, my mind wandered, yearning for an escape. I wanted to see my friends. Sometimes, I even wanted to go back to doing my homework. Most of all, I wanted to spend time with Ma and Ba. From my corner, I heard families laughing, having their dinner out together. That was something we never did. We never could do. I tried imagining what it would be like. But it was a life that was just too far out of reach on the other side of the wall.

One night, I decided I'd tell my parents. In the kitchen, Ma hunched over the sinks, washing piles of dishes by hand. Our family didn't believe in dishwashers, even though we had one. It sat idle as extra storage while Ma scrubbed fast and furious.

I sidled up to her and whined that I wanted us to leave. Making suds fly everywhere, she snapped, "If you don't help us out, you'll be stuck here forever!" That was the last time I said such a thing. Filled with disappointment and a tinge of shame, I sulked back behind the wall to the basket of chopsticks I was wiping dry.

* * *

In my busier years of school, my evenings were filled with after-school activities, so I had an out. But that meant there were days when I only saw my parents fleetingly in the mornings before school and sometimes late at night when I stayed up. If I came home in the afternoon, they'd be taking their precious naps in the brief break they had between a day of prep at the restaurant and dashing back to work at night. I knew they worked non-stop so that I could have the opportunities they never had. I was reminded of this even more at concerts, debates and matches where all my classmates were surrounded by their families. But no matter how busy she was, Ma always found a moment to ring me on those nights. In the minutes we had, we'd clumsily tell each other how much we loved and missed one another. I could hear how apologetic she was that she couldn't be around more. I just hoped she couldn't hear how much I resented the restaurant for taking her away from me.

When studying the Australian identity in one of my high school English classes, we discussed some of the stereotypes surrounding different cultural groups in Australia. My teacher said that for the Chinese, it was that they were cooks. I suppose it was now more of a historical narrative than a stereotype. The origins of Chinese restaurants in Australia can be traced back to the gold rush of the 1850s when Chinese migrants opened cookhouses on the goldfields to serve meals to both Chinese and Australian miners.[1] As Chinese migrants moved around the country, they opened restaurants in cities and rural areas. By the 1890s, a third of all cooks in Australia were Chinese.[2] But when the *Immigration Restriction Act* was introduced in 1901, Chinese migration had come to a halt. During the time of the White Australia policy, for those who ran businesses in Australia while supporting their families in China, life could be lonely.

Our family was lucky to have found firm friends in Brisbane's Chinese community. Even in Goondiwindi, we could count on those who ran Chinese restaurants in nearby towns. But the demanding lifestyle of running a small family business was still isolating at times, especially for my parents whose families remained in China. And when you run the local Chinese restaurant, that often means there's only one of you around. I now know that was probably a good thing for keeping business up. But to my teenage self, that was just another way I was different. I remember telling my English teacher we were that family, and she was very apologetic if she'd offended. She certainly hadn't, but I just didn't know how to feel about it then. About being Chinese. By that point, my Cantonese was slipping away, leaving me fumbling for words in my calls with Ma. Perhaps our restaurant was the thing that kept me tied to my cultural roots.

Growing up Asian in Australia often meant negotiating an identity in the grey space between two cultures and communities. Too different to be Australian but not alike

---

1   O'Connell, n.d.
2   O'Connell, n.d.

enough to be Asian. But when I was younger, it felt like growing up in a Chinese restaurant only amplified that even more.

* * *

As I grew older and taller than the dividing wall in our dining room, I began working front-of-house. Finishing school and starting university too meant a more flexible schedule and with that, more nights at the restaurant again. By now, I knew that there was no point wishing myself away; I was going to be there helping whether I wanted to or not. Around this time, my sisters had also begun the full-time grind in their careers, so sometimes it was just me and my parents at the restaurant. When I began to work more closely with my parents, I saw the physical toll that running the restaurant had taken on them. But they carried on tirelessly, as they did for almost three decades.

In 1934, the Australian government changed the laws to allow Chinese restaurants to bring in chefs and workers as temporary labour from China.[3] Although they were not allowed to, this was an opportunity for restaurant owners to bring their families over, using different names to avoid being caught out. Many of these "cooks" had no kitchen experience. To stay, they learnt on the job.[4]

My parents came to Australia in the later waves of migration, when Asian immigration was encouraged after the White Australia policy was amended in 1966[5] and eventually

---

3   Nichol n.d.
4   Nichol and Stacker 2016.
5   Noone 2018.

renounced. By the time they arrived, there were Chinese restaurants in every city and in many small towns. But in a new country with a new language to learn, they didn't have much of a choice of what they could do for work. Neither Ma nor Ba were chefs but like those who came before them, they saw that running a restaurant was how they could survive here.

One night, as I was bringing in more dishes for her to wash, Ma stopped me with a soapy hand and whispered, "Study and work hard so you can choose not to be here forever."

Coming to Australia meant putting aside any dreams and leaving behind what was familiar. When they got here, my parents knew that the restaurant life wasn't going to be easy. But they took on the challenge willingly. Fervently. Lovingly. They worked hard in the hopes that my sisters and I wouldn't share their struggles. In the hopes that we would only know stability and fulfilment. In the hopes of giving us what we needed so we could go far in our lives, further than they had. All in the hopes that my sisters and I could choose our own futures.

And here Ma was, reminding me that I should want to leave.

Life with a restaurant was all I had known. Up until that moment, I hadn't really thought about life after the restaurant. Deep down, we all knew that my sisters and I wouldn't take over the business – nor did our parents want that. It was only then that it sank in that soon, this would be over for all of us.

All this time, I'd failed to see that our restaurant was more than just a place we worked in to feed hungry mouths. My parents had taken every hardship that being an immigrant family had thrown our way and built something special out of it for all of us. Our restaurant had become the heartbeat of our family – the cornucopia that kept us going. Instead,

I'd childishly let the misunderstanding manifest over all these years. The guilt stung. Sometimes, appreciation was easier in hindsight. And now, I wasn't sure if I was ready to just let it slip away.

* * *

But that wasn't the end just yet. We still had a few more years in us, at least until when I would finish my degree. In the time we had left, I wanted to help my parents out more; I wanted to understand what I had missed all along. From the front counter, I started to see the things I'd never noticed before about the restaurant – things I had only heard fragments of from the other side of the wall. Our restaurant drew in a crowd of locals and newcomers – from those who sailed into the bay for a takeaway on their trips to those who knew exactly which table they wanted to sit at each time to look out over the bay. Learning the patterns of our restaurant was like watching the tide come in and out. Sometimes, something unexpected would wash ashore but for the most part, the nights thrived in their rhythmicity. And this time, I paid attention.

Over the years, there were many orders we looked forward to seeing. Luke came early each Wednesday for a fried rice with no prawns and a chicken and cashews. Jess rang most Fridays for a Family Pack B and a bag of prawn chips. Adam walked in for a table or takeaway three times a week. Although I couldn't predict when or what he'd order, he would always show up. Just as many others did, even throughout the pandemic.

Gradually, our family would get to know the people behind these orders. Our menu barely changed over years and featured all the Chinese restaurant classics so through Ba's cooking, many found comfort in familiarity. Each plate of honey chicken came laced with nostalgia, taking people back to their childhoods, and they would pass on their love of sweet and sour pork to their children. Everyone brought a different story about their Chinese food memories to the table, but often they would all end with deep-fried ice creams. Through these stories, we came to know the families who grew up celebrating their birthdays and special occasions at our restaurant, the friends who caught up over a monthly meal and the local businesses who hosted parties in our dining room. Each time I passed a bag over the counter or circled their table, I learnt a little more about them. But what made my nights at work was when they asked about us too.

Our customers cared a lot about our family, and many would become our friends. They'd stay around to chat with us when we had a quiet moment, keen to hear how we were doing or to wish us well on our cultural holidays. Kids made us drawings that Ma proudly stuck on the fridge and many regulars brought us presents at Christmas. We felt so loved by our community, and Ma and Ba always returned their affection in the ways they did best as Chinese parents: with an insistent willingness to help others out, immense generosity and lots of free food. Here in our restaurant, kindness was in abundance, and it brought us closer together.

There was a group of people who helped us make this all happen. In the dining room were a team of wait staff, many of whom stayed with us for years. Ma gave many their first casual jobs, mentoring and guiding them. Together, we not only learnt how to write orders while adding up at the same time or balance full trays of drinks, but we also learnt how to work with the occasional irate customer and through the inevitable mistakes that happened. We had each other's backs on difficult nights and shared the successes of the good ones.

And when they moved on, they brought their siblings and friends to help us in their stead. Working alongside Ba were our kitchen hands. Like my parents, they too had migrated to Australia. They spent more time with us in the kitchen than with their own families overseas, so we became their family here and they became ours. In working together, our restaurant gave us all a sense of purpose and belonging.

But after twenty-nine years of Ma and Ba putting their hearts and health into our restaurant, the time came for us to move on. The hardest part of it all was leaving the people who had welcomed us and our food.

I came to realise that our restaurant was a place for compassion; it bridged the gap between our two cultures and communities. Built on tradition but forged through adaptation and resilience, our restaurant showed me what it meant to be Australian Chinese. It's the long-lasting legacy Chinese restaurants around the country leave to the generation who grew up in them, and I'm proud to have been a part of it.

* * *

In September 2021, shortly after I graduated from university, we sold the restaurant. Now that we finally had the time, we decided to take a road trip out to Goondiwindi. It had been at least a decade since we'd last visited. As we drove through the small towns along the way, Ba pointed out the places where there had once been Chinese restaurants. Wistfully, he told me of the friends who moved away to the big cities when their children had finished school. When we finally arrived in Goondiwindi, our old restaurant was no longer there too. My parents had heard about it earlier from the locals we kept in touch with. Seeing it gone made it real.

Standing outside the shop, Ma and Ba talked fondly about our time running a restaurant. They told me about the things that photos couldn't capture of our first restaurant. And then the things that kept them going for all those years. Seeing my sisters, and then me, grow up. Meeting and befriending our regular customers. Sitting at the round table in our dining room with our staff late at night for post-work dinners. As they passed these stories onto me, I caught a hint of pride and relief in their voices. When we walked away, there was a lightness to them, from the load they had now let go.

I was glad to see there were still Chinese restaurants – two in fact – that were thriving in Goondiwindi. And our restaurant in Manly is still going strong. Chinese restaurants have survived over 150 years of history in Australia, and they are here to stay for many more. But over time, like the yachts that we watch come and go in the bay, so too will the families that run these restaurants. As we "restaurant kids" grow up and leave, it's important we keep these stories alive for our families and for our restaurants because they have shaped us into who we are today.

* * *

On our final night at the restaurant, once the last table had slowly filed out after many farewells, I bolted the door shut and let out a wistful sigh. A new life breathed into our kitchen as my parents set into action cooking our dinner, like they did at the end of each night. We would always eat together with the kitchen hands, although the wait staff went home earlier when their shifts finished. It was a time for us to finally sit down, relax and reflect on the night's happenings. A good night of work was often enough to warrant a feast, but this was a night to celebrate, however bittersweet it was.

While the round table in the dining room was usually set for five, we always managed to crowd more around, elbowing each other as we tucked into bowls of steamed rice. The array of Cantonese dishes on the table included steamed whole bream, pak cham kai (white-cut chicken) and stir-fried choy sum. Much to Ma's dismay at it being too *yeet hay* (heaty, or unhealthy), Ba sneaked a honey chicken in the spread as a treat for me and my sisters. As we passed around dishes, we laughed loudly and soaked up each other's company in our dining room for the final time before the new owners would come to run our restaurant the next day.

After the table was cleared and cleaned, it was time to switch off the lights and wander down the stairs one last time. With hearts fuller than our stomachs, each of us walked out with a takeaway, packed lovingly by our family. These takeways were filled with memories and experiences that would continue to feed us in our new lives – ones enriched by the time we had together in our restaurant.

Bibliography

Nichol, Barbara. n.d. "Sweet and sour history: Melbourne's early Chinese restaurants." *Memento*, January 2008: 10–12. http://www.multiculturalaustralia.edu.au/doc/ Nichol_MelbChinRest.pdf

Nichol, Barbara and Stacker, Julia. "A Sweet and Sour History." Interview by David Wong. 20 February 2016. https://www.nla.gov.au/sites/ default/files/transcript-sweet-and-sour-history.rtf.

Noone, Yasmin. 2018. "Why does every town in Australia have a Chinese restaurant?" SBS Food. https://www.sbs.com.au/food/article/ why-does-every-town-in-australia-have-a-chinese-restaurant/ pkyzdbo35.

O'Connell, Jan. n.d. "1847 Chinese labourers arrive in Adelaide." Australian Food Timeline. https://australianfoodtimeline.com.au/ 1847-chinese-labourers-arrive-adelaide/.

Pages of Time

Komal Gupta

I've been running through pages,
one to ninety-nine.
Running through them my entire life.

Running from pasts and running through presents,
running towards the future where endpages lie.

I stop.

I breathe.

The memories of childhood, where the salty warm breeze and
    sand meet, we fill up
buckets of sand and make castles out of them, some of us run
    to the shoreline to collect
water for our moats, some of us collect seashells along this
    shore, some of us taken aback by
the bleeding sky while we lie buried in the cool sand.

I stop.

I breathe.

The hands relaxed in grainy sands now hold papers and pens
    as college days begin,
writing non-stop with anxiety till the timer stops us. These
    hands chug drinks after to
cheers to exams finishing, and after month by months going
    by, we now wear robes of black
and toast off our final sips goodbye.

I stop.

I breathe.

Leaving the doors of college times and entering through doors
    of parenthood, swapping
beers for tea and coffee, having added stresses to look after in
    the form of a baby, zines from
the past replaced with large print newspapers, changing
    lifestyles so that the kids could lead
their own successful lives.

I stop.

I breathe.

* * *

I inhale a deep breath as I come to see a dark, box-like archway
    in front of me.

It reflects a golden colour,
golden arms come out to reach me.

I guess I have no choice but to accept I am near my end,
left at page ninety-nine, I look again to pages I leave behind;
the soft playful pages of childhood,
the rough and studious pages of college,
and the hair-torn pages of stressful parenthood.

They all flicker and rustle toward me, with faces of friends and
    children peering, waving
back at me.

I pause.

And take one last big breath overfilled with emotions.

Seeing these faces makes water race down to the ends of both
    of my wrinkled cheeks as I
try to make myself leave this world and enter into the arms of
    a golden fate.

As I am grabbed by this golden force, I feel my body start to
    become brittle and to dry
out, becoming pieces of golden flecks.

I float and disperse into golden ideas in the universe,
floating around till a gravity pulls me in;
and once this gravity starts pulling me in, I become a new
  story,

Newly written and sewn.

Shelter

Tom Evans

You grow up wide-eyed and in awe of the world and those around you.

Of the warm embrace of a hug, light rain on your skin or the rays of a spring sun on your face. A mum walking a dog or a dad kicking a ball with his kid in the park. An old couple walking down the footpath, slowly with hands clasped and smiles on their faces. Fresh linen to wrap yourself in during a cold night, soft sand to lie in at the beach filled with laughter and crashing waves.

Observing and learning the art of noticing, something that can last a lifetime.

There are not many issues for a person like you going through school. A brief playground confrontation or a failed romance with that person in Year Five who you shared a single kiss on the cheek with. The lowest of lows is a poor result on your assignment or losing by a goal on the weekend. You take the sense of security for granted at this age. This is the world you know.

Sometimes you hear in the playground that a friend's parents are fighting or even separating – but these things are far removed from the love you've known. Whispers in the classroom: he or she has to live in two different houses. To you it is a foreign world, a life away from the shelter of two parents under one roof.

Moments of fracture come when a parent or friend loses a loved one. But you still have all four grandparents, and any illnesses are close calls or quick fixes. The big C lingers when Mum's friend succumbs to it, but people move on and Mum hides her tears from her children, so you return back to your bright and cheerful life.

And this continues, for many years. You finish school and finally get to explore the world, to find yourself in your studies and work, in friends and partners. Your world expands when you're out of your comfort zone. Even when you finally move into that share-house with your friends, the shelter is still there.

In your childhood home, with your loving parents, the air always feels lighter, and breathing is easier. The green tapestry of garden bends and towering trees replace bright white streetlights and sirens. Your shelter is within the gate that opens with the press of a button and alerts the dog that still remembers you. Cousins, an auntie or uncle and even grandparents pop by. Life seems so much simpler there.

And then it happens. The illness of a loved one gets more severe. You wouldn't believe what is happening because you've never had to experience this so directly. Parents that previously hid their tears and pain from you, can no longer hide as grieving takes hold.

The funeral. Black suits and dresses, lowered gazes, the rainy day filled with tears and sniffling noses makes it all real when it's Mum's friend. And then it's a friend's mum, another friend's dad. A grandma and a grandpa. Loss seems to come in waves as your happiness ebbs and flows. No longer is life as simple as it once was, you think of those early years as a prologue to your life.

You still take each day with a smile and process pain with a positive attitude, able to feel deeply but also bounce back from loss. You read more, begin to finally appreciate walks in the park and days without drinking. You begin to appreciate a home-cooked meal and a daily journal more than beers with friends and a club every Friday night that follows with a hangover all weekend.

But each heartbreak and loss build up until your foundations begin to crumble. There are accusations, developments in relationships and illnesses that affect your immediate family. They slowly chip away at the shelter that you thought would never fall.

The walks through the park becomes a necessity, as do the gym routine and a healthy lifestyle. Sad songs begin to have new meaning; you put that piano piece on repeat and even shed a tear at the lyrics of an old tune you used to smile to.

You accept that this is what growing up is, this is what being an adult means. It's hard to keep the optimism and curiosity of your previous self, but you trudge along. Taking each day as it comes, you live in the moment rather than dwelling on the past or worrying about the future.

You listen to a podcast, watch a video and then another that the faceless digital man serves you in order to motivate and inspire. In your partner you find someone you can trust, and in each parent, you find a glimpse of a shelter that you now cherish as a memory from what seems so long ago.

Still, there will always be moments when you're in the shower, and you'll let the warm water run for a little longer as you stare at the droplets race down the fogged-up glass. And there will be times when you need to put that piano piece on repeat for a couple of minutes before bed.

As each year comes and goes, as friends move overseas or settle in to make families, shelters of their own, you begin to realise that childhood was a prologue to your life, as a forerunner to growing up. A prologue not unique to you, but a reality shared by being human

This part of the story after the prologue is the most important. It's where you find out who you truly are, what really means the most to you. You start to see the importance of doing the job you feel real meaning in, dating the person who makes you better and inspires you, reading books that make you laugh and cry. You go to the movies alone or consider getting a coffee with an old friend for brunch. And eventually you start to enjoy each day because as the overused adage says, it's all about the journey and not the destination.

Shelter changes as you do. It was constant when you were growing up with two parents, siblings and a dog but now it's something transient, coming in all shapes and sizes. A share-house in the inner city, a team you can laugh with at work, your local bookshop or supermarket. Even the knowledge that you can confide in a best friend, over the phone with mum or a beer with dad.

And you know that in the end, everything will be okay. This story is yours to live up until the epilogue when you are surrounded by the ones you love, and you think back to the times when you felt most safe. You think of your shelter. There are so many moments to cherish in life; every day is a gift. Even when life seems to slip away, there is always another day. Another chance, another moment to remember.

For I am large, I contain multitudes of moments to cherish.

Seashells on Sand

Eeshita

I sit in a quiet room that echoes with the keyboard's *tap tap tap* ...

There are days when the words rise and ebb like the Indian Ocean that foams against the sandy beaches of Sydney. Then there are nights when it's all still and too quiet.

Growing up in the north-western state of India, Rajasthan, home to the Great Indian Desert, Thar, I have always felt an affiliation with the sun-kissed dunes. For me, sand encapsulates the vast endlessness of my childhood days. Running barefoot in the sandy backyard of my grandmother's house, leaving behind a trail of small footprints soon to be licked away by the arid summer winds. I have spent many vacations there, making sandcastles that looked more like caves and lying underneath the cool shade of our old Neem tree with my back against the warm sand. I could spend hours watching the sun peak in and out from between the serrated leaves overhead, casting diamond-like shadows upon the sand.

One day I decided that I needed the desert for more than what my limited holidays allowed. So, I poured some sand into an empty glass bottle with a blue turban-like cap and packed it with my luggage to take back home to the city. You can't hold time, they say ... but whenever I opened the bottle, letting the sand loose into my palms I was transported back to the desert. Once again watching the sand sparkle in the sun like galaxies of the faraway sky.

People say that every desert was once a sea. Now, all that remains is the ever-shifting wave-like patterns. Once on a school trip to the Thar Sand Dunes, as the sun blushed over the horizon, I could almost see the sea flicker in the golden grains before me.

Then the hourglass turned and by destiny's design, I found myself in Sydney to study writing. Whenever I remember the uni days, the memory overwhelms me before disappearing like a pebble in quicksand. It's so surreal and fleeting that I can't help but wonder if it really happened or if it was all just an elaborate dream. But then my eyes find the little paper package placed atop my writing table. I smile, reassured.

Wrapped tenderly in a piece of paper are a few seashells with some sand still stuck on their smooth surface. Proof that it was real. When I first arrived in Australia, I visited the beach on my third day because it seemed like the rite of passage. The glistening waves rushed to my feet like a greeting, only to take away the sand beneath my toes. It reminded me of the desert. The sand felt the same under my soles but everything else was intimidatingly new.

No wonder I got lost on my way back. The Opal card I'd borrowed from a friend had only two dollars left, and I took the wrong bus due to my confusion over the Sydney bus routes. Finally, after pleading with a driver, who was kind enough to let me ride the bus for free, I managed to get back safely to my university accommodation. The second my lost eyes found the warmly lit glass windows of the building, it felt like coming home.

The new place was different, yes, but also similar in a comforting way. The sun blazed with familiar fierceness, and the silver moon still peeked into my window like it did back home. As months passed, I slipped into the ease of being in a foreign setting that had started to feel like home. Nevertheless, the sand in the hourglass ran out as it always does, and it was time to say goodbye. Before leaving, I visited the beach again, only this time I looked more closely, watching how the sparkling water played with the gazillion grains of sand. As I walked along the soft edge between the two, I found my memorabilia: seashells. Thus, with luggage made heavier with add-on memories I returned home.

Today, as I sit here with a degree and an experience, technically I should know more. Yet ironically, I've never felt more lost. As if learning 'Writing' has pressed the backspace button on my understanding so far that the page has turned blank again. Awaiting another story. I continue to write; of course I write, what else can I do? Still, most of my pages remain unread, uncertain ... unpublished. It makes me wonder: if no one knows I am a writer, am I still one?

The cursor continues to blink anxiously ... waiting. The sand and the seashells hold their breath in anticipation. I don't look at them anymore. Because when I do, they ask questions I don't know the answer to. *So what now?*

While the winds blow, the sand rises and settles on the waves, the dunes shift and the water cools, the question remains. *What now?*

And I sit quietly in my room and wonder if I should just google it ...

Nocturne

Phil Nondum

When on high the moon whispers
its faint light like a scree,
and wrinkles a ladle of satiny sky –
that film of jellyfish blue
begins to shift, stray *aurora australis*
takes me to my dead fish and
the fawn bricks of my primary school –

I was never good at maths or holding urine,
or standing up for myself – rather, I sat,
peering as wind pummelled the trees
beyond the false azure; aloof from symbols
on the chalkboard, I found them in nature,
and kneaded my future with as much vigour
as wind kneaded those leaves. I caught the sun in flight,
saw it tint the ginkgo, and mangle the cirrus –
at twilight the dust had made me teary,
– air soaked through with PM 2.5 –
and when over that cypress-horizon blessed
with a thousand crimson deaths, the sun,
brittle with age, stumbled on to its fate,

I found my *waxwing slain,* parched
on the windowsill.
I still believed myself the Son of God though
I couldn't save a fish.

Here the newborn sun drowns two hours sooner
in winter hills whose gnarly branches
cradle its fall, though they say the moon
is everywhere the same.
Before the days of jasmine and ashes,
the air has an icy gravitas –
like a ferry tethered to a port,
waiting, waiting ...
Ethics turned me from meat, but occasionally
I still eat fish – and I still wonder
if you had tasted the brew of Lady Meng
when Styx ripped you away. I remember
only in dream, of the sky and the cirrus
on my transpacific flight – I don't know where
to visit when I return, nor how to face the relatives'
saintly exigent hospitality. Cold drops
on the runway, stars climb high –
no storm in sight. My home
is a streak of triturated dusk.
I've learnt to play handball and Galois theory,
though not yet to fork lightning.

Tim

Josie Lu

Prologue

I liked Tim even before I saw the books on his shelf: classics like Austen and Tolstoy, contemporary works by emerging international authors, the occasional science-fiction novel found somewhere in between. Sydney was a new and scary city, its streets unfamiliar and its residents foreign, but in the bookshelf of his childhood bedroom, I knew I had found a new home.

The three of us ate dinner together that night – Tim, me, the mutual friend that introduced us; my high school classmate who was the only person I knew in the city I had moved to for university. Tim's family was away, leaving the house empty, so he invited us over and cooked for us, preparing Vietnamese rice paper rolls with the carrots sliced more finely than I had ever seen.

Tim was two years older and he already seemed to know how the world worked: the sort of people he liked hanging out with, what to wear while interning at a big tech firm, how to prepare a dinner for new friends and make conversation flow the whole evening. Before we left, I asked Tim if I could borrow one of his books, making sure I had a reason to see him again. It was the first time ...

On the adjacent page, Isabelle's name is written in black ink, the e's and l's looped in her signature style.

She adds a smiley face next to it, like she always has, when it comes to Thomas.

"Did you ever think you'd see me like this?" she asks, closing the book and handing it back to him.

"You were always going to make it," he says. "I just don't think you saw it in yourself back then."

"It's funny, isn't it? How life works out sometimes." She looks down at her expensive persimmon red dress, the belt buckle shiny and the fabric stiff against her skin.

"I can't believe you're here though. It's been what, seven years? How did you even find me?"

He gives a wry chuckle, one that sounds almost wistful. "I got an ad about your event, I guess the Instagram algorithm works in mysterious ways." He looks down at the book in his hand, mesmerised by the cover as his voice comes out nonchalant. "Realised I was in Sydney too and thought I'd stop by to say hi. I'm looking forward to it, by the way. Reading your book."

"Oh." She smiles bashfully, colour flooding her cheeks. "It's a little weird to think about all the people who now have access to these thoughts I've kept inside for so long. But maybe it's a little freeing too, to finally have them out in the world."

There was something else, but she couldn't bring herself to say it.

He smiles. "Well, you were never one to keep your thoughts to yourself." He pauses to examine the book in his hands again. "It's what I liked about you back then."

The moment settles. There, he said it, breaking the barrier that was keeping the past so firmly guarded from the present.

"I … that was only for you though. Now it's for everyone," she manages to say, trying to stop the memories rushing in now that the floodgates have opened.

"I just think it's kind of crazy this is all really happening, you know? Back then I never would have thought my life would look like this. Like, what is this?" She waves her hand emphatically, gesturing at the posters around the bookstore with her retouched face and the stacks of books with her name on the cover.

"If you had told me back then that I would be a writer someday, a *writer*, I never would've believed you. But I do think it all really did start then, you know what I mean? Like, every little choice I made, every step I took, somehow landed me here, and now I can't imagine my life any other way. Or at least, I try not to."

The words somehow come out all at once, one tumbling over another, fighting to be said.

Before Thomas can reply, a sales assistant walks over and taps Isabelle's shoulder, letting her know it's time for the book signing. A line has already formed at the table, stretching past the door and onto the street outside.

Thomas turns to look at the people waiting. "Well, I guess you better get to it. Are you free for coffee later, maybe?"

Isabelle nods. "Sure, it'd be nice to catch up." She makes her way to the table, where her books are piled onto both ends.

It was a brilliant debut novel, they said. Heralded by the press as "a new voice for a new generation," speaking to Gen-Z and millennial anxieties like no other. The novel created frenzy in the literary world and then permeated the wider culture, with eight companies battling for the rights to produce a television series inspired by her work. Deeply personal, semi-autobiographical and profoundly moving, one critic wrote. A stunning examination of the choices we make under capitalism; the tradeoffs between money and things we truly want, is how another described it.

The fans are enthusiastic, clamouring over her every word, desperate to dig a little deeper into the vulnerabilities she has excavated onto the page.

"You wrote my father," one woman says, clutching the book to her chest. "Thank you for putting those feelings into words."

Another steps up to the table. "Tim's the one that got away, isn't he? He made me think of someone, and I'm dying to know more. Will you ever write more about him?"

Isabelle feels grateful that these people, that so many people, somehow care about her, but the thought is simultaneously oppressive. Here she is, a single person, amassing something so much larger than herself, letting her most personal ideas foray into the world, wildly outside of her own control. It's an exercise in trust, in believing these words will be used to connect rather than divide, in allowing others to welcome and not ostracise. She picks up another book, signs her name on the inside cover in swirling black font, then hands it to the girl in front of her. The girl makes eye contact, holding the book with both hands. "Thank you. Truly. Your writing saved my life."

The phrase is simple, but it strikes a chord somewhere within Isabelle. This is why she writes. This is why she is willing to dredge up her most painful memories and arrange them into words that make some sort of sense to another person.

"That's all I can hope to do. Hang in there."

The line eventually dwindles, and Isabelle is left feeling both satisfied and hollowed, like she has been turned inside out and emptied all over the desk. From the corner of her eye, she sees Thomas slip in through the bookstore entrance, quietly browsing the bookshelves with her novel still tucked under one arm. He does look different now – older, sure, but more so the air around him feels different. Maybe it's simply that she no longer sees him in the way she used to.

When her last fan exits the bookstore, Thomas is still standing by the door, reading some book he's taken from the shelf. Isabelle gathers her belongings, thanks her event organisers and the assistants who will help pack up, then walks over to Thomas and tells him she's ready to leave.

The sun is bright but the day is unusually cold, so as they step outside, Isabelle unfastens the strap of her coat and pulls the fabric tighter around her body before tying it back into place. Glebe is busy – it is a Saturday afternoon after all – and there are still people lounging around on the seats outside cafés. Thomas asks her where they should grab coffee, but Isabelle suspects he already has a place in mind.

"Glebe Village Café? For old time's sake?" Saying the name reminds her of moments she thought she'd forgotten: mornings studying together with their drinks on the table, coffees they vowed they would not finish until their work had been done for the day.

"That's literally what I was thinking," Thomas says.

So they make their way to the café, where she orders a latte with oat milk, as she always did, and he orders a large cappuccino, as he always did. While they sit down at a table and wait for their orders, she tells him about the local restaurants that closed during COVID lockdowns, how they're lucky this one is still here. She is grateful Glebe Village Café remains, that within the sun-streaked brick walls of this place, she can cling onto some semblance of happier times. On the windowsill are two bobblehead figurines: a smiling cat and a frowning penguin. They used to joke about how he was the cat and she was the penguin, and these figurines still remain. She is surprised to realise how much she cares.

"So how has Hong Kong been?" she asks. "Are you still living there?"

"Yeah, I'm still living there. It's been good."

"So what's it like? How's work?"

"Work's fine, long hours though. The city's great too, lots to see and do and the food's amazing. Sometimes it gets tiring, but that's only expected I guess. Have you ever been?"

She has been planning to travel somewhere now that she has savings in her bank account and an advance for her next book. The last few years were rough, juggling three part-time jobs while carving out time to write in the tiny room she paid two fifty a week for. Now, for the first time in what feels like her entire life, she thinks she can let herself exhale slightly, take a break somewhere. Perhaps Hong Kong could be her first destination.

"No, but I would love to go sometime. What should I see there?"

"Actually, I have a whole guide written about things to do in Hong Kong, I send it to all my friends who come and visit. I can send it to you later, if you add me on Instagram or give me your email or something."

Just then the coffee arrives, sharply aromatic like it had been all those years ago. The waiter places down their drinks, and Isabelle looks over at the cappuccino in front of Thomas, the royal blue mug it's always been served in.

"You know, I haven't been back here since you left. I pass by every now and then though."

Thomas looks at her, his eyes scanning across her face and taking in every detail.

"What about you? How have you been?" he asks.

"Oh, you can probably kind of imagine, a life in the arts and everything." She smiles, but her lips only move slightly. "It's been stressful. Exciting. A bit of an adventure. Sometimes I can't really believe these past few years have actually happened."

Thomas nods slowly.

"Was it worth it?" he asks.

She feels her expression change as thoughts race through her mind, trying to choose one interpretation out of a million possibilities. "You mean, like, pursuing a career in writing?"

"Yeah, I guess so."

"Definitely. I don't think I can see the world in any other way. Before I found writing, everything was grey, colourless. I thought it was worse than not living."

Thomas looks out the window and watches some cars drive past, but his eyes look distant, the way they do when he is in one of his pensive moods.

"So when did you find it? Writing, I mean."

Isabelle ponders this question, drumming her fingers on the wooden table. "It must've been a year or two after you left. I mean, you know what I was like back then. Always jotting things down, always telling you random observations I had. But no, I never thought about writing as a proper thing until way after you left. It was just an outlet at first, and then suddenly I had all these stories I wanted to tell. Before that, I didn't have a clue what I wanted to do with my life."

"Does anyone know what they want to do with their life?"

"I do now," Isabelle says. "Do you?"

Thomas picks up his cup and moves it in circular motions, swirling the remaining coffee left inside. "That's a hard question to answer," he finally replies.

The barista has begun wiping down the coffee machine, and clattering sounds can be heard from someone washing dishes in the kitchen. Isabelle takes her phone out of her bag and glances at it. "It's almost four. We should probably go, before we hold them up any longer."

They leave the café, stepping out into autumnal air that chills Isabelle's bare neck. "Do you want to walk through Victoria Park?" she asks. "If you feel like it, of course. I think I might warm up if we do." Thomas agrees, so they cross the road and enter the park, walking down a path that branches into two, the right side leading to stairs going towards the university campus.

Isabelle chooses the other option. "Let's not go to campus. I already go too much when I tutor for writing classes." So they turn towards the jelly-bean-shaped pond, the one filled with murky water and ducks swimming around, surrounded by tall fig trees and their luscious draping branches. The afternoon light is hitting the water at a low angle, and everything sparkles under its honeyed glow.

"Look how pretty it is," Isabelle says. She stops walking and brings out her phone to type some notes. "Sorry, I just have to write it down before I forget." She takes in the ducks swimming, the rippling patterns dancing across the surface of the water. There's something beautiful about it, about how emerald green the grass shines under sunlight, how happy the toddler chasing birds around the pond looks.

They stand at the pond's edge, Isabelle typing into her phone, Thomas watching the toddler on the other side. "Do you remember how scared you were of the birds here?" he asks. Isabelle smiles at him. He used to chase them away for her. "I'm still terrified actually. They're good for writing though. I was just making some notes about that one."

"What about it?"

"Oh you know, its beady eyes, the evil secrets it must be hiding. I'm thinking about trying fantasy sometime, and that bird could turn into the next monster haunting your nightmares." Thomas suppresses a laugh, and Isabelle realises she can still hear what it sounds like inside her head.

When she finishes typing they continue walking along the water's edge, then wander further into the park. Dried leaves crunch under their feet, flattening into the dense earthy path underneath.

"So what brought you back to Sydney?" Isabelle asks.

Thomas says he's visiting family, how it's been a long time since he's seen them with all the border closures before.

"How are they doing? Your parents? And your sister?"

"They're doing well. I helped pay off the mortgage mum was so stressed about, so they're retired now, just relaxing most of the time I think. And Taylor's happy too. She got into her dream school, and really likes America apparently."

Warmth fills Isabelle's heart, and it reaches her eyes. She had been by his side during late nights when he laboured over coding questions, and she told him he could solve them when he wasn't so sure himself. "That's amazing," she says. "Taylor's tuition must've been so expensive, and I know how stressed you were over it."

"She got financial aid as well, but yeah, I helped out a little. I'm just happy she's happy."

"Stop downplaying yourself. You worked so hard for that job, I know you did." Isabelle laughs. "Look at me – I still make my parents worry. They're always going on about art not being a stable career and asking if I'll ever meet a guy who makes it past three dates and when I'll grow up and settle down. At least I have the money to take them travelling now, I guess."

"Hey, they don't need to stress. I'm serious. Why would they ever need to worry about someone like you?"

Isabelle doesn't know how to answer, so they continue walking in silence. The path is now concrete and leads them to an open field, trees no longer shrouding them from above. Here the park slopes upward, and the central business district comes into view as they walk to higher ground. In the distance, lights are starting to turn on in the cluster of buildings forming the city skyline. The clear sky from earlier has given way to pastel colours, a gradient of pinks and purples and greys that blend seamlessly into each other. Against the sky, the city lights look almost magical, like fireflies illuminating a mystical faraway land.

Isabelle turns around to admire the view.

"Remember how magical the city used to feel? All those lights, and people, and things to do."

She used to drag him around the city, curious about some event she found online or some new musician busking on the streets. It really was kind of magical, all the pockets of wonder and possibility she found hidden within the crevices of the city.

"Yeah. I miss that feeling." Thomas brushes the hair falling in front of his eyes.

"Can I ask you something?" he says. "The book's about me, isn't it? I started reading it while I was waiting for you earlier."

Isabelle doesn't say anything, stands completely still, then pulls a face at him. "How conceited can you get? Just because you have some fancy job doesn't mean everything in the world is about you, you know."

Then she sees Thomas's stricken face, how he wishes he could take back his question, and bursts into laughter.

"I'm just kidding. Of course it's about you, or partly inspired by you at least. I had to do something with all my bottled-up emotions after you left."

The tightness releases from his shoulders and he chuckles softly. "You almost got me there, but I knew it. I mean, how can anyone date someone as perfect as me and not write a book about it afterwards?"

Isabelle smiles and punches his arm lightly. "I wonder what made you turn out this way," she jokes. "How was I ever with someone like you?"

Thomas falls quiet, his mind having drifted off somewhere. Isabelle wonders if he's thinking the same thing. How did they end up here? Standing together, in this park they used to frequent, years of lost time between them.

Eventually, he replies. "I mean, it's like the prologue of your book right? The night we had dinner together for the first time? Isn't that where it all began?"

Isabelle thinks about his question, staring at the city lights and drawing lines from one memory to the next. She finally comes up with an answer.

"Can we really tell where things begin? Maybe it was dinner that first night, or maybe it was when I hopped on a flight to Sydney, or maybe it began when you bought your first book and started filling that bookshelf of yours I loved so much. Every moment is so interconnected with all the other ones, so how can there be any actual beginning, aside from the ones we make up for ourselves?"

She pauses and takes a breath before continuing on.

"I think that's how I got into writing. I needed to make sense of things by giving them beginnings and endings, by turning them into chapters of a book I could read and then move on from. It's my way of getting through life, the good times and the bad."

"I'm glad you found writing then. I'm glad it was there for you when I wasn't."

Neither of them know what to say, so they look down and avoid making eye contact. Finally, Thomas breaks the silence. "Do you ever wish things happened differently?"

"Sometimes I wonder if I would be a writer if I hadn't met you. Or what our lives would look like if we hadn't left each other. I don't know, I can only imagine."

The book is still in his hand, now cold to the touch. "It's like the epilogue of your book, right? It's set in an alternate world, isn't it? One where they made different choices?

Isabelle blushes, her cheeks warm against the darkening night.

Thomas continues on. "That wouldn't be your epilogue if we stayed together. I don't think you would've seen me that way, had we really spent months and years together after university. Maybe it's better this way."

"Maybe," she says, the wind blowing her hair and coat around as she stands beside him. "I guess we'll never know."

Life in a Museum

Isla Scott

Oh, wouldn't it be simpler if a comet wiped away the past,
    instead of just killing the future?

Let asteroids be black and white,
their craters cleaning slates to shine like new.
Make meteors just rain straight down
on all the fossils holding awkward truths.
No more mud and grey and wavy lines,
where you loved me and changed your mind,
we grew apart and didn't try.
We never even said goodbye.

If all that's left of us is fossils,
I don't want to dig them up.
It's so much easier to leave them lying,
hidden underground, in the dirt.
Let's pack layers of mud on our skeletons
so I can just pretend it wasn't real.
You never cared.
Doesn't that make more sense?
How could there have been a world of greenery and dinosaurs
    and laughter, if it no longer exists?
Tell me the trilobites were never anything but rubble,

and I'll be absolved.
Let the relics gather dust and lie simple.

Oh, but isn't that past worth preserving?
Even if it's over?
Isn't it worth remembering the truth?
Maybe it's easy to be cynical and bitter,
to shove all of your bones into a box.
But just because it's gone, or just because you lie about it,
doesn't make that history unhappen.
The dinosaurs are dead, that's never going to change.
But they lived, and they loved,
and their fossils deserve life in a museum.

Dead Things in the Dark

Samantha Bowers

The skipper hoists Sal up so that her legs are dangling, her eyes level now with his. He smells of coffee and cigarettes.

"Do you believe in God?" His voice is narrow and insistent, and even though she's seen him go through this routine a hundred times before, even though she knows it's a game and the other kids are already shrieking delightedly in the water, perfectly safe, suddenly Sal can't tell if he's serious or having her on.

It doesn't matter what she says, she knows. The result either way will be the same. Yet suddenly she wants to get down, to get as far from the creek as she can. Suddenly the right answer seems crucial.

"Do you believe in God?" His voice again. The sun glares off the creek's surface, making her eyes water.

She thinks of Sunday mornings, standing stiff and frilly beside her older brothers in her best white dress, her slip-on shoes, the ritualistic parade down the aisle, forgetting which hand to layer over which to take Communion. Then after, probing the roof of her mouth with her tongue to peel the stiff wafer away from her palate. She imagines the priest, holding his hands to the sky, singing in his off-key baritone *have mercy on us*.

A cloud passes over the sun and she meets the old skipper's eyes suddenly and fiercely as she gives her answer, screwing her fists into balls.

* * *

Outside a wind has whipped up and Lisa can hear the dead leaves in the courtyard skitter across the paving. The sky is grey and threatening, the forecast has been rain for the past two days, but the ground remains dry.

In the kitchen, she plucks the egg carton out of the fridge, and opens it. Two of the new dozen she bought yesterday are cracked, their thick yolks oozing out of them. She picks them out, and dabs at the residue they have left behind. Paul is careful with her allowance, and he will know the carton is new. He has warned her to always check the eggs before buying, and she normally remembers, but yesterday she had been in such a hurry at the register. She had seen Becky, an old school friend, and was trying to avoid a conversation.

Lisa rinses the egg yolk down the drain, watching it slide through the cracks in a thick mass, then carefully wraps the shells in old newspaper and crushes them in her hand. Paul doesn't go through the garbage, but he does sometimes peer into the can.

She selects two more eggs, unbroken, from the carton and lowers them carefully into the saucepan of water on the stove. She watches them bobbing around, bumping clumsily against one another, softly and irregularly at first, and then more frequently, more violently, as the water comes to a boil. Out the window, she can just glimpse the curve of the creek.

The kitchen timer goes off, startling her. She spoons the eggs up, one, two, into the egg cups that came with their wedding china. Baby blue flowers adorn the edges, fading in places even though it's only been three years. She had loved the set when it was new.

By the time Paul moves down the hall, Lisa is setting the eggs and toast at his place at the table. She shimmies his chair out, so he will be able to sit, and seats herself in front of her cold cup of tea, barely touched, but too late now to re-heat it.

"What will you do today?" he asks.

"Oh cleaning, probably. There's the bathroom to do."

He slices the top off his egg. "Will you go to the library?"

"Not today." She thinks about Paris. What it would be like to live there.

"You sure?" He fishes a library slip out of his pocket and places it on the table between them. "Your books are overdue."

She takes the slip and pretends to be surprised. "Perhaps I will go, then." She looks out at the lawn, sipping her cold tea. A magpie is hopping about the grass, stabbing its beak into the earth, looking for beetles.

"I was thinking, actually," she says evenly, as though it matters very little, "that I might try a different library, sometime. Ours never seems to have the books I want."

"Plenty of books at ours," he says, dipping his toast into the egg. His voice is smooth, but she can feel the air tighten, the static of a storm brewing.

* * *

Sal feels a snatch of panic as she is released, then a sudden weightlessness, strange and welcome. She hits the creek's surface, backside first, and shrieks at the shock of the water, still cold from winter. A giggle bubbles out of her as her life jacket prises her back to the surface. Water streams down her fringe into her eyes, her nose. She kicks her legs and rolls over onto her back.

Overhead, on the branch of a scribbly gum, a kookaburra throws back its head and laughs and laughs.

Later, she and Shelley pick their way along the dirt track by the creek's edge, dangling their shoes by the laces. They've pulled denim cut offs straight over their swimmers and the water has bled through, making them both look like they've wet themselves. Late afternoon sun slants into their faces and Sal has to squint to see.

"Come on," she says, charging ahead through a patch of mud that oozes black between her toes.

Behind her, Shelley screams. Sal jumps, "What?"

"I saw something," Shelley whimpers. "Something dead."

"Where?" Sal feels goosebumps prick deliciously, like the time Tim caught a huntsman in the dunny and convinced her to let it crawl up and down her arm.

* * *

Lisa rehearses it in her mind, *I'm leaving, I'm leaving, I'm leaving.* It sticks in her head some days like a nursery rhyme, until she thinks that it is about to burst out of her, like a champagne cork out of the bottle, and it will be done, the decision made for her. But then Paul will look at her the way he did when they first met or rake his fingers through his hair to give her a lopsided grin, or pull her to him and kiss her slowly, slowly, until she burns, until she finds herself saying something else entirely.

At the library, Claire, the woman at the loans desk, smiles and says it's been too long and has she been sick or something?

She says *or something* carefully, looking at Lisa's face. When Lisa opens her purse to pay for her overdue books, Claire says *keep it,* and waves her away.

Lisa browses the fairytales like she used to when she was a child, tracing the filigree letters on the front covers with her finger, tucking her legs under herself and reading in the children's corner while around her the afternoon sun grows weak.

That night, as she is making dinner, Lisa takes a swig of the cooking wine, and then another, and thinks she will tell him tonight. The rain has finally started. It slants against the windows, battering the agapanthus and churning the garden bed to mud. She will go and stay with her sister, she thinks, until she can find a place of her own. Maybe she will even go back to college, finish her nursing degree. She kept a little book, when she was a girl, on how to be a nurse. She laboured over drawings, labelling equipment neatly in pencil. Syringe, bandage, thermometer. She even wrote to hospitals, for brochures. It was the only thing she'd wanted to do when she grew up.

* * *

Shelley shakes her head, her eyes large and frightened. "In there," she points into the thick basket grass close to the water's edge. "I want to go home."

"Don't be a baby," Sal strikes out decisively, ignoring the sting of the grass blades against her bare calves. "Come on."

She can hear the rustle of Shelley following. She doesn't look back.

"Jenny Radcliffe said she once found a dead person down here," Shelley hisses. "A lady."

"Jenny Radcliffe's a liar."

She strides ahead, more confident than she feels, and stops just shy of where Shelley has pointed. Shelley peers over her shoulder as she parts the long grass with a stick. Sal's breath is in her throat, her stomach feels red-hot.

The skin is wrinkled and pruned, like her own after a bath. Dirty white fur sticks up in little spikes at the neck, as though someone has grabbed it by the throat and squeezed. A purpled tongue lolls out of the little blue-pink mouth, which is twisted into a shape almost human.

"It's a cat," Shelley edges out from behind her.

"Duh."

"Poor thing."

There is rot in the air. Sal looks into the creature's eyes. One has rolled up into the back of its head, the other stares straight through her. *Do you believe in God?*

* * *

Lisa's shoulder aches, and she can feel the bruise through her nightdress, like a stain. She knows better than to touch or even look at it. A wince, a sigh, these are all mortal slights on him. He lives in two bodies – the one that strikes her and the one that never would. It would kill him to admit that they were one and the same.

She pulls the sheets down on her side, and rearranges the pillows quietly, easing herself into bed. Beside her, Paul is already asleep. A three o'clock shadow blurs his jaw, and his eyes are puffy from crying. His features always settle disarmingly back into boyhood when he sleeps, and she loves him so fiercely in those moments that her heart feels too big for her chest. She will trail her fingers, sometimes, along the line where his hair curls around his ears, and he will smile in his sleep, and take her hand in his and not let go.

* * *

"We should bury it," Sal says, and Shelley nods.

They scoop the mud in thick handfuls, until it is under their nails and in their hair and on their faces. Sal nudges the cat's bloated body into the hollow with the stick. It slides down to rest in the dirty water, and they pat the mud back down quickly, trying not to look. The grave is too shallow, and they both pretend they cannot see the dirty white fur poking through. The sun behind them is crimson and gold; it is that moment before sunset where the light burns briefest and most bright.

The earth smells black and viscous, and the air is growing crisp.

* * *

He follows Lisa to the creek, pushes her face into the mud, she can taste hair and dirt, there is no air. She tries to say help or please, she tries to explain that she is leaving, that she is going to be a nurse, but the mud is thick in the back of her throat.

The rain is coming down in sheets now, and the sun is behind him so that she cannot see his face, can only feel his fingers gripping her, digging into the soft flesh of her arms. She writhes to free herself, wrenches her head to the side and feels the hair in his fingers tear out of her scalp. The grass is rough against her skin, the mud is under her nails. She kicks and connects with something – his face? His groin? – and he releases her with a grunt. She thinks she is saved, she thinks thank god, she tries to scramble to her feet but the ground is slippery and she falls on her back into the mud.

She sees him raise his hand, a rock in his fist, as she spits mud and muck and tries to scream.

The sun is sinking on the horizon as he brings it down, and the sky blazes red and gold.

* * *

Sal feels Shelley's cold little hand in her own. "Do you think it was her cat?" Shelley asks. "The lady Jenny Radcliffe saw?"

"I told you, Jenny Radcliffe made that up."

"Maybe we should say something, like at a funeral."

"Do you believe in God?"

Shelley shrugs, "I dunno."

In the distance, the kookaburras are laughing, their voices layered over one another, echoing across the creek.

By the water's edge the girls stand together, shadows gathering behind them, holding hands and thinking about dead things in the dark.

Protanopia

Jannet Xie

two goodbyes i wish i'd given him, one new beginning i saved for you:

1. i shouldn't have to beg for your love / only receive it when you glance at the bottom of an empty wine glass / when you slur your words together and somehow "I need you" is supposed to make up for forgotten love / when you look into my eyes and all i find is a whisper of lust and a blurry outline of a girl you wouldn't say a sober mouthful to.
2. you are a scar that will never fade – refuses to leave / like a dirty red stain from a blossoming woman's cotton / you took away the last piece of my softness so i'll carve my teeth into your heart as bitterly as you tore mine.
    (don't yell when i bite back)
3. you changed how i see the world grey-blue-dreary; shades of pale yellow, red no longer bears pain, but slowly seeps a deep ochre, who am i to say it's only me who suffers when you, who has suffered more, only serve to soften my edges; hold me down as i wail heaving sobs that turn into soft whimpers; i just want to be held close and closer by someone i trust with my whole being, my whole heart, until silence seeps into peace and i am no longer afraid of the aching dark when i know you are with me

Special Intimacies

Sally Chik

For Q.

There's something incredibly intimate
about the first time you fart
in your lover's presence,
a gross gateway to a jungle of special
intimacies reserved for accidental participants,
unashamed exhibitionists and lazy people,
a weird prologue to a romantic conversation
that somehow keeps going
it's no longer caring when the surprise
flatulence gets you while reclining
I catalogue your soft sounds as
you ready for the day:
the zip of the pants going up instead of
coming down for fun times,
a splash while you're brushing
your teeth that isn't the tap.

My favourite special intimacy is when we both
jump in the shower, after,
I look down to see two pale golden
streams swirling together down the drain
gross, you say
and I laugh.

Stitched

Jannet Xie

it's different with you
he made me wilt but you make me melt like soft buttery honey
there are no commands, no musts
he made me fracture until i mirrored his agony
but you stitch me with tender forgiveness and glue me with
    new beginnings
i unfurl my beauty and we stand side by side, hand in hand –
two broken beings; imperfectly whole at last.

Climax

Mabel G. Rytmeister

This girlish delight
at the curl of the hair
beneath his arm.
She trembles for the almostness
of this illusion.

She is looking for a love story,
so falls for the first boy she meets.
There is still no better way to say you love life
than to say you love another
so she does.
Casual words of careful selection,
the story comes crashing down
with his chivalrous rejection.
He is blasted away into pieces.

I plunge into the real.

This eternal internal narrator is a liar.
She writes this story,
the prologue to the next one,

the eulogy to the imaginations,
and the burials of the hypotheticals.
Such a great output of art from such a minute exchange.
Perhaps these are the multitudes we are said to contain.

Mio Babbino

Katherine Rosonakis

Prologue

The theatre has a familiar smell, a funny mix of colognes and wine-breath. And some high-class cleaning agent, only used in fancy places. One of those smells that is so subtle, you can hardly tell if you can smell it at all. The orchestra is tuning up, and this sound too, is familiar. The sound is nudging at something. A memory on the periphery, trying to come into view.

The curtains open. I feel my eyelids flutter and I peel forward in my seat. My eyes dart from fabric to prop to face. The costumes are spectacular, taking you to another time. The nineteenth century maybe? I'm not sure. I haven't read the program. But they are those old-style dresses: tight corsets, fine fabrics, with the hugely exaggerated bums and hips that poof out audaciously from the waist. The conductor is vigorous, his whole body in convulsions. But when I realise that I know the melody. That I can sing along. That's when I feel the tears.

I have always hated opera. It has been in our family lore for as long as I can remember. There were the adolescent early mornings, when Dad, half-deaf, would blast warbly voices through the house.

Mum and Dad met on the queue for the opera and were both opera fanatics. They both grew up working-class with aspirations for refined tastes. While I, on the other hand, grew up middle-class and had more bohemian aspirations. I wanted parents who listened to Jimi Hendrix and Janice Joplin. The type of music that sixties and seventies parents were supposed to listen to. The kind of Woodstock heroes of my long-haired-washed-up-drummer-high-school-music teacher. But my musical inheritance was opera.

Now here I am, in the Joan Sutherland Theatre. As a favour to a friend who recently had a tragic break up and needed someone to use the extra ticket. How long is it since I've been to the opera? I strain to remember. Was it adolescence? Maybe once in my twenties as a kind gesture to Dad?

As the drama unfolds on stage, it's like I'm him. Like I'm Dad as he was, as a young man. And I can see for the first time what moved him about these soaring violins, these over-the-top declarations of love in song. I feel the pang of it.

The strings start rising to that familiar melody again. I am singing along with Violetta in my mind. And it comes to me: his hand in mine, the warmth going from his body. The orchestra plays the refrain and I can see him: eyes closed, a faint smile, head swaying, moving in indiscernible shapes with the strings. And I wonder now what he saw behind his eyes, what pictures, what memories. I wonder who he thought of in that gentle reverie.

The injustice of it rises in me. I was too young to really know him. To really want to know him.

* * *

Seven

As a little girl, I thought that my dad was the tallest person in the world.

I can see him as I did then, coming home from work, his head almost touching the door frame. He has these skinny long legs that seem out of proportion with his broad shoulders and slightly protruding belly. His legs are tanned from weekends at the beach and they are covered in long curly black hairs that feel prickly to the touch.

As he comes through the door I see his massive smile, which raises his bushy moustache into his nostrils. I wonder what that must feel like, and it gives me a tickling sensation inside my own nose. Sweeping through the door he lifts me up onto his hip and kisses my cheeks. He groans every single time.

"Ooouuugh! You are too big for this! I'm not a young man you know!"

"Daddy! I'm not that big!"

I hook my legs and arms around him tightly, so that he can't put me down.

He has been trying to teach me Greek. But we never speak it enough for me to really pick it up. Mum is not Greek, and Dad's parents, my *Yia Yia* and *Papou*, died long before I was born. Dad was born in Australia, as were his two siblings, and our big family gatherings with the Greek side are all in English. There are just two uncles who were born in Greece. They have the best Greek of anyone, but I only ever hear snippets. They look so proud when us kids manage basic things like *Christos anesti* or *Kala Christougenna*. All I really know about the culture comes from food: red eggs, spanakopita, koulourakia, dolmades, tzatziki, souvlakia and baklava.

I learn the Greek alphabet at school. Dad sends me to the "native" Greek classes, but this feels silly because I speak little more Greek than the Italian, Vietnamese or Bengali kids. After dinner each night (after Dad does the washing up, because this is always his job), I curl up in his lap and we read Greek picture books together. He always says that I'm too big to sit in his lap, but he never makes me get off. The books we read are for much younger kids. I can sound out the words slowly, but sometimes I forget some of the Greek letters. After every page Dad will ask me what it means, and usually I just make it up from the pictures.

Whenever I get the chance, I make Dad tell me stories. Over dinner, on a long drive, while we wait in the car for my brother to finish his piano lesson. He tells me his favourite stories, of Ancient Greek myths, Shakespeare plays, operas and ballets. These become my favourite stories too, full of drama and larger-than-life characters.

One night, Dad takes me to see *Madame Butterfly*. It's probably not the first opera I was taken to, but it's the first that I recall clearly. I love the story: it feels exotic because it's set in Japan. And I think Madame Butterfly is so beautiful, in her red robe, with white flowers in her hair. I get all dressed up in my long purple velvet dress. I feel so elegant and grown up, and Mum even lets me wear some of her red lipstick. I have a small black handbag with a long gold chain, which my Aunty Trish gave me. I keep my Maltesers inside, that Dad buys me at the interval. When I eat them, back in the theatre, I take them out carefully one by one, so I don't annoy the other people with lots of rattling.

My Dad in 1993 with me and my brother, Andreas.
(Photo courtesy of the author).

Thirteen

Dad has this unique gift of making me want to die in a hole.
It's the worst when we're out in public. At restaurants and

cafés he's always asking them to turn the music down. And he doesn't ask politely either.

On one occasion, we go to a café in Bronte, just Dad and me. The waiter is stupidly hot, and I try hard not to stare. I can't help looking at the fit of his jeans, they are so tight you can almost see everything. He walks over to us and takes Dad's order, and his voice is velvety with the swagger of an unfamiliar accent. Some kind of European, maybe? While he's turned toward Dad, I'm trying my best not to look at the contours of his legs. Suddenly he looks at me with this smile you could die for and says, "And what would your granddaughter like?" I'm so mortified I can't speak. Dad looks amused and is about to intervene when finally I splutter, "Ah... chocolate milkshake." I had this whole plan to pretend that I drink coffee so I might seem older than I am. But I'm so startled by the whole thing that I order a milkshake like a little kid.

My Dad is *fifty-one* years older than me. Sometimes when I look at him, he seems ancient. He is fully bald on top with this strap of curly greying hair wrapped around his ears. He looks like an old man, and everyone can see it. It's even worse when he's out with just my younger brother, Andreas, who still looks like a little kid. Dre gets the grandad comment even more than me. I can see how he longs for the kind of Dad who will kick a ball with him. He is in total awe of our family friend's dad, Graeme. When we visit them in Orange, Graeme makes us a fireball, which is literally a ball of wool soaked in metho that we light on fire and kick to each other through the night. Graeme shows the boys how to use power tools and takes us all out for drives in the back of his ute. Last time we went to visit, he gave me my first driving lesson in the paddock. He said the boys were still too young. Dre was seething. When we visit Orange, Dre follows Graeme around like his border collie.

Dad was born in 1938, which puts him before the Second World War. He even has this story about the day the war ended. He was a little boy, and his uncle, a shop owner in Grenfell, threw lollies like confetti in the street. Dad is sixty-four, which makes him closer in age to my grandma, who is seventy-five, than to my Mum, who is forty-five. Sometimes I can't imagine what my Mum would see in such an old man, and such a grumpy and inflexible one at that.

Dad retired a couple of years ago, so he is always around at home, telling me to clean this, do that, turn the music down. He is so conservative that the things he says sometimes literally offend me. He voted for John Howard and can't even see what could be wrong with that. He likes saying semi-racist things, just to annoy me. Then afterwards, he'll say, "I knew that would get a bite!" and throw his head back in this evil laugh, like Greek Mr Burns.

Seventeen

I unlock the front door, itching to get out of my uniform, my armpits sweaty and prickling.

"Hello?" I call out, and there is a vague murmur from the back room. Dad is in that armchair again, elbow on the armrest, head resting in his hand. He offers a weak smile as I walk in. It's all aged him like a decade or so, since Mum left him. The edges of his mouth seem to droop lower and the frown lines look like a sculptor has scraped them in deep with a scalpel. It feels like years that he's been in this same chair, head in hands.

"How's ya day, Dad?"

"Oh, fine."

"Did you get up to anything?"

"Oh, you know ..."

"Okay. Well ... what should we have for dinner?"

"Oh ... umm ... isn't there some chicken curry in the deep freeze?"

The fucking chicken curry. One of three things he knows how to cook. And it's not really like he knows how to cook chicken curry either. It's basically just chicken, curry powder and onion cut way too big. I make a beeline for the kitchen and rifle about in the freezer as if I'm looking for the chicken curry, so that I don't have to think of anything else to say. Then I heap Milo in a glass, top it with milk, shake a generous serve of Jatz into a bowl and head upstairs. In my room I strip off the uniform and pull on trackies and a hoodie.

I still haven't told anyone at school that they separated. It happened almost three years ago now, and I just said nothing. How am I supposed to explain that Mum still lives here with us half the time? She moved into the single bed in the spare room upstairs, then half the time she lives in the apartment in Surry Hills with her new partner Ruth. All their furniture is red, and it looks gaudy. We all knew Ruth for several years as Mum's new best friend. They met singing in the Sydney Gay and Lesbian Choir, so we probably should have cottoned on sooner. But Ruth had a husband and kids as well. We'd even been on family holidays with them all. I don't think this eventuality occurred to any of us. Except Mum and Ruth, I guess.

They told me and Dre after Christmas, just before I turned fifteen. Dre sat in the corner of the room and begged Mum not to leave us. I will always remember the corners of Dad's mouth when they told us. They were so low on his face, almost like a cartoon sad face. I was sort of fascinated that a mouth could be that droopy in real life. A few months ago, I overheard Dad's cousin in the lounge with him, suggesting that maybe it would be better if my Mum moved out. Ever so gently, he asked Dad if he'd ever thought about speaking to a counsellor. My Dad just stopped talking to him after that. Never took his calls again.

Upstairs in my room, I pull Jeff Buckley out of his case, stick him inside my little blue stereo, skip to the second track and turn the volume right up. I flop onto the bed, stick my legs in the air and strum along messily, scream-singing: "Wait in the fire, wait in fire-iiii-iiii-iiiire!"

Twenty-One

I cycle down Avenida Chapultepec from uni to my white house on Calle Puebla, which snuggles between the two larger houses either side. I love the vintage bike which I found in my first weeks here at a sprawling second hand market and it astounds me that I've never commuted by bicycle in Sydney before. I love the little life I've built here in Guadalajara. I feel weightless.

That's been interrupted somewhat by Dad's visit. But thankfully he is staying in his own hotel, and I still have my uni classes to myself. During the commutes on my beloved bike, I can mull over all the new people and words and ideas. I can feel my Spanish improving every week – every day, even. When I first arrived classes were a blur, but now I understand seventy-to-eighty per cent. As I pedal, I try to think in Spanish, circling back over past conversations, imagining future ones. But even in my thoughts I still stumble over words, hesitate to find the right conjugation, pause on unknown vocab and make a mental note to look the word up later.

I know that I'm not quite fluent yet, but Dad has been so impressed with how I speak to people in the world. To waiters and taxi drivers and to Julio at the corner store. I think he's disappointed that I never learned Greek, but I can see he's also chuffed and bewildered that I speak this whole other language that he doesn't understand. He jovially tries out phrases here and there, but they are actually just bits of Italian that he knows from opera. He acts as if they are basically the same language, and something about his eagerness means that everyone seems to humour him anyway. I don't remember the last time I've seen him so cheerful. I try to focus on this, and not on all the parties I'm missing while he's here.

Twenty-Six

I am sitting in the office of the geriatrician with Dad, Dre and Mum. The doctor has asked Dad to bring his family along to the appointment, which doesn't seem like a good sign. Mum has offered to come along because she's an aged care social worker and understands more medical terminology than the rest of us. Dad doesn't seem to mind.

The geriatrician is an older man with a kind face and one of those South African accents that makes everything sound a little condescending. He tells us that Dad's brain scans show a stroke. A frontal-lobe stroke. That it's historical, but they don't know how historical. It might have happened a year ago, maybe two, maybe three.

"... This kind of stroke affects short-term memory and higher order functioning, things like decision making, sequencing tasks … This kind of stroke we often call a silent stroke, because the effects are sometimes subtler, and patients can cover them up well, and they usually have no insight into their own condition."

The doctor asks Dad to step out of the room, explaining that this is a standard part of his process, to speak to families alone. Dad obliges with little protest, which feels out of character, and then the doctor asks us if we have noticed any changes with Dad. We recount some vague observations about Dad being a little more forgetful in recent years, perhaps. We thought it was normal getting older stuff, we say weakly.

"Mmmm," the doctor nods and starts prattling on about My Aged Care and carer support and getting Dad a driving test, but I am hardly listening now. Guilt churns. I strain back, trying to think of when this memory thing might have started. But it's mostly blank. There is just him watching his DVDs, him doing the shopping, him making his porridge with cinnamon, him reading the newspaper. I can't put my finger on anything specific. He stopped swimming laps a while back, which he had done religiously three times per week since his twenties; maybe that should have been a sign. Honestly, I probably haven't been paying much attention.

"… do you understand? It might not be safe for him to drive or to cook by himself anymore."

The guilt slides quickly into despair. My dreams of working overseas start crumbling around me.

Thirty-One

It's funny how quickly it becomes normal to wipe his ass and change his nappy. The hospital calls them "pads", which seems like a stupid name because they are clearly just adult-sized nappies. I guess the older folks that still have enough marbles to care find it more dignified.

I sit with my friend Nicole in the sun on the deck, painting rocks. I paint trees and sunsets, while Nicole, who is more artistically inclined, devises strange mythical creatures with dolphin tails and lion faces. The baby monitor sits in front of me, so that I can watch Dad while he naps. I'm on the late afternoon shift now. I was on night shift last night, and I'm so drowsy now that I can hardly hold a conversation. Nicole puts on the kettle to make us lemongrass tea.

He is in end stage renal failure. This time, the hospital has given us a clear prognosis. He has one to three months to live. Dre and I joke that, knowing him, he will probably drag it on to six. We keep telling each other that if it gets too miserable, drags on too long – there's always a nursing home. But unspoken between us, we know it's a non-option. COVID has been tearing through the nursing homes, and so many old people have died alone. Worse, we would be petrified that *we'd* be the ones to give it to other people's parents and grandparents. On and off, during the lockdowns, visitors have been banned from nursing homes altogether. For the three weeks Dad was in hospital, we weren't allowed to visit him at all.

The sleep deprivation is the worst part. Dre and I have both stopped work to care for him. Between us we do a twenty-four-hour roster. Mum comes to help a few times a week as well, but Dre doesn't like leaving Mum alone with him, because she's not really strong enough if he fights or has a fall. When the hospital first told us he would need twenty-four-hour supervision, we didn't really believe them, but within a day or two at home, we could see they were right this time.

He is so unsteady on his feet, and his dementia is bad enough that he thinks he's fine to walk on his own. Every time he needs to pee, he shoots up quickly. He doesn't remember that we need to help him with toileting and bathing, so every single time he's angry and embarrassed anew. Sometimes, when he's particularly frustrated, he'll physically fight against us when we try to help him with toileting. Even though his muscles have wasted a lot, he is still six foot and surprisingly strong. Trust him to still be feisty on his deathbed. One time, he is so angry and determined that my brother has to forcibly restrain him when he tries to get up and walk to the bathroom.

Yesterday morning Mum came over and he was in a good mood. He's often in a good mood when she comes; I think he might have forgotten they're not still married. The three of us were in Dad's room. Mum sat on his wheelchair, I sat on the futon and Dad was sat up in his hospital bed, peering out the window to the street. Mum started singing *Yerakina*, an old Greek folk song that I knew vaguely from childhood. Dad joined in, word for word in a croaky voice. I found a harmony line, half making up the sounds of the words.

Epilogue

In the weeks after he dies, a new picture of him emerges. In small glimpses, the fuzzy picture of ancient film. Other people hand over memories like small gift-wrapped boxes and they wind tentacles around my own sense of him.

On the day of the funeral, I wear a black dress covered in white and yellow daisies. It is the first funeral I can remember where I don't worry about what to wear. This is *our* funeral and we set the tone. My friend Sarah, who used to work for a florist, has made a spray of native flowers, which sit atop the coffin, as they carry it from the hearse to the chapel. Mum has told us how Dad used to hate the garish flower arrangements at wog funerals.

Dre and I stand out the front of the chapel as people arrive; everyone hugs us, but the whole ritual feels awkward. It is the fourth death in around two years on the Greek side of the family. The fifth will come two months later. Dad's sister. There is a little shrine of funeral leaflets on the bookshelf at home. The big boisterous crowd that was the Greek side feels meek and emaciated. We are back here again, at Botany Cemetery, and I can't help but feel that it's a repeat of my aunty's funeral a year ago. We congregate in the same car park, and later we will have the same "Greek Feast" in the function room across the sea of graves. Except that my aunty was only fifty-two, the baby of her family; she passed after a decade with a rare cancer. Her husband is here, a humongous Aussie man of almost two metres; he looks gruff and hunched in his suit. Her sisters and brother are here too. All over again. Compounding. Surely remembering. There is not a hierarchy of grief, but also, there is.

In the week before the funeral, as I'm writing the eulogy, new stories emerge. The stories that I already know twist in shape and perspective, I see them suddenly as an adult. And there are new stories that I've never heard before. It is hard for me to remember my father, before he was cloaked in depression and then dementia. But there is another man in other people's memories, a man I saw glimmers of, but he always felt far away. A man who was passionate, intelligent, generous, vigorous and bright.

I sit with Mum before starting on the eulogy and she tells me again, the story of the day they met. It was 6 am in the middle of winter and they were number one and number three on the queue for opera tickets. Mum says she can't remember who the number two was, because she only had eyes for the tall, dark, lively and enthusiastic man who was head of the queue and knew absolutely everything about opera. They got to know each other slowly, as they were both quite shy. Dad would always say that before meeting Mum, he'd been a "confirmed bachelor". He'd been very unsure about having children, worried about being too old, but my mother had brought him around, in her gentle way. I'd seen him softened by her many times, seen him melt under her persuasion, and I guess that this was no different.

Mum says that Dad took to fatherhood straight away. There is a story she always loves to tell me on birthdays, about how I was tall from day one. She would say, "When you were born, your father was down there watching you come out, shouting up to me: It's still coming! It's still coming!" By all reports, Dad was a doting father. In the photos from when I was a baby, I can see the joy and pride in his face; this silly grin, hidden under an eighties moustache. I imagine that he didn't have the fear or insecurity of a young parent and was probably old enough to really appreciate the blessing of a child. By the time I was born he was well settled in a successful accounting career and in a beautiful house with a large garden that seemed endless, because it backed onto a golf course.

Days before the funeral, a few of my girlfriends came over to help digitalise the family photo albums for the slideshow. There is a staged black-and-white baby photo where Dad sits on a table in a little white dress and white booties; he has a mop of curly hair and huge ears which remained all his life.

There's also a family shot, taken on the rocks at Nielsen Park. A young teenage Dad sits in the front, knees curled to his chest, his face looks tiny peeping out from his large afro and huge ears. There is some budding fluff on his upper lip.

Choosing the songs for the funeral feels impossible. At home there are two entire floor-to-ceiling walls covered in his CD and record collections. Dad grew up with *Rembetica*, often called the "Greek Blues", a music of deep female vibrato and tinkling bouzouki melodies with an Arabic flavour. He first discovered classical music in high school, when he figured out that he could attend symphonies instead of doing weekly sport. From there he fell in love with opera and became absolutely obsessed for life. The love of opera led him to meet my mother, and to meet most of the major friends of his life. But he loved all classical music, some jazz as well as music from old films: Nelson Eddy and Paul Robeson.

While drafting the eulogy, I talk on the phone to Dad's elder sister, my Aunty Mary, who's in her late eighties. She brings some colour into the hazy ideas that I have of their childhood. This conversation will become unbearably precious because two months later, she will also be gone. I will be gutted that I didn't record the conversation. Or find time to have it in person.

She is the holder of the family stories. Here's some of what she tells me on the phone that day: Their parents, my *Yia Yia* and *Papou*, were among the earliest Greek migrants to Australia. They grew up in Smirni, and fled the *Katastrofi*, a war between Greece and Turkey. My grandfather could not get a visa for the United State of America, where his older brothers had gone, but did make it into Australia. A few years later my grandfather sent for the girl next door, literally his childhood neighbour, but she didn't want to go and so her younger, more adventurous sister was sent instead. The younger sister became my grandmother.

Dad and his siblings grew up in the family businesses: fruit and veg shops, a milk bar and eventually they added a lolly counter. One of the favourite childhood stories that Aunty Mary reminded me of was the time that some young Aussie customers were going out hunting and my grandfather told them to bring him back a rabbit, because he knew the Greek way to cook it with all these delicious spices. Instead of the expected hunted rabbit, the boys appeared with a live pig, who then lived for many happy months tied to the hills hoist in the backyard. One day, they heard a spine-tingling scream from the lady next door. The pig had escaped and come up behind her while she was doing laundry. Eventually, having had enough of the pig and its antics, my grandmother served it up for dinner and my young father looked across the table to everyone in disgust and said, "How can you eat that!? You cannibals!"

For the funeral service, we decide against the whole Orthodox thing. We are not really sure what Dad would have wanted. He was not really religious, just Greek Orthodox by culture. Instead of the priest or the rituals, we fill the service to the brim with words and music. But as a nod to tradition, we decide on burial rather than cremation, even though it's three times the price, and it pains us to give any more money to the funeral industry. We do know that Dad (or at least earlier versions of him) was attached to this particular aspect of tradition. Greeks are not cremated; Greeks are always buried.

We ask Trish to speak at the funeral. I call Trish my aunt, even though she is actually my first cousin. In the past two years Trish has lost her father, her husband, her baby sister and in two months, she will lose her mother, Aunty Mary. She wasn't able to speak at any of the other funerals and we are so moved that she agrees to speak at Dad's.

For Trish, Dad was the young, adventurous, cultured uncle. Trish was born when my Dad was just seventeen, his first niece. Dad used to take her and his other nieces to the ballet as children, and this was a tradition they continued until the year he died. This was huge for Trish because she became a dancer and later a dance teacher. While his older sister Mary married at nineteen, and started a family, Dad travelled the world and sent back letters squished to the brim with facts about the history and museums and ruins.

In 1963, at age twenty-four, Dad set off for London: a six-week trip on a huge ship, the *Oriana*. Trish says in her eulogy: "In one of his letters I recently found from London, he wrote that during his first nine days there he attended seven plays, four operas, one ballet and four art exhibitions." He lived in London for four years, and he was in heaven, seeing some of his heroes perform live: Arthur Rubinstein, Rudolf Nureyev and Maggie Smith. He was also the first to reconnect with the relatives in Greece who the family had not seen for a generation. In my favourite story of all, he took a six-month trip in a kombi van with his friend Hugh, visiting every country in Europe, including all those in Eastern Europe, behind the Iron Curtain. While I was writing my eulogy, Aunty Mary reminded me of a story where Dad nearly got them both arrested in one of the communist countries: he was taking photos illegally, and then he argued with a gun-wielding communist policeman until they gave his camera back.

As we walk from the cars to the burial spot, we play the aria, *Softly Awakes my Heart*, sung by his beloved Lauris Elms. We selected the burial spot days before. It's in the Greek section, close to a stream and some large trees, and a stone's throw from the graves of his own parents and his brother-in-law, Uncle Ross. My brother Dre, his three best friends and two of our cousins carry the coffin over the fresh dirt. The sight of this ritual, the brawn and the solemnity, has gotten to my aunties and uncles: they are sobbing. The final song, a Rembetica classic called *To Minore Tis Avgis* (Dawn in a Minor Key), plays as the coffin is lowered, and in my memory the scene feels almost comically operatic. We scatter white petals over the coffin as the anguish in the bouzouki melody builds, as Haris Alexiou's sultry contralto sends involuntary tingles. And I know that somehow he's showing me that sometimes, life really can imitate opera.

My Dad (right) in the late 1950s with his brother-in-law, Ross. (Photo courtesy of the author).

A Ghost's Rumination

Maysa Amy Sarkis

I have stopped tumbling
and now flow freely

Replacing tangibility,
embracing impalpability

Rather than being,
I watch and observe
memories and predictions

These moments flutter by, quick fire
blurs I am unable to touch
but understand them all –
the pain, the pleasure, the love, the loss
moving between each instant,
collecting the remnants
and coalescing

No longer is there a:

then
and now,

before
and after,

prologue
or epilogue.

I am everything, everywhere, every time

The transcendental phantasmic
discarnate that escapes shackles and
chains

Free to be
Omniscient
Omnipotent
Omnipresent
Forevermore

The Philippine Eagle

Harold Legaspi

A dark face stares at its fate
Far, through the thick jungle, it woos
The solitary way.

It stoops upon its nest
Heavy legs hooked
By sharp, attacking claws.

It bites a snake into half
Eats a monkey raw
Drinks fresh water, preys on flying lemurs.

Feathers form a mane-like crest
A high-arched beak, bluish grey
Spreading its wings to balance the easy breeze.

Whistling to the golden light
Kuk-kuk-kuking to the pulse of skies
Silence, magenta jungle eyes.

The bird is not a bird, but a species hunted, endangered –
It soars weeping jungles in the islands
And whirls the measured clouds.

Revived through song, twisted oaks
Accompanied by feet
A modest house in every tree – pride, aristocracy!

Ágila's flight is agile
Háribon's flight is fiery
Banog's flight is fearless, sheer beauty!

Shimmering Tears: Unveiling the Teardrop

Janika Fernando

Foreword

This is a fictional reimagining. Prince Vijaya, upon discovering Sri Lanka and the inhabitants of the Veddas, planned to assimilate them to the ways of the Sinhalese and Tamils, including the children. They invaded the village by crossing the bridge and then built a stronger steel marvel. The Veddas lost their customs. Eventually, the jungle and the village became the place where the Mahiyangana Raja Maha Vihara temple was built. Only a few Veddas remain.

Prince Vijaya

Water churned, rocking the small boat violently. They struggled to move in the knee-deep water and avoided slipping off the boat. The prayers they prayed to Buddha could not save them from such horror, no matter what they thought. It was clear that the thunderstorm thought otherwise. With every rock, the boat was tossed like a cork on the waves. The thunder continued until Prince Vijaya[1] and his descendants believed the end was near. The numb perception pierced him as if it were a dagger, and he drowned in it. All his descendants were pushed deep into the Indian Ocean by the tide.

Vedda

Against the clear river below, the bridge arched elegantly with high sides. The river was serene and peaceful but underneath lay a different story, a story that only a true Vedda[2] could comprehend. There were stories forbidden to children under the crystal water, savage currents that would speed away anyone who dared disturb them. Only this bridge could cross the deadly river. They had built it. The Ancient men. They had built the bridge to access the land by gathering wood from the trees and tying it with coconut palm rope.

Crossing the bridge was the only way the Vedda could reach his village and the dense, susurration of leaves in the forest ahead. The village itself seemed to be shrouded in obscurity. Shivers swept down his spine as he sensed evil emanating from the area. He was also uncertain about the accuracy of the ripples he read in the river as fortunes. He believed as any Vedda would in Animism and the power of nature. There was a special connection in worshipping spirits, where the spirits of the water were speaking to aid him in the journey through life.

Their mother, the land, had given them solace for all these generations.

---

1   Prince Vijaya – name of a legendary king of Sri Lanka – 6 BCE.
2   Vedda – term that refers to the Indigenous people of Sri Lanka.

"Eththo!"[3] he called, as the village chief sauntered towards him. He adjusted his posture as he remembered he was in the presence of a god-like figure. It was necessary to maintain such formality. The bridge rattled with coloured locks bearing the names of the Kekulo[4] and Kekule.[5]

"Esamaya[6], Thisa Haroiy," the Vedda said.

Thisa Horoiy's gaze drifted to the river below them as he asked, "What do you see?"

The Vedda shook his head and stared at the water. "Nothing, Thisa Haroiy, nothing I don't know of," he said. Truth was not something he wanted to hide, but the truth he saw in those waters created barriers of fear and confrontation. Until those fears and doubts formed a bridge, the Vedda would keep them locked up in his heart.

"I must be informed if you see anything. It is our duty to protect the village, yes?" Thisa Haroiy asked.

"My duty is to protect this village, Thisa Haroiy," the Vedda promised.

With that, the Vedda left his Thisa Haroiy to ponder the safety of the village. As he left, his eyes looked into the river's gaze, an immense feeling emerging. Despite the beauty it reflected, the river could not be trusted. The Vedda knew that danger was slowly approaching the island that they had known all their lives.

---

3   eththo – Vedda term for people within the tribes, slang for what they called each other.
4   kekulo – Vedda term for boy child.
5   kekule – Vedda term for girl child.
6   esamaya – Vedda term that means "yes".

Prince Vijaya

A sudden shiver spread throughout the entire earth. Vijaya shuddered, shaking his shoulders after emerging from what he thought would have been eternal sleep. The surface on which he lay was shaped like a teardrop. But he didn't know that. Nobody knows that. Not yet, at least. His descendants had not come with him.

The island seemed strange yet intriguing to the mind, body and soul. His mind wandered to the possibility of building a temple here. His cascade of dark hair waved endlessly as he planted footprints into the soft golden sand with his bare feet. A sweet, cold breeze drifted from the now gentle waters washing the shore. Awestruck at the beauty surrounding him, he inhaled a deep breath and exhaled. The island looked like it was made of gold.

The dazzling blue of the ocean shimmered in the sunlight that surrounded the island, the immaculate golden beach, the greenery of the forest in the distance. His mind was filled with thoughts of soaking up richness, of creating his own dynasty so he could worship Buddha along with many Sinhalese and Tamils.

This is what Prince Vijaya believed Buddha had led him to, and he could not contain his excitement. His people could preach and live Nirvana's simple way on this island of renewal. The Sinhalese and Tamils would soon converge on this land, and soon it would be a hub of activity.

His gaze flickered back to his descendants who had not yet awakened on the shore. Turns out they were not lost in the depths of the Indian Ocean. It was not his intention to make them shiver and bother them during this quest. Vijaya had a great appetite to roam, reign, explore and discover the depths of this great island, to map out the temples that would become sacred to those back home in north-west India. After plunging into the abundant greenery behind the shore, he did not even glance back.

Vedda

"Where are you going, Apache?" the young Vedda asked, tugging at his father's scratchy beard while watching him rummage through their straw hut. He had just come back from visiting the chief.

"To hunt, we need food," the Vedda told his son, tying a barkcloth around his waist.

"Can I come?"

The Vedda patted his son's shoulders gently and chuckled as he said, "Kekulo, it would be better if you stayed here. There are all kinds of evil out there."

"What kind of evil?" his son asked curiously.

"I don't know yet, but don't worry, I'll be back and I'll keep you safe," the father assured.

"Bring me back a coconut palm frond, Apache."

"I will bring you back one of the finest," his father affirmed.

After kissing his son, the Vedda slung his bow and arrow over his shoulder, slipped out of the straw covering of the hut and into the open, smelling the sweet and musky aroma of the forest.

Outside the hut, he greeted the other Veddas, "ye, Eththo!" They cautioned him to be careful.

The Vedda nodded and slowly crossed the bridge, the locks shaking with every step. These locks belonged to children. His face shone with an appreciative smile as he saw the name, Kekulo, encircled in a love heart. They knew how lucky they were to have children. That was the second best of the gifts they were most thankful for. The island, of course, came first, as it was the essence of how they lived.

A Vedda would never take and go. A Vedda would return to nurture every delicacy of tree and water that extended island life's inexhaustible variety. Coconut palms were the only way to create huts and the only way to make rope for the bridge that connected them to their means of survival. There they are. Hot and still, the forest's myriad of noises became ancient music to the Veddas' eardrums. No breeze stirred and the silence brought serenity and peace, as did the river.

The Vedda climbed the tree and used the sharp edge of an arrow to cut down one coconut palm frond before shimmying back down. As he had already fulfilled his son's wish, he only required venison meat and firewood to complete his hunt. Just then, a sound pierced his eardrums. An animal? No. He shook his head, it cannot be. The sound echoed evil, just as he had sensed at the bridge.

Prince Vijaya

Coconut palms loomed above, failing to block the heat and humidity. The aura of the jungle, of a million wild souls, was as tangible as water when bathing. It was another sense, one that came to the heart rather than the eyes, as rich as they were.

Brutal branches bruised Prince Vijaya's dark, tanned skin. Teardrops of sweat trickled down his cheeks as he trod. The virescent hues were in the foreground, the background and as high up as you could see. Mosquitoes, leeches and stinging ants had attacked him, of course. But the snakes and scorpions did him no harm at all. His arms and legs were swollen, but that did not stop him from cutting his way through the suffocating vines and the vast canopy of leaves. He found what he needed to find.

His moral compass was as true as the ten virtues Buddha had enlightened him with. The jungle had a voice of its own. Prince Vijaya followed nature's symphony; the sudden screech of a parrot, the flicker of a monkey swinging on branches.

Deeper and deeper he waded into the land, further away from the shore where his descendants had hopefully awakened by now.

His foot tangled with some shrubbery and he stumbled over. His mouth was full of the virescent leaves that the ground had given him. As he struggled to steady himself, his eyes widened. A thin line between awe and fright emerged. Just a few metres ahead of him was a wild man. The wild man was elegantly poised with an arrow nocked to his bow. There was nothing covering him except the barkcloth tied around his waist. The wild man's skin was darker than his was. Above all, he seemed ready to shoot that arrow and kill him.

But he couldn't really, could he? He is one of us, right?

Vedda

Frightened and bewildered, the Vedda decided to close in with his bow and arrow as if a predator about to pounce on its prey.

This man's shirt is ripped. His face is so beautiful despite him cowering in fear, but who is he? Eththo? No, his skin is lighter than mine. How strange.

He had to protect his village. He didn't know what this man knew about the place, let alone how he found it. However, he knew this was what the river had foreseen. Evil had come from the waters. As the Vedda held his weapon, his eyes met the distant shore where a broken boat was lying recklessly. How many others are there?

This boat and its evil stench last for miles. Thisa Haroiy would know by now. His thoughts raced again.

The Vedda felt that the man did not have good intentions and was still a threat even though he was on the floor. There was no way he was a brother. His son was waiting for him to return. The coconut palm frond he had collected was now down on the ground and more lay high up in the trees.

He had to alert Thisa Haroiy. The time had come, the good had to face the evil that lurked on the island. He had to run back and rattle the locks. The shore was no longer safe. What were they looking for? Coconut palms? The man was lying on the floor in what seemed like agony, but if he was in agony after falling, what would the Veddas have to face?

Prince Vijaya

Holding the bow and arrow steady, the wild man stayed in that position. The silence was so surreal that, as the cocoon of noises grew faint, Prince Vijaya both heard and felt a teardrop from above land on his forehead. He shivered again, as his life flashed before his eyes.

"maṭa anukampā karanna!" Prince Vijaya cried out for mercy.

He should not have to die so soon. At least, not by the hands of some wild man who appeared almost naked by the eye. He was a prince for Buddha's sake, destined for greatness on this island. To rule and roam.

The wild man had no reaction, no response, no reply to the mercy he had asked for. Can he not understand me? Is he not one of us? Is he a Buddha follower? These questions swirled in his mind, unanswered continuously.

As if his prayers to Buddha had been answered, the wild man gently lowered his bow and arrow. His eyes were still fixed on Prince Vijaya as if he were a piece of venison ready to be cooked. Their eyes locked with such intensity that Prince Vijaya remained intrigued to learn his story. But the trance broke and the wild man retreated, the barkcloth around his waist riding up as he ran to who knows where, leaving Prince Vijaya in the heart of the jungle inhabited by wild men.

This wild man, standing in my way, my way of the temple. I will teach him how.

hatching

Jem Rice

The bushes are cut
by a hand I never see
into neat little purse shapes
uncanny in their charm

These days are a project of knowing
I can stop to note a place
in all its facets:

here cockatoos flock to the housing estate
and windows are left open like cameras
and ground is shored up
in yet another
        name

Two years ago I walked this park
in a line as aimless as it was
straight,
my thoughts spider eggs
finding crevices and
settling

Today I'll let them hatch
before I hunger –

These days are a project of knowing
I can stop to help the others
turn the soil:

it's easy to think yourself
the only witness,
harder to listen and wonder
whether they, too,
watch English roses wilt
in the sun of calm November

These days are a project of knowing
we can stop keeping safe our forgettings
and learn what we have to remember:

Losing The Blue Lotus: A New Year

Janika Fernando

It happened. Like every year, it happened for a good reason, to bring prosperity, hope and positivity. *Aluth Avurudu*. Sri Lankan New Year. There would be a long night before the New Year rolled around.

The village was cloaked in darkness, and all that could be heard were the sounds of her in the kitchen. It was common for her to spend hours in the kitchen, cooking while her lover slept. Deep-frying *kokis* were her task: the crunchy deep-fried snack made with rice flour that looked like milky batter, shaped like a butterfly ready to flutter away.

Getting the *aasami* right was another culinary battle worth winning. Usually pink or brown, the gooey-sweet toffee-like confections were honeycomb shaped and covered in caramelised sugar syrup. Her batter was made with rice flour, *kurundu* – a cinnamon-flavoured coconut milk – and sugar. Once it had been fried a second time, she would sugar it. She stirred it continuously over a large pot until it was gooey, separated the oil from the mixture, and then sliced it into pieces.

For the *Dhana* the following day, she was making a rich saga of deliciousness. Temple almsgiving would not be complete without the traditional *kiribath* and *luni miris*. In the morning, she would steam raw rice with coconut milk and a hint of salt over a sputtering open fire, then pour it out onto a large tray and cut it into diamonds. A *luni miris* would be prepared along with it. The paste was prepared with dried chillies, salt, onions and dry fish.

There is nothing like the fusion of creamy rice and spicy *lunis muris*. There can't be anything more Sri Lankan than the food this New Year, with these sweets, bananas, *kiribath* and *luni muris*. In the teardrop-shaped country they called home, she and her love had grown up celebrating Sri Lankan New Year this way.

* * *

She wore her classic white dress with flowy sleeves made from batik fabric, and next to her, he wore a white sarong and shirt. She packed the food she had prepared for the *Dhana*. It was a long drive to the temple, and this time of year it would be packed. The long drives meant something to her, this sense of spiritual connection, not just because they were both Buddhists, but because they both loved their culture and everything that unified them. Like the golden centre of a lotus flower, this sense of understanding and love was unparalleled. It bloomed during the day and had star-shaped flowers, as if it could predict fate and destiny for them both.

After they reached the temple, he stepped out of the car first, and opened the door for her to jump out of the Jeep. Once they had taken all the food to the temple, they held hands and walked further and further, admiring the rich tapestries and the carvings on the temple walls. Lotus drawings had always intrigued her; the golden centre and blue petals capturing her attention. They glowed for her, and she looked beside her and saw another pair of eyes glistening too. It was him. It was his love.

Visiting this place had a special meaning for her. Something about it just felt right. Someone, rather. She craved something beyond the Bo tree, beyond the white abode, beyond the traditional flags and beyond the statues of Buddha, though it was always near her. When they entered the sacred place, the wide entrance, where only Buddha's eyes watched from the statue above, her love's brown calloused hand gripped hers. *This is home.*

* * *

Ceremony had begun in the room. Their eyes remained closed. As the monk in the orange saffron robe spoke, he instructed their hearts to look within, seeking wisdom and hope. Her hands were held with a soft grip, making her feel at ease. A smile spread across her face. Inhale. *The lotus can be found within yourself if you look within. In there, you will find peace of mind.* Exhale. The moment she opened her eyes, it was as if his eyes had never left hers.

When the ceremony was over and they had finished meditating, they went to the hall where the food was laid out and began preparing it together for the people to eat, especially the monks, as well as all their aunts and uncles, who reminded them of their parents in many ways. The night before, she had prepared a feast of the finest foods. As the aunties, uncles and monks tucked into the food, her husband, grateful that she had made it all, kissed her hand and never left her side. The *luni miris* and *aasami* were made with the right amount of sweetness and spice and were both complimented by the people. She smiled. He smiled.

* * *

Sitting on the swing near the hall, which was made especially for the little monks, reminded them much of their childhood, and gave them a sense of peace. He fed her pieces of *kiribath* and *luni miris* from his paper plate. She always liked when he fed her, even though she didn't like chilli much. It felt good to eat with him. The two of them chuckled when he missed and bits fell to the floor, and she would feed him back in return. When he thought of wasting food, he would roll his eyes. Because wasting food was a bad thing, and Ammi and Thathi knew they would both say the same thing. They laughed and ate the rest, and by the end, every crumb was gone from their plate. Empty.

* * *

At temple, another way to ease the mind was circling the Bo tree, venerating in the sacred presence of Buddha. Tall in nature, its virescent leaves extended over the branches. They gathered little, black clay pots and filled them with water. In tandem, they carried the clay pots around the Bo tree ten or so times until each felt fulfilled for the richness of their lives. Being together made it richer but having their culture's life and blood made it grand. All together.

   She noticed something poking out of the tree after they finished wandering around it. A small message was written in Sinhala wishing a happy New Year, while another seemed to plant a small blue flower, with a golden centre. *The Blue Lotus.*

She felt him reach out to grab the lotus from the tree and closed her eyes as he placed it in the strands of her long, black hair.

"You are the flower now, dear," he said.

Laughter echoed through the temple, a happy memory of love. A love that would last as long as the lotus did, for it symbolised hope, purity, a rebirth, a sunrise she never wanted to end.

* * *

They had just returned from the temple. It was a long drive back home. They had all the empty plates and boxes in the back, along with *kawm* sweets, coconut cake and some leftover *kiribath*. They decided to make another *luni miris* when they got home, so they could eat some for dinner the next day and enjoy the sweets for dessert. He could not keep his eyes on the road; he kept one eye on his lotus and the other on the road as they drove past the temple and all the way home. With every smile she returned, he knew. He waited. He hoped, and was always patient with her.

The night was calm. In the kitchen, she hummed a happy melody, much like the smooth tunes they would sing together over the radio. It was melody of love. While she made the luni muris for their left-over *kiribath*, he came up behind her and wrapped his arms around her. Although he was tired from driving and her muscles ached from the night before, being in his embrace made everything so much more meaningful. As long as he was by her side, she felt loved, and nothing could ever rob her of that feeling. Playfully teasing her, he grabbed the blue lotus and placed it exactly where she had left it in her hair.

"You're never gonna let go of this flower," he teased.

"Why is that?" she asked in frustration and annoyance, snapping at him with her fingers and almost hitting her head with the clay pot rolling pin she was using.

"This lotus is one of a kind, and it will last forever in your hair ... and in your hear –" He staggered a little, hand on chest, and her whole being stopped.

After opening and closing her eyes, she awoke to reality, rushed before he could fall, and sat him on a chair. In her mind, she could make it better. But she couldn't. She stayed by his side that night, lying in his arms and holding his hands as his eyes closed. Fearing that his eyes would stay closed, she was afraid to close her own. He reassured her that he would always be there for her, and kissed her head that night and told her they would close their eyes together.

* * *

She opened her eyes the next morning to see sunlight beaming through the window and casting shadows on their faces. As she waited for him to wake up, she nudged him. She was sure he had a pulse, she had felt it. Again, she tried, splashing him with water. But the lotus flower in her hair was rotten, a brown colour, and no longer glowing like she wanted it to. It had been tossed on the floor, falling apart and fading. He was gone.

* * *

Three years had passed.

This time, it wasn't like every other year.

Different things happened.

This gesture was full of love, hope and prosperity. *Aluth Avurudu.*

The night was long, but her delicate hands brought her ever closer to him and the experience they shared. Like always, she made all the sweets and food. At her side was a miniature version of him, watching her and trying to eat free samples, which made her laugh. In every way, he resembled him, from his walk to his speech. Their *putha*. It had never been more important to her to be with him at this moment. As if he were his father, he was so reminiscent of him. Whether framed by her bedside or living in reincarnation like their son, this portrait wouldn't fade.

It was her turn to drive them to the temple. The food had been packed. She opened the door for her son, and they unloaded the food together and walked side by side, his little hand gripping hers with a sense of tenderness and sweetness that made her heart melt. Home.

While she engaged in the meditation and ceremonies, his son joined her but never closed his eyes, keeping them open, looking at his amma, just as all sons do; because there is always a special connection with your mother that cannot be denied. After the ceremony, her son helped his amma set the table and prepare the meal until he ran to play by the swing. Swings always drew his attention, and Amma smiled.

"*Ane, duwa*, how are you doing?" The aunts condescendingly asked.

"I am fine," she replied, smiling with reassurance. The others exchanged smiles too, while others whispered as if she were dying. It was not that she was dying, but rather that she was living. Does it feel like living without him? Not at all. He was living within her.

With her paper plate of *kiribath* and *luni muris*, she fed her son, much to his reluctance – he just wanted to play – but he eventually gave in and the two sat on the swings together. After filling their clay pots with water, they walked around the Bo tree with their pots. As they were about to leave after circling quite a few times, her son pointed and yelled.

From the tree, he saw something emerging. He begged Amma to get it for him, and she did. She held a blue flower with a golden centre in her hands. It glowed again. Taking her son's hand, she placed it in his.

"The flower is a blue lotus. You'll always keep it close to your heart. Just like *him*," she replied confidently. She hugged her son as tears streamed down her cheeks in joy and sadness. He hugged her back. As a gust of wind swept through the temple, the Bo tree's leaves shook gently, offering a calm and peaceful breeze. It was as if he had never left. This New Year, the Blue Lotus remains. As it always has.

The Waterbearer

Holly Ford

The room is infused with the glow of possibility. Sand particles stir, set adrift by the warm breeze ambling through the window. Everything holds its breath: the closet, the walls, the cracked, crooked mirror. They all wait for the boy to awaken, for the world to change. What lives will transform, what ripples emerge, from an ordinary open window?

The boy moves! His sleepy eyes scrunch against the glow of the sun. Dragging himself from his foetal position he reaches up and swings the window shut with a groan, halting the dance of the sand.

Emerging from his room, the boy sits on a small, rickety stool at a small, rickety table. On the front doorstep, his father sweeps away the sand that invaded during the night. Sweat already stains his ratty shirt as the hours leak towards the hot, sticky part of the day. His mother has left for work. She will not return until evening, but her absence will be made up for by her wages: a full jug of water. They are more fortunate than most.

Yesterday's wages are on the table. The jug is almost empty. The boy grasps its handle, ready to claim the last silty dregs. But as he lifts the jug, something cool dribbles down his hand. The boy's brows knit and his mouth falls open. The jug is not empty ... it is full.

Summoned by his child's expression, his father abandons the broom. He cannot fathom the clear droplets spilling over the rim, trickling down the curved side and tracing tracks through the dirt on the boy's hand

Brow still rigid with confusion, the boy reaches for his cup. At his touch, as though a seam has split at its base, the cup fills with clear, unfathomable water. A grin spreads across his father's face. He knows what this means. Just to be sure, he takes the cup from his son. In three gulps, the water is gone, but the grin has endured, even deepened.

It only takes a few steps for his father to reach the door. Hands on either side of his mouth, his yells reverberate off the sandy street. They echo off stone walls, absorbing into ears only to reappear on dry, cracked tongues. As the cries of "Waterbearer" spread, they summon a crowd to the doorstep. All have tingling tongues; some have jingling pockets. The latter is all that matters to the boy's father. Naming his price, coins are raised next to buckets and boy becomes saviour.

* * *

The Waterbearer, now a gangly youth, pulls at his collar as he waits. He wipes the sweat meandering down his neck and curses the sunlight filtering through the tent. The inviting glow that it casts fails to distract from the stifling heat. More stifling are the rumbles of the crowd outside. The voices blur together and seep into the tent, guaranteeing long lines and thirsty customers.

Through the din of the crowd, the Waterbearer hears his father summon the next customer. The sharp clinking of coins pierces the white noise and the tent flap is lifted. A woman, eyes downcast, shuffles inside. The Waterbearer can't help but lean back at the sight of her flaking, sunburnt skin as she places her bucket on the table before him.

Retreating a few steps, the woman wobbles to her knees. She winces as the sand coating the floor grinds into her legs. The Waterbearer rolls his eyes. He brushes his fingers against the bucket's rim. It takes only seconds to fill and overflow.

At his word, the woman – eyes still fixed to the floor – rises and hefts the bucket into her arms. She does not spill a single drop.

When she is finally gone, the Waterbearer meets the eyes of his father who holds the tent flap open. His father winks and shakes a bulging pouch. The Waterbearer winks back and smiles.

* * *

The Waterbearer, now a man, stumbles through the dunes. His scarf is pulled tight, shielding his face from the sun which sits two finger-widths from the horizon, teasing ever towards the relief of night. No matter how well the scarf protects his skin, the Waterbearer's eyes are left to the sun's mercy. And it is not merciful. He squints against the glare of the sand, raising his head to survey the horizon. Disappointed, the Waterbearer walks onwards.

When his father strode into their villa that morning, neither the Waterbearer nor his mother could have guessed his news. When he divulged, silver forks clattered to plates and servants were ushered from the room. The conversation that ensued was swift and decisive. If rumour, a day wasted. If real, a day in exchange for eternity. He must go alone – he couldn't risk another claiming this gift. And if he left now, he would arrive before any who had overheard.

Mounting the next dune, the Waterbearer grasps his waterskin and takes a long, gluttonous swig. By the time he ties the skin back to his hip, it is once again swollen with water. He sighs at the coolness that emanates from it but is quickly distracted by the outline of trees on the horizon.

Night has arrived by the time the Waterbearer reaches the oasis. Palm trees loom and the crisp chirping of crickets emanates from the darkness. The only illumination comes from the window of a small shack, nestled between two palms. The golden square draws the man near, promising warmth, comfort and so much more. This is the place.

After knocking, the Waterbearer is greeted by a stranger. His skin is smooth and unblemished, but there is a weight behind his eyes that hints at wrinkles unseen. With a resigned sigh, the stranger steps aside. No words have yet been exchanged. There is only one reason for such a visit. If the rumours are true, that is. Gesturing towards the floor, the stranger and the Waterbearer sit. Only by descending into this lower realm does the Waterbearer feel fit to break the silence.

"Rumour has it you are a god."

The stranger's reply is calm and unsurprised. "One with no power apart from longevity."

"Is that not just a curse?" The Waterbearer hopes this does not sound rehearsed.

The stranger chuckles. "I find myself thinking that rather often, young man. Often enough to start thinking that another might be more worthy of my gift." He raises an eyebrow. "I may even have taken steps to ensure his arrival."

"So *you* started the rumour?" The Waterbearer abandons his script. "Then, is it true that you wish to give up your immortality? To give it away?"

His triumph is near.

"That's what I told your father yesterday," the stranger says with a wink.

There is no need to prolong their conversation. A consensus is reached and they rise. The stranger looks older than he had on the Waterbearer's entry. Something in those old eyes has bled into his countenance. There is only enough time to notice this detail before the stranger lifts his hand to cover the Waterbearer's forehead as though taking a child's temperature. The discomfort of the clammy touch is quickly eclipsed by an intense pull inside the Waterbearer's chest. It feels as though a stylus is inscribing onto his very soul, overwriting the original script, making room for something new. He cries out and his vision fades.

The sun has risen by the time he wakes. Its rays tentatively enter the hut, casting a warm filter over the sparse furniture. There is no sign of the stranger. He is gone.

The Waterbearer rises from the floor and replays the events of the night. The corners of his mouth creep upwards as his memory returns. His excitement builds and his hands go to the back of his head. He spins. He yells. He cries. Laughs. Gasps. He is not just a saviour; he is now a god. Eternal. Endless!

He pictures his father's face as he tells him the news. Pictures him letting out that deep-bellied laugh and embracing his son. He pictures the people, with their deep pockets and purses, celebrating long into the night. The servants will bow. The people will cheer. The water will flow. Endlessly.

There is no need to worry now.

Only when his initial excitement has settled does the Waterbearer notice his thirst. His jubilations have tired his voice and parched his throat. A jug rests on a table in the corner, promising sweet relief. The Waterbearer grasps its handle and ...

... nothing.

The jug remains empty. His breath catches and his left hand joins his right on the handle. There is no gentle tinkle, no gain in weight, no water at all. He stands frozen. His mind swirls as his father's laugh turns into a cry and the people's cheers become slurs.

His hands start to quiver.

They will revile him, curse him, scorn him. And then they will forget him.

He does not remember crumpling to the floor. His body rocks as he clasps the jug to his chest. He cradles it, breathing in heaving, guttural sobs. The water he so desperately seeks leaks mockingly from his eyes as he realises that he is the Waterbearer no more. He is just Endless.

* * *

His scarf wrapped tightly around his face, the Endless Man keeps to the edges of the crowded street. Where once this piece of cloth protected him from the sun, now it protects him from the stifling gazes of others. But in the end, it is the scarf itself that gives him away: too fine, too well embroidered. Such a broadcast of wealth draws beggars near, until a faint spark of recognition in one ripples outwards to encompass the rest.

At the news of his return, men and women run into homes and emerge with buckets and jugs. They crowd around the Endless Man, pushing and jostling so that his vision is filled with a sea of grimy faces. They hold their buckets and coins out to him, but he has nothing for them. He brushes off their pleas and walks onwards. The crowd trails desperately behind, scrambling for his attention, his blessing, until one woman – more brazen than the rest – pushes her pitcher into the Endless Man's arms.

He freezes. The crowd draws a breath.

Nothing.

The Endless Man drops the pitcher and its hollow knell resonates through the street. Buckets are lowered and sideways glances are exchanged as the same question circulates through the murmuring crowd.

The Endless Man sees the moment when realisation dawns; a gasp sounds from somewhere in the crowd and a voice yells, "He's lost his powers!"

As one, eyes widen and the murmurs transform into yells. The sound batters the Endless Man, pushing at him from all sides, making him feel small. He raises his hands in a calming gesture but the crowd seems all the more incensed.

They surge against the Endless Man, demanding answers, demanding water. He can provide neither so he retreats. But the crowd has him surrounded, leaving him nowhere to run when the first blow lands. The Endless Man's head snaps to the side. He stumbles against the crowd only to be pushed back towards the offender. There are more than one now, and the Endless Man wears their blows. None of their punches bruise; his new gift ensures this. The Endless Man whimpers all the same.

In the flow of the crowd, a gap emerges. He takes his chance and stumbles away from his aggressors. Like a snake weaving through boulders, he squeezes through the crushing crowd and takes off.

He does not stop until he reaches the edge of town, but he can still hear the yells of the crowd in pursuit. Looking out towards the desert, at the dunes with their ephemeral ripples, he knows there is one escape. He sets off. Away from the crowd, away from his family's ruin, away from his own disappointing legacy. Towards the one safe haven that he knows: a hut in an abandoned oasis.

* * *

The desert moon casts the dusty street in a gentle, cool aura. Inside houses, residents sigh as the heat of the day is drawn from their bones. No such relief is felt by the figure slinking through the shadows outside. He knows there is no need for such discretion, there is no-one left who could recognise him. Yet he trembles.

Sand chokes the street, laying siege to sagging stone walls as though no time has passed at all. Such sights tease the Endless Man, making years of solitude seem soft and dreamlike. But he will not allow such fantasies to distract him from his purpose, make him forget the curse that his gift has become.

Something clatters ahead. The Endless Man freezes. His stomach turns to ice and a cold sweat layers his skin. His mind cannot help but stray to his last encounter with the residents of this town. Flattening himself against a wall, he watches as a beggar stumbles from the darkness of an alley, leaving long, dragging footprints as he makes his way to the end of the street.

Only when the beggar is gone does the Endless Man notice another sound. He glances to his left. Someone has left their window open. Its hinge sighs in rhythm with the gentle breeze. Inside, a boy sleeps by the window, the relaxed lines of his face betraying a foreign peacefulness. The Endless Man had hoped to find someone older, but it is as though fate itself has left this window open. Or so he tells himself as he glances again at the footprints and a shiver runs down his spine.

Reaching through the window, the Endless Man places his hand on the boy's forehead. He has only experienced this once before, but when he closes his eyes he knows what to do. Reaching into himself, the Endless Man drags something free, like prising a nut from its shell. He pushes it through his arm and into the boy before pulling his hand from the window. He can already tell that he has failed; that the script of immortality still scratches his soul. He can feel it. If this is the case, what gift, what burden, has he just bestowed upon the boy? He thinks he knows.

He considers trying again. Just one touch and this will all be over. But his curiosity has been sparked. He needs to know how this will play out, whether his actions were inevitable. Hope ignites at the thought; this might not have been his fault. But to find out, he must be patient. Setting his back to the window, the Endless Man retreats down the street, towards a desert marred by the past and a little oasis that hides in its dunes. And there he waits.

* * *

The room is crowded with the glow of possibility. Sand particles stir, set adrift by the warm breeze ambling through the window. Everything holds its breath: the closet, the walls, the cracked, crooked mirror. They all wait for the boy to awaken, for the world to change. What lives will transform, what ripples emerge, from an ordinary open window?

147

My Grandfather the Soothsayer

Sharmila Jayasinghe

"*Divihimiyen sanda nobalan badada*," Grandfather warned us all. "For God's sake do not look at the full moon on a Wednesday." Grandfather was full of wisdom based on folklore that he was never shy to share.

Though he lived in a village a six-hour train ride paired with another two-hour bus ride away from our house in the city, most years the bulk of our April New Year school holidays were spent at his house. There, we ran in the paddy fields, swam in the river and had mud fights with the neighbourhood kids. On quieter days, when the April heat was too much to bear, we loitered around the house watching Grandfather do what he did. It is then that he imparted these pearls of folk wisdom on all of us kids. "Cover all the mirrors in the house at night," he would say, "never walk under a clothesline and remember never to wash your hair on a Tuesday. Tuesdays are not auspicious enough days to embark on something new. Wait 'till it's Wednesday. Retreat your step if a gecko clicks or squeaks when you are about to leave the house."

Though my foreign-born, westernised children find it humorous, I have never, to this day, forgotten to cover the mirrors in our house at night, looked straight at the full moon on a Wednesday or started anything new on a Tuesday. When vacationing in a tropical place, I make certain that I haven't heard a gecko chirp when I step out the door.

My extreme traits have made me the butt of many a joke, once even having been mentioned in a speech my son gave at school. But I would never in my wildest dreams risk it – take a risk by doing what I was asked not to do, despite not really knowing what would happen if I did. Once when I was still little, a curious sort, I asked my grandfather what would happen if I looked at the full moon on a Wednesday.

Grandfather was kind. "Would you like to know?" he asked. "This coming Wednesday is a full moon. Do you want to look at it and find out?"

Though I accepted the challenge enthusiastically, the excitement of finding out dwindled soon, and when the full moon Wednesday approached, I had already chickened out.

As a habit, Grandfather woke up long before the moon recognised the sun. Early morning, he could be found in ceremonious circumambulation, traveling clockwise around the house, chanting prayers and sprinkling *pirith pan*, or holy water, off a brass vessel. It is fair to say that my grandfather was a religious man. The distinct scent of incense and camphor floated through the house when Grandfather stood at the three-tiered shrine erected in a corner of the lounge room, softly chanting Buddhist prayers in worship morning and night.

The lanky man with skin as dark as ebony was never a social being. He rarely went out, but people often visited him. They came in hoards, bearing gifts and sheaves of betel leaves. Grandfather consulted their birth charts, named their newborn babies and discussed the compatibility of marriages.

People in the village regarded him with veneration and were afraid of him. Not because he had an intimidating presence or because they thought of him as violent or strong, but because they believed Grandfather to be a magic man who could see the future and the past and change the present.

Grandfather predicted the future, retraced the past and advised on how to change the present.

"There is no magic to my art," Grandfather often said. "It's the planets, moon, the sun and the constellations that tell me what to expect, what has passed and what changes can be made to prevent malefic. This is a science of the light. The connection between astronomical bodies and our destinies are undeniable. I am merely reading."

Having seen him exorcise the devil out of a young man, I couldn't but help side with the village people in believing Grandfather to be a mystical magic man.

It was one of those scorching April days that was designed to boil us alive. Abandoning our play, all the kids lazed around the house, bored to their wits end. Mid-afternoon the fun began, a commotion rolling in through the open gates. Women were weeping, men were grunting and, in the middle of the group, a young man was dragged, literally dragged, on the gravel ground. Clad in denim and a graphic T-shirt, the young man was frothing from the mouth, growling like a rabid dog. Grandfather sprang to his feet, grabbed a small bottle off the window ledge and jumped out to the yard. There he stood towering over the young man, commanding him to be still as Grandfather recited an incantation in a melodic high-pitched voice. The weepers and grunters took a step back while the grandchildren of the soothsayer marched to his side with shoulders squared and chests puffed. Soon the young man started to violently shake, causing our jaws to drop and goose bumps to form. Grandfather's chanting reached a crescendo, the shaking and shivering of the man sprawled at

Grandfather's feet intensified. All of a sudden, an almighty, throaty scream escaped from the patient and, as if the earth had stopped spinning, everything came to a halt and both the man and Grandfather became silent and still. Moments passed before Grandfather sprang back into action; taking the small bottle he had grabbed off the ledge, he spilled a few drops on to his finger and rubbed it gently in circular motions on the young man's forehead – and that was that. The young man joined the dispersing crowd after they had all paid obeisance to the one who performed the miracle.

I was left as confused as I ever was.

I have no way of proving or disproving my grandfather's abilities, or to say if what conspired around Grandfather were coincidences or not, but there was something to it. The gifts and sheaves of betel piling up on the veranda and snaking around his house were a statement to the success of Grandfather's art.

The first prediction I can remember my grandfather making about me was soon after my puberty celebrations. "The daughter," a concerned Grandfather warned my parents, "has a dark time ahead. She will meet with a terrible accident that will cause her a disability," he said, kneading his forehead, "but, those dark times too will pass." He advised my parents to do good deeds to lessen the impact of my unfavourable planetary alignment. Hundreds of magpies were fed, thousands of flowers were laid at the foot of Buddha, many thousands of lamps were lit around the sacred Bo tree and a gold amulet was tied to my waist, but as predicted, misfortune struck me in my mid-teens when I least expected – an unfortunate accident leaving me with a dislocated spine and a paralysed side. But as Grandfather had predicted, the dark times passed and I was soon on my feet again.

As I grew up and became deeply devout in my own religious beliefs, Grandfather and his magic took a back seat. I started becoming less astonished and less convinced of my grandfather's abilities. He was left in the village with the villagers who venerated him, and I was busy with my city life.

During one of my last visits to his house, Grandfather sat me down and said he had couple of things he needed to reveal about my future.

"I won't be living too much longer, and you won't be visiting me again before I die," he said, "so, daughter, this will be my only chance to share these with you."

Half-heartedly, I indulged.

Sitting at his writing desk in his usual white sarong and white national shirt, my grandfather listed the future events of my life that I should be aware of in no particular order; you will leave your homeland in your mid-twenties and settle down in a foreign land; you will fall into a creative path; you will be the mother of three kids, a son the youngest; you will die on the 2nd of December 2023.

Grandfather died of a massive heart attack soon after he'd shared these predictions with me. I had been overseas for work when he passed and, as he had predicted, I wasn't able to visit him again before his demise.

As for the rest of the predictions he left me with, I did leave my homeland and made a home in a foreign land. Despite having been diagnosed with endometriosis and medical doctors advising me of possible infertility, I am now the mother of three beautiful kids and, as Grandfather predicted, my youngest is a son. With two published novels, several published short stories and a novella launched, I can easily say I am on a creative path.

Grandfather's predictions have been spot on thus far. All that remains now is his last prediction – my death on the 2nd of December 2023.

Ipomoea Alba

I.C. Kaluza

Winter sighed into the night,
fogging the windowpane
where streaks of rain weaved
like the veins of a leaf.

It was there that I eased into the embrace of darkness
as gentle as a rolling tide,
becoming lost beneath the starless sky,
caught by her bright, ivory eye.

Dreams fell through me,
whisked away by Winter's breath.
I could not escape it –
the Raven of Death.

A dark, lonely veil fell over me,
a lick of ice that glazed my skin.
Shivers danced in its wake
as it fed the hollowness within.

Ipomoea Alba

And so, with the rain,
I fell to the earth
and wept for the shadow
that has now departed me, too.

After Samara

Tara E. Berg

3 February

Dear Samara,

Today I tried going for a run. It was horrible. Was it always that bad when you used to go? I suppose you always had more natural athletic ability (and, let's be honest, smaller boobs) than me, but still. It was 4 pm, the sun was still aggressive as anything, and it felt like there were people everywhere, watching me – judging me? Maybe I'm just being paranoid, but it felt like people kept looking at me whenever I went past them. There was a pervy-looking old man who was wearing a shirt, woollen vest and coat but with SHORTS. Please note it was over thirty degrees today. I'm fairly sure he was looking at my chest as I went past him. Either that or he was compelled by my new Nike tank top (a treat to myself to motivate me to try and run), which is a ravishing shade of navy blue. You know this is daring for me seeing as my wardrobe mainly consists of black. I still haven't quite found my personal sense of "style" like you.

There was also this other woman with bleached blonde hair walking her toy poodle who gave me a very encouraging look when I went past her. It was disturbing, she was definitely giving "wow how brave of you to run, as a woman over a size

10!" vibes. I was worried she was going to try and talk to me but luckily, she didn't. I really don't know how you used to do it. All I could think about was if people were wondering why I was wearing leggings in the heat, or why I didn't invest in a better sports bra, or why I still used earphones that had a cable instead of AirPods. My left calf hurt and I could feel the backs of my knees getting sweaty, which I hate because they always get itchy after that.

How long does it take to feel the runners' high? How long does it take to get fit enough that you don't hate it? How long does it take to block out all the people around you? I thought later that maybe some of these people were the same ones you would see when you went running. Maybe you even saw them on your last day. It made me feel closer to you. So maybe it's worth trying it again. I'll need at least a day to recover though.

All my love,
Katie

4 February

Hey Samara,

Wow, maybe I did experience some kind of runners' high yesterday after all – I went for another run today! For some reason this afternoon I felt a strong urge to go again. A small part of me tried to protest and say that hmm, perhaps it is not the best idea for a total beginner. Give my muscles time to recover, etc. Did I listen to that small part of me? No I did not, and off I went running again, this time in an oversized old SpongeBob SquarePants T-shirt (honestly, I was setting my expectations low and only purchased one exercise top) that was nowhere near as breathable as my Nike top. I ran for maybe 200 metres before the pain in my left calf returned, which then made its way somehow around my leg to my shins. So when I say I went running again today, I mean I ran for a couple of minutes, then walked the rest of the way, and "accidentally" ended up near the bubble tea shop we used to go to every weekend, and well, I was already there so I had to stop for a roasted milk tea with pearls, half sugar, less ice. I almost got a passionfruit green tea with rainbow jelly (full sugar, extra ice) in your honour but you know I never liked those much. The friendly woman with the purple streaks in her hair was there and she asked where my friend was. I just shrugged, not wanting to correct her that actually, you were my sister, not my friend, though of course you will always be my best friend. I hope she didn't notice the tears that were filling my eyes as I left the shop.

Okay, this time I will really try and take a day or two to recover. I think.

Love,
Katie

25 February

Dear Samara,

Sometimes I wonder what you would be up to now if you had survived the fall. Maybe it would've made you reconsider your boring-as job in accounting, seeing as you never seemed to find it fulfilling or even mildly interesting. I know you did it to make Mum and Dad happy, but maybe a near-death experience might've helped you realise how short life is, and that you should've pursued your true passion. I'm not sure if you ever got to tell Mum and Dad that you wanted to be a chef and have your own restaurant. I don't know if I should tell them. It might make them too sad.

In saying that, I've barely seen them the last few months. They were pretty work-obsessed before, as you know, but since you left us, they've been even worse. I guess their method of dealing with grief is just to work and work and not talk about anything. They've both been bringing extra work home and hiding in their respective rooms – Dad has taken the study and Mum has taken their bedroom. I guess there's always something to be done when you're a lawyer. Other nights, they both just collapse into bed, even if it's only 7 pm. I think we've had one family meal in the last four months. I never realised it was your cooking that brought us all together at dinner time.

I haven't tried running again in the last couple of weeks. I've been using my sore calf as an excuse, but maybe it's time to try again. I bought a massage gun as a gift to myself so I may as well make my muscles sore so I can get some use out of it.

Love,
Katie

28 February

The question that swirls in my mind, over and over, is: Did you mean it?

1 March

Samara,

Terrible news. Rani's is closing. I couldn't believe it when she told me earlier tonight. I stopped by for a quick dinner after my shift at Coles; Mum and Dad were working late again.

I hadn't been back since we went there for my twenty-first last year. Remember how Mum and Dad were running late so we ordered that mixed naan basket and "accidentally" ate all five naans? Between that and the huge jug of mango lassi Rani gave us, we could barely fit in the curries. You said it would be an insult to Rani's cooking to not eat everything. I had wanted to go out for drinks afterwards, but I could barely walk by the time we'd finished eating. Remember how we lay on the couch, and I could barely breathe because it felt like my stomach was so full it was compressing my lungs? You just laughed at me and said it was worth it for the best malai kofta in Sydney.

When Rani told me tonight, I burst into tears. She looked a bit shocked, especially when I blurted out, "How could you? This was Samara's favourite restaurant!" She pulled me into a hug and explained that she and Ajay had saved enough to retire on the Gold Coast. She said if I was ever in Queensland to visit them, she'd make me some malai kofta. It's hard to stay mad when they're so bloody nice, but it's still not fair.

8 March

Dear Samara,

Today I had an awful realisation: I think I may be more like Mum and Dad than I thought.

Uni went back today. I can't believe it's my last year already. I don't know if I'm ready to go out into the real world and get a job (that isn't being a checkout chick). Maybe I should do honours, and then I can do a PhD, and maybe a master's too … Though I'd have to pay for that I guess, so maybe not. In any case, the longer I stay at uni the better.

Anyway, it was this line of thinking that made me realise just how similar to Mum and Dad I might actually be.

Everyone was pretty excited to be back in class (what a bunch of nerds), and the tutors had to keep shushing us during the lab. I guess that's the nice thing about doing a science degree, we've all been together for the last three years. People were already talking about graduation (!) even though it's a year away. We all have to pass the bloody course first.

Amy was saying that her family is already planning their trip from Hong Kong to come to the graduation, and John's family in New Zealand are thinking of taking an extended holiday here for the last few months to "be with him while he finishes off the degree". The conversation turned in my direction, and you could almost see them all remembering what happened to you. Everyone was looking down at the desks or was suddenly very interested in what the tutors were trying to teach us. Amy said, "Well, at least your parents will come, right?" I didn't want to get into it too much, so I just smiled and nodded.

The conversation really should've moved on according to what I thought would've been mutual social understanding, but then John goes, "You know, I can't believe you just kept studying after your sister ... yeah, after what happened with your sister last year. I don't think I could've kept coming to uni."

"Gee, thanks, John. Make me out to be some kind of fucking unfeeling monster." I thought I had said this in my mind but turns out I hadn't because everyone turned to look at me, eyes wide. Amy said, "What the fuck?" and I wasn't sure if it was directed at me or John, or just generally at the situation. John at least had the decency to look remorseful while he tried to get out some half-arsed apology. I gave him the finger and moved to the front of the class.

Am I an unfeeling monster? When you died, it was the middle of semester. I know there are probably things I could've done to get special consideration or permission to suspend my studies or whatever, but honestly, at that point, some of the only comfort I got was from studying. I could throw myself into preparing for labs and doing experiments and studying for tests. It gave me somewhere to be and made me get out of bed, made me keep getting up each day and interacting with other people. If I had had no obligations, I honestly don't know what I would've done. Maybe it would've helped, to have the time and to sit in the grief, fully absorb it and not suppress any of it, just feel whatever I felt. But there wouldn't have been anyone at home with me; Mum and Dad took a couple of weeks off work and that was it. I would've just been by myself all day, in a house with constant reminders of you. Throwing myself into uni work seemed like the best idea at the time. I guess I just never realised I was basically doing exactly what Mum and Dad did. A pretty daunting thought, when I think about how critical I've been of them. But it's different. Isn't it?

Love,
Katie

14 March

~~Samara,~~

~~Sometimes I wonder if it should've been me. Maybe it would've been better for everyone. Maybe you and Mum and Dad would've stayed together better than me and Mum and Dad have.~~
~~So... how's the, uh, afterlife?~~

20 March

Hey Sammy,

I caught up with Gemma today. It was nice, actually. She's been trying to get me to go out with everyone for a while now. You know that by "everyone" I mean me, Gemma, Kei and Indigo – not exactly a large group but I've been spending a lot of time with uni friends, so my social battery has been a bit drained, and the first few weeks of semester always take some adjustment. Well, okay, I will admit these are partly just excuses. I love my friends dearly, but things are definitely strange in the group, since you left us. I'm not sure what's worse: when people like John say things like what he said the other day, or people who just act like it never happened. There must be a happy medium, right?

If there is, Gemma is probably in that happy medium. When I was putting off catching up with the whole group, I think she caught on and suggested the two of us meet up for brunch. I can just hear you, "Where did you go?" – always asking the most important question. A new café opened up down the road where the old Chinese takeaway used to be. It's a Japanese-Lebanese fusion, which I was a bit sceptical of at first, but the food was great. I was sold as soon as I tried the edamame falafel with yuzu hummus. It's definitely your kind of thing, I wish you could've seen it.

Anyway. Gemma specifically asked how I was coping, which meant a lot. I get tired of the dancing around and the "so, how are you holding up?" line of questioning (through bones and skin and muscle, that's how – don't ask a biology student that kind of question). I told her I'd tried to take up running in your honour and she didn't laugh! In fact, she even encouraged me and said if I wanted, we could try going together. I'm not sure I'm ready for that but I appreciated the sentiment. It was really nice, my uni friends are great but we do tend to mainly talk about, well, uni. Gemma told me about the new girl she's dating, Sarah, and the spontaneous trip they took to Cairns. I was so jealous!

We ended up sitting there chatting for almost four hours, I couldn't believe it. I actually had … fun, for what felt like the first time in a while. Then I felt guilty for having fun. Are you allowed to have fun within the first year of your sister dying? It doesn't seem like it should be allowed, but I know that's not the most helpful way of thinking. You'd want me to continue living my life, blah blah blah. It still just doesn't seem right though.

Missing you and not having TOO much fun.

Lots of love,
Katie

22 March

Dear Samara,

I was inspired by Gemma and tried going for a run again today. It has *not* gotten easier. Seriously, how did you do this?! I managed to get to the end of the street but was huffing and puffing by then. At least it wasn't as hot today, but still. I went for about four kilometres, but it was probably about thirty seconds of running, five minutes of walking each time. It's a work in progress, I suppose.

I saw the pervy old man again, though he didn't seem to be looking in my direction this time at least. Today he was wearing a T-shirt and shorts, but with a scarf around his neck and a beanie with a cute pom-pom on top. Truly, he does not seem to have any concept of weather. It's fascinating.

To celebrate my run and "recover", I made a huge pot of pasta – your favourite, pesto gnocchi. I didn't hand-make the gnocchi like you used to though, and I'm sorry to admit it but I didn't make the pesto myself either. Do you think I can be bothered grinding all that basil and cooking the potatoes? I don't know how you made such elaborate meals each night on top of working a full-time job. I guess it made you happier than most other things, so it was always worth it.

Anyway, you'll be happy (or sad? I don't know) to know that the gnocchi was too hard, and the pesto was nowhere near as garlicky as I like it. Mum and Dad didn't eat any, so I just sat at the dining table by myself, thinking of you.

Love,
Katie

2 April

If you meant it ... how could you? How could you leave me behind like that?

Why didn't you talk to me?

Why couldn't you talk to me?

Why didn't you go to therapy or something? Why couldn't you suck it up like I always do? Was it really so hard to go on? Did you even think about how it might affect me?

WHY DID YOU TAKE THE EASY WAY OUT???

4 April

I'm sorry. I know it isn't the easy way out. And that's if you did actually mean to do it.
I guess I'll never know.

10 April

Dear Samara,

I went there today – the place where it happened. I haven't been back since. How could I? How could I possibly face it, knowing what happened to you there? I'm not sure why I went. It's the long weekend, and I wanted to get out of the house. It's been about six months since you left us, and I miss you every single day. I think writing the letters has helped. That's why I have kept doing it, I suppose.

So, I went to the cliffs just south of the beach. The waves were crashing against the rocks, and it was cloudy today, so the water was that opaque, dark blue colour it goes when it's overcast. I sat there for a long time, Samara, and I thought about you, and I thought about what must have been going through your mind before it happened, how scared you must have felt. You always loved running along here, feeling the salt from the sea on your face. It had never occurred to me that something like that could've happened. I wish I had thought about it a bit more, and maybe warned you not to run along the cliffs, especially in the evening. Would you have listened? Probably not.

I found myself yelling, screaming at the water below me. I was angry at myself for not thinking to warn you. I was angry at the stupid rocks for being slippery. I was angry at Mum and Dad for not being there for me, or for us. I was angry at the universe, for taking away my best friend. And ... I was angry at you. I'm sorry, and it feels awful, but it's true. I'm angry at you for leaving me. We were meant to be by each other's sides forever. We were meant to have each other's backs when Mum and Dad were being annoying, and we were going to travel together, and have families around the same time, and our kids were supposed to grow up together. We were meant to all gather at your place every weekend and you would cook us a three-course meal like it was nothing. You were meant to be here, with me.

The waves kept crashing against the rocks. The frothy whitewash went back and forth. It was impossible to see anything. There was a part of me, a tiny part of me, that wondered what it would be like to jump. To be smashed against the rocks, for the whitewash to carry me back and then to ram me into the rocks again. Eventually, I'd be taken out to sea, and I would feel nothing. The urge passed as quickly as it came, but the feeling terrified me. I'd do anything to be with you again, but I like being alive. I am in pain, but I like being alive.

I sat at the top of the cliffs, and I cried and cried.

1 May

Sammy!

High Intensity Interval Training boxing class, can you believe it? As someone who can barely exercise for more than ten minutes, and is painfully self-conscious while doing so, it seems ridiculous that I would go to a group fitness class voluntarily.

It was Gemma's idea. I met up with her over the Easter long weekend, after I'd been to visit the cliffs. She could tell I was off straightaway, and I told her everything, about the letters and our parents and how angry I felt. When I told her the running wasn't exactly working out, she told me about the boxing classes Sarah's really into. Apparently Sarah has been trying to make her go for ages, so Gemma suggested we all give it a go together.

It was glorious. The interval training was indeed highly intense, but somehow it was a lot more manageable than trying to run for five kilometres. We would do quick bursts of running or squats or whatever, and then we'd be on the punching bags, hitting it as hard as we could for thirty seconds. Then the instructor would do some sequences with different kinds of punches, so I really had to concentrate. It was all women, and there was no competitiveness – just everyone letting out whatever they needed to, in a healthy way. And no one looks at each other, really, because they're all so focussed on what they're doing. I loved it, but Gemma hated it! So, Sarah and I will just go together, I think, it will be fun.

After the class the three of us went out for dinner and then I stopped by Rebel sport on the way home to get myself some boxing gloves. I bought some cute red ones! They had bright pink ones, but I thought that was a bit much, probably more your style than mine. Red seems like a nice pop of colour without being too bright.

It was only one session, but I honestly feel better already. I guess the pain will always be there, but I can at least let some of the anger out. I never realised how badly I needed to punch something until tonight. I don't think I can be a runner like you, but still I hope you would be proud of me.

Love,
Katie

30 July

Samara,

I found myself at the cliffs again today. It's been a couple of months since I last went there, but I have been going to boxing class every week, and as of a couple of weeks ago, I've been seeing a psychologist as well. She was so happy when I told her about my letters to you. I miss you every single day, but things are getting better. It's winter break at the moment so I wanted to get out of the house a bit before uni starts and I get busy again. It will be my last semester!

I was sitting on an ornate wooden bench that overlooks the ocean in the small park near the cliffs. I think it got installed not long before you died, one of those ones that has the small memorial plaque on it. Guess who came and sat next to me – the pervy old man! I noticed him straight away, seeing as he was wearing bright orange trackies, a tank top and the same beanie with the pom-pom. I thought about leaving in case he did anything weird, but I decided I had as much right to be there as him.

I was so deep in thought I almost didn't notice when he started trying to talk to me. All I heard was something about the bench.

"… built in memory of my wife," he was saying. "She died about a year ago."

"Oh, I'm so sorry," I said. "I lost my sister almost a year ago too."

"I'm sorry to hear that." He looked genuinely sad. "It's so hard, isn't it? You get used to having someone around every day, and then they're just gone. My wife used to pick out my clothes for me every day. Now I can barely see what I'm putting on in the morning."

That explained a lot. Part of me wanted to make a joke to lighten the mood a bit. "I love your beanie," I said instead.

"She made it for me." He gave a small smile. "I can't see it, but I know the feel of the wool and the pom-pom. She was always knitting."

We chatted a bit more and he told me more about his wife and I told him about you, how you liked to run along here. Eventually the conversation tapered out, and we just sat there, looking at the ocean as the sun was setting behind us. When it got dark, we both headed home.

Love always,
Katie

Lost Boy

Samantha Bowers

I looked for you
afterwards –

in your childhood toys, the clothes you used to wear,
I couldn't find you

– instead, shadows licking corners in your empty room,
spiders stringing lace across the shelves, your running

trophies. Do you remember winning?
You went so fast.

I saw you once in winter,
take off your shoes and socks

and tread a pilgrimage through frost-kissed grass,
each step transforming icy white to vivid green.

You were always pressing beauty
into ordinary things.

The Story That Ends Before It Begins

Jennifer Scarini

They sat silently as she stared out the window. She tapped at the radio several times, before slapping at it to extinguish its unwanted prattle. She had a pain in her pelvis that was not expected; it wasn't something she had been warned about. It was a dull dragging pain in her arse – a punishment. She was bleeding steadily but not excessively. The pain and the bleeding would become an uncomfortable reminder of what she had just done for several years to come. She bore the pain without complaint. It felt deserved.

"Can we go to Waverly? I want to check out the fabric shop." She wasn't insisting, but she knew they wouldn't be coming this way again anytime soon and a stroll through a decent fabric shop was one of her favourite things. She had been dreaming about pink and green fabrics for the past couple of months. She'd thought it was a sign at first, but it was no longer helpful to look at, or for, any signs.

She felt empty, emptier now than she had ever felt before. Another piece of fabric might fill that void.

The prospect of walking around with the pain didn't stop her from wanting to wander around all the textures and colours. She would look for silk or some other distraction.

He didn't want to go. He wanted to eat. He always wanted to eat. Food was never far from his mind. It annoyed her now, but she knew there was a great vegan restaurant at Waverly and used it as a carrot to make sure she got her way. "It's not just a restaurant or food," she said, "it is a religious experience."

How could he eat? She may never eat again. He hated the vegan food, and she couldn't connect with anything in the fabric shop. She didn't buy silk. Nothing was going to fill the empty space.

Three hours earlier, they had both walked into the clinic to nudge the course of history, punch a small pinprick in time and break her heart forever. She was blank, expectant, ashamed. She let the desk monitor know she had arrived and was asked to take a seat. She looked around the clinic at the other exhibits, wondering if they too felt shame. Eyeless, headed beasts camouflaged in the pink, beige sadness of the waiting room. All shapes and sizes, ages and characters. She gave them all lives; it entertained and calmed her.

A bright, friendly woman approached them with some paperwork and a genuine smile. She didn't deserve the smile. She noticed the woman's shoes. Red T-straps. Vintage probably. The shoes soothed her. They too seemed terrifically friendly.

She appealed to "Red Shoes", a subtle appeal, but an appeal nonetheless. She'd met Red Shoes a week prior, when she had decided against changing the course of history, reversing time and breaking her own heart – when they had impulsively decided to forgo the procedure and leave, not before thanking the desk and being buzzed out. It had seemed like such a grand gesture at the time. A decisive moment of sureness, joy, relief even. But then the morning sickness nagged at her again. They'd stopped at a factory outlet on the way home that day to buy a much-needed lounge. Before the lounge had been decided upon, she was already doubting her grand gesture. She bought the first lounge they looked at. The salesperson had discounted it heavily.

"What are we doing?" she said out loud, head in hands, as the salesclerk rang up a further discount at the cashier's desk. Another sign, perhaps.

A couple of months earlier she had laid in bed while her tummy glowed with something she had never felt before. It was as if she had been visited by a spirit of some variety. A warmth or vibration rang out across her body like ripples in a pond, as she half woke from a peaceful sleep. She consciously thanked whatever it was that had come to visit her on that day. It was a serenity she had never experienced before. A gift. She thought at the time it was like being visited by an angel and wondered if a friend who had passed recently had called on her. She now knows it was probably a conception. The body's unrestrained response to its own cleverness. Joy. Later that same morning while walking through a sunlit lounge room, as Bob Dylan blared out in the background, she stopped to take a moment to notice just how happy she felt. It was an unmistakable, definable bliss. It washed over her, permeating every one of her cells – she had never felt it before; it was unfamiliar. She took the time to notice it, to really feel it. It was the single most peaceful moment of her entire life. She has searched for that feeling many times since, without success. Not even Bob can bring it back.

Just a few weeks later when playing at a park with her two young children, in between making calls for her work and organising appointments, without warning, one of those early signs of pregnancy launched from her mouth. Her eldest, a sweet and loving child expressed concern for his sick mummy. She reassured him she was fine. She had the car being serviced that morning and was due to collect it, but she picked up a pregnancy test on their way back up the street to the mechanics. She thought she felt the clerk's disapproval, looking at her like she was some kind of creature from the black lagoon. It wasn't the test that the clerk wondered about. It was the fact that she had walked into the chemist wearing the fabric hat that, minutes earlier, she had used to clean down a swing set and then placed it back on her head. She looked as if she had just slipped out of a skip bin.

Later that same night, she waved the unmistakable stick with the two little windows in front of her husband, interrupting his troll through the newspaper. His initial expression was one of elation, until he saw her face. She complained there was still so much to do, and she worried she would never finish her degree, plus there was the prospect of going skiing with Kat that winter, and then there was the job she hated that she wanted to leave. In reality, the job was not likely to stop her from having a baby, nor was the baby likely to stop her from leaving the job. They were all selfish reasons – she knew that, but so too was having a baby when she was already spreading herself pretty thin with the two boys under five, work, study and him. She was exhausted just thinking about it. The degree was almost within reach. She could almost touch it – just six units to go. She was so close, and she genuinely believed it was going to propel her into other opportunities that she had set her mind to.

It was Christmas Eve when they mutually decided it was something they needed to think about. Just think about. No pressure.

The doctor had told her not to wait too long to decide when handing her the brochure for the contraception clinic. They had thought about it too long already. She was so busy with her job, the study and the kids that she hadn't even noticed the missed period. She hadn't noticed the sore boobs. She was exhausted.

There is a beauty in having a small person growing inside you that cannot be explained. It can only be felt or understood from within. There is a stillness, and maybe even a slight sense of superiority – being able to create another living thing inside of yourself. It's the stuff dreams are made of, quite literally.

There are also the vile horrors that trick you into wanting to escape a pregnancy. The morning sickness, a constant nagging and churning of the stomach that even water cannot snake past. Exhaustion, and for those that have already experienced the joys of childbirth, there is the ever-present knowledge and vision of stretching one's poor vagina well beyond reasonable girth with the inescapable exiting of a four-kilogram baby. Memories of sleepless nights still haunted her. The twenty-four-hour care of another human being. The lunging out of bed in the middle of the night to catch an invisible baby that slept peacefully on the other side of the room. The constant feeding, the cracked nipples, the mastitis, the boob swapping for the first six weeks to get the bloody supply pumping and the inevitable feeling of being a surrogate for the rest of the family, so they can play with a baby while you play cow to it.

The relentless and ceaseless worries of protecting and keeping that human, or humans, safe was still ever-present with the two they'd already brought into the world. Not that any of this truly bothered her – she'd always found it a blessing. She loved her children. She loved being a mum and was pretty damn good at it. But some of this gnawed at her, and the nagging came with a little voice that tricked her into thinking that aborting her baby might be the best option.

Red Shoes collected the forms, returning to her a minute later to advise her to wait for the counsellor who would like to have a quick chat with her before she went ahead with the procedure. It hadn't gone unnoticed at the clinic that she had popped in the week before, left, and now here she was presenting again with the same wishy-washy intent. Perhaps Red Shoes had noticed her appeal after all.

The counsellor was a very small, unassuming woman with a contradictory big head of the most beautiful curly hair. Apologetic in nature, "Unassuming" motioned her to enter the lift, shyly waving her in, eyes down, also having some difficulty connecting by sight. She felt it – that shame again. Tears sprang from her face. She did wonder many years later if only Unassuming had been less polite, less apologetic, more of a bull. Not to lessen any of the responsibility she felt around the abortion, but just to give meaning to Unassuming's important role. There are so many things we dance around in this life, in the name of treading lightly on other's toes. Some things are worth stomping for, and some things are worth raging about – or at least a spirited tirade.

The lift was steamy and dark – the morning sickness didn't help. The conversation was immediate, as if she had started the "little chat" before even getting to her office. Unassuming expressed her concern about the fact that there was clearly some doubt in her mind after having visited the clinic just a week earlier, and now she was back again holding back tears in a lift.

The conversation continued when they got to the counsellor's office, and she did express some trepidation about proceeding with the termination. Unassuming told her it was her decision to make, her choice to make. She detailed the many women she had seen over the years that had later struggled psychologically post-procedure, but also those who had felt an immense relief. She admitted to Unassuming that she had doubts, but it could have been shame that encouraged her to do this – she truly wasn't sure what or how she should be feeling. Her husband was quickly called for and was ushered to Unassuming's office by none other than Red Shoes, still smiling, bubbly and happy. The hide.

An argument quickly broke out, between Unassuming and her husband. He insisted it would do no good; they would simply get home and she would want to come back a week later, and the longer they left it, it would be too late. He was angry. He didn't like someone questioning his beliefs or his wife's. It isn't clear, but she thinks he did this to protect her in some way. When she eventually verbalised that she still had some doubts about the termination, he protested and re-directed his anger at her instead. Unassuming asked him to leave. When he was out of the room and out of earshot, she said, "Do not have any more children with that man." Seeing her husband's anger, his outrage at her taking her time to mull over this decision, she couldn't help but agree with Unassuming's assessment. The meeting or chat was over.

She returned alone to the waiting room where he was waiting for her. They were promptly ushered to an in-between room where gowns and other provisions were made in readiness for the procedure. Her own clothes were placed in a plastic bag with her shoes.

They sat together in the room – let us call it purgatory, where the gown did little to sure up her confidence. Throw-away foot covers, fear and indifference filled the rest of the space. More painful minutes prevailed. She appealed to him to help her to feel like they were doing the right thing. He continued with the line of "this is the right thing to do". More eyes that did not wish to be met, as he looked away from her, down, up, but away. She was summoned from the room by another cheerful nurse.

Post-purgatory was a surprisingly ordinary-looking space. Almost office-like, not that "clinical" looking, but bare. A man that looked like a used car salesman told her not to worry, that "this won't happen again". She buzzed for a minute. What does that mean? Not happen again. What does that mean?

She was helped onto the bed. The nurse held her hand while another man entered the room. He was orange and looked very much like someone had taken the version of Beaker from The Muppet Show and tried to fashion a human from him. She gripped the nurse's hand tighter, as tears flowed from her eyes, and no sound dared escape from her ungrateful mouth.

As she counted back from ten, still gripping the nurse's hand, she wondered if her unconscious, slumbering head would wail as they suctioned out her womb.

Waking what seemed a second later, her new reality settled in, though she did not want to acknowledge it. A reality where an important part of her had been lost forever. She had just murdered a vibrant part of herself – never to be seen again. The Bob-Dylan-bliss part. Gone. And while she had made the decision herself, she struggled to feel truly content in it.

She rolled back over and pulled the blankets over her head; she did not want this new reality, not right now. It was too much right now. She did not like this new reality. She told herself she deserved it though.

A much less cheerful nurse berated her for being too slow to rise. She gripped tightly to the blanket, pulling at it, while she tried to disappear, spiritually trying to reverse what she had just done. The nurse continued with protests to get up, and then asked her a few questions as she got herself up and out of the bed. She was surprised that her clothes were back on as she sat in a chair at a nearby desk where the nurse was completing some paperwork. After a few questions and the rejection of the ultrasounds she'd brought with her, she was free to go.

He was waiting for her in the public waiting room.

She didn't look at him, nor him at her. They walked out. Buzz. Click. Air, sun, grief. No protestors, no colour, no nothing. Just a heaviness.

The fabric shop was not going to fix this, but she did try. Nothing there. Nothing. The food at the vegan restaurant tasted like water to her. The morning sickness had kind of hung around. The optimist in her wondered if maybe they had forgotten to do the procedure while she was out cold. The realist in her laughed its sinister laugh in her racing head. They got in the car to drive home.

The body has a memory that we cannot explain nor fathom.

Her body played nasty with her head, while a part of it searched in vain for the little bit of bliss that was now missing. Screaming at her, "Have you seen my baby ... have you seen my baby". She tried to ignore her body as she looked out the window, tears flowing slowly down her reflection.

The drive home felt longer than usual. The pain was still there, dull and constant.

He made small talk, which was usually her job. He must have been feeling the way she normally did when she made small talk, unsure if she was trespassing on his solitude. Unwanted. Lonely.

"Got your appetite back yet? What do ya feel like for dinner?

"How's ya bum, still sore?"

"Oh Mum rang while you were in the … in the, the thing
… She said Beth will be at the caravan on Monday if you want
to wait until then to pick up the boys, that'll give us a couple
more days to ourselves."

She wondered what he was really thinking. She yepped and
okayed every now and then as she wriggled around in her seat
to trying to escape the persistent pain, hoping he would relax
and allow the silence. Reluctantly, she settled herself into her
uncomfortable, unfamiliar new normal.

She watched the hills sweep by kilometre after kilometre,
the scenery not changing a great deal. Then at one point, she
noticed a strangely shaped tree in the distance, and seconds
later, a second tree, an exact replica of the first, except it was
on another hill some distance to the right. She referred back
to the original tree, which was still in sight. She checked them
again. Back and forth until she had verified the likeness of the
trees. There was little doubt in her racing mind that the trees
were the same, just on two separate hills, she estimated about
a kilometre apart. Same tree, different hill. Was she dreaming?
No, no she wasn't.

Maybe … She contemplated the idea that this was all just
some artificially constructed world she'd now found herself
living in. Not precious enough for a real world, maybe she
had now been relegated to live in Fakeland, seeing as she had
exposed herself as the metaphorical scissor-wielding destroyer
of the… fabric of time. Floundering in some giant cosmic
nerd's railway model that he was constructing in his giant
cosmic man shed, just beyond the realms of reality. Maybe it
was all just one big computer simulation.

Still waiting to wake up from the nightmare she had found
herself in, she entertained herself with her "maybes". He was

still making conversation with himself in the background. She empathised with him.

She thought about the odd philosophies she'd read about over the years and considered the notion that she had no free will and was simply following a set of pre-ordained conditions or instructions that some coder had typed into computer program many moons before. Fucking prick! She mentally berated the coder. Tell a different story arsehole! Where is your imagination – your compassion?

Of course! That would help her make sense of the decision she had just had to make.

She gave energy to the question in her mind, of what kind of monster would force this choice upon her. She could see her reflection in the window as she lost focus on her replica tree discovery. She was the monster. It was her choice and she assumed that one day she would forgive herself for it. She felt the pain, the physical and emotional pain. How do the philosophers explain that? The pain of childbirth, is that an illusion or some part of a simulation? The joy of it even – how could joy be constructed with a binary code?

01001010 01101111 01111001

Joy is not two-dimensional. She would argue that childbirth "joy" is more likely six-dimensional. Abortion sorrow, therefore, would follow a six-dimensional path. For others it might be an eight-dimensional relief.

She stopped looking out of the window and questioning herself about reality and tried to sleep, still praying she would wake up, and it would all be a bad dream. She closed her eyes and dozed. Not a bad dream – reality and everything that was awful swimming around in it just kept coming back to her.

She silently wept at night, as he snored. He felt it too, he had to be feeling it. His snoring was simply a mask to hide his inescapable grief.

Betrayed by her mind, she slowly began a year-long quest to loathe herself to death. She felt relief would never come. Then one morning, her youngest son begged her to get out of bed, as she tried to spend another morning dreaming herself free of the living nightmare she'd found herself in.

His face was so earnest, so beautiful. She wondered how much he would suffer if she didn't drag herself out of the hole she had dug. She got out of bed, organised breakfast, and cleaned up the dishes left by her husband and number one son, before they had headed off on their days and sat and watched number two … live.

He played happily, oblivious to his mother's state of mind. He chatted, giggled and smiled away, changing the world, saving hers.

"Come and play, Mummy, let's go sailing today." He upended the lounge cushions and attached a toy vacuum to the end of it, bouncing through the very same loungeroom her bliss was once found in. She joined him on the upturned cushion, played and bounced along, dodging the imaginary waves. Catching the imaginary fish, waving at the imaginary whales.

Later that morning, she walked into the bathroom, took the hair-cutting scissors from the drawer and began cutting off her hair, rather resolutely. It was a small act of self-mutilation, but it seemed to do the trick to reset her, on her way in this new reality.

She lived happily never after, but her surviving children did. She made sure of that. That would be the legacy of the red shoe silk bliss baby.

She would go on to lead many lives fearlessly, and this moment, this lesson, was just one of them.

Transformed

Memi Adams

Transformed
by the spirit-filled truth,
torn from the blackest night.
Breaking through chains of darkness,
the scales fall from my eyes
and my heart sings a new song.
Transformed
by a prayer of hope,
the unspoken pain of loss
that lingers on my silent cries of despair
– and yet dissipates as He tends to the callous cuts of grief –
as the waves of grace wash over me –
I am transformed by His light.
Redeemed by grace –
forever changed.
Transformed.

A Mercurial Ending

Emma Murphy

You can hear the sadness.

It rings like an ignored
phone call
that you should answer,
but talking
is just too much effort
right now.

You can hear the sadness
rushing towards you
like a speeding car
on a freeway
past a dreadful corner
littered with dying flowers
and sun-bleached
photographs.

Sadness is loud,
pressure
too much,
yet so little.

A feeling created in your mind,
but you can feel it
in your gut,
your stomach,
your eyes.

It rings for me
far too often,
it seems to be the only phone call
I get these days.

After stringing out
every sad thought
from my head
and into my poetry,
I yearn to replace the melancholy
with happiness and change.

But you can't create mercurial thoughts
without mercurial moments.

You must keep living
until you've lived every
whimsicality

and every sadness
you possibly can.

The sharp ringing will sometimes dull
and become elevator music
drowned beneath the background's surface
by the sounds of
laughter
and enchantment.

In time, you'll be surrounded
by a solar system
of delicate prose,
eternity,
the feeling of "enough".

Death & a Projector

Matthew Platakos

shadows dance orange & orbital
light-painted moons – cosmic chandeliers
slice through dark & onto off-white wall

death watches life floating like flowers in a fountain
she has seen nascent skies & serene evenings
& geiger counter midnights

immortality means infinite procrastination
train watching from a terminus
the rectangular projection of a billion psyches –

> ... *an orange sun diving into clouds*
> *dripping cherry-blossom raindrops*
> > *red ink on paper-thin earth ...*

> ... *first kiss under the eucalypts ...*

> ... *gang wars & dance floors ...*

... smiles through fruit juice smears

rolling & muddied through the leaves ...

... intercontinental/generational ballistic
traumas ...

... yearning for warmth
burning touch of the heart ...

... inventing god & holding him close ...

... conjuring music from
lips & fingertips ...

... holding each other
as the asteroid
breaks atmosphere ...

reels end in filmic flapping
a beat as the universe sighs

she flips the earth on its ecliptic –
the shadows dance again

A Poor Substitute

Michael Kowalczyk-Barker

Act 1: Blind Insight

The rain was smattering upon the roof, and the lantern cast a barely visible outline of the desperation that lay beyond. The mud underneath was churned and ground and repulsive. What sad people lay in the village ahead! Hopefully few to be encountered, even less to be engaged. These were the thoughts that ran through the mind of the Emissary as he checked the flint that lay next to him and felt for the hidden dagger. A small peak through the curtains was all that was needed to confirm his worst suspicions about what lay ahead. He leaned back with a sigh of indignation. It was difficult to cuddle up to warm thoughts of Viennese streets and Habsburgian splendour when the creeping frost of the outside was mingling with the growing trepidation from within. *What a punishment for me to be sent here,* he thought. The Empire wanted to teach Meaning to their new subjects, but all they brought was credulity and superstition.

The horses dug their hooves into the sodden mud as the carriage ground to an undignified halt. The shock brought the Emissary back from the misgivings of the past to the unease of the present. As the carriage door opened to the gloom, his quick eyes noticed that none of the other parties had arrived. One particularly absence was that of the armed escort. *Perfect,* he thought, *I am to be fed to the wolves.*

Ever since the Empire had expanded to the former lands of the Ottomans, all sorts of tales had reached the capital. Attempts on the lives of villagers by monsters that fed on their very essence. It was told that they were more adapted to the harsh life of these near-pagan lands than the victims they preyed upon. Before long, expeditions were sent to investigate. One of these monsters was encased in a hut, towards which the Emissary had now begun his slow and wearying slog through the mud. The subdued light from the window was soon enveloped by a shadow as the door was opened and entrance permitted. This monster, the Emissary had heard, was not like the others. It didn't feast on blood, but knowledge. A true Parasite.

The door swung closed with a muffled squelch that smothered the pounding rain and desperate voices. Water squealed from his boots as he took commanding steps towards the candlelight. The water that swished off his coat landed on the wooden floor with a rhythmic drumming that matched his well-timed strides. In one hand he gripped his rain-catcher hat, in the other the frigid handle of his supposed protection. The flint barrel was sodden, the powder no doubt ruined. *More useful as a bludgeon now,* he thought grimly, *but I have my dagger, so no worry.* He felt the sheath near his breast, and the confidence in his heart. Any attempts on his life will be met with swift retaliation. For that is the guarantee of Empire: Security for all.

"So far, so good," mused the omniscient director, watching the opening act with great satisfaction.

Inside the Emissary's contact greeted him courteously and pointed at the wretch.

"Why this one?"

The Emissary shone the question at the hunched figure which had sagged into the stool that, apart from the small table, made up the entire contents of the room. The figure's arms splayed dismissively across the table, and a dribble of despair ran down its panting cheeks. This forlorn image was complemented by the musky odour of wet fabric from its person. The water-logged environs beyond fused with the misgivings from within as the Emissary fashioned a smile. Nothing was more frigid than suspected warmth.

"This," the self-appointed Gaoler proudly announced, "is the village idiot."

"And on what grounds was he detained?"

"Well, during our last village gathering, he raised many interesting and insightful points. So, we confined him in this room immediately and have been keeping a watch on him ever since."

The Emissary rubbed his head in a futile attempt to understand the situation. He had been brought all the way out here because a man could *think*. How he yearned for coffee. He could not recall if the Turks had introduced it to Europe yet. He should have checked the date before embarking on this adventure. *She* should have checked for inaccuracies, but it was too late for such considerations. For the story had already begun, and only the right question remained. Everything else was set dressing.

He turned to the figure, "So, why were you, uh, feeding off the thoughts of others?"

"Simple," the figure replied, "to remove from them the fog of ambition, and reveal the desolate landscape of stigma and responsibility."

"I see," said the Emissary, and looked to the Gaoler for clarification. He did not receive it.

"No, no, no," she exclaimed, "wrong question, wrong answer. Quickly, for I can hear day breaking!"

The Emissary cleared his throat, placed his hat on the table, and began again.

"Do you enjoy stealing human thoughts?" he asked blandly.

The figure shrugged its little hands, its little eyes, its little mind.

She watched in disbelief at the lacklustre display. The interactions were so wooden; they may as well blend into the furniture. "These actors are even worse than before," she maligned to herself, "not worth conjuring!"

The questioning continued. More mundane clichés directed at the prisoner, more platitudes, vagaries, and philosophical convolutions served back at the interrogator.

Each brought a moan of despair from the one watching and hoping for the right answer, but she could feel it slinking away. She had spent too much time creating the setting, feeling and mood, and not enough time on the characters! If she wanted real representations of genuine human interaction, then she should have created more than just receptacles and mouthpieces of her own thoughts. Plus, names – names are important. Laziness was the cornerstone of ingenuity, but this was just lethargy on stage, and she knew it.

Ask the right question!

But it was too late.

The ball had dropped. Bright, beaming, and completely out of place. The three characters looked with great alarm as it rolled uncaringly through her lavishly generated set.

She panicked, and almost pulled back the curtain.

With great trepidation, the Emissary reached down and then gently held the ball up for the others to see.

By the time they came to an understating, she knew it was over.

* * *

She woke to the rain lashing at her windows and the cold creeping in. Looking over her bed, she noticed her dog in a state of irascible animation. The mutt had dropped his tennis ball again and was frantically searching for it under and around the bed. Why he would be playing with it at 2 am (according to her trusty alarm clock) was beyond her understanding. So was her own mind, for that matter. That's what this exercise was all about, but there was only so much she could learn from a dream. She looked beyond the shadow of the history books by her bedside and to the rain drenched windows beyond. All she could focus on now was the chill gathering outside.

Act 2: The Mountain

The mountaintop provided a horizon of beautiful austerity. Countless peaks of similar height and individual sculpt, spread out across a windswept skyline of deep, swim-through blue. The base of each neatly organised mountain disappeared into the deep fog of unimportance. Only the projected image mattered to the climbers and the hunters. Each peak was accessible, each difficult, and each a worthy challenge to those who had an interest in such things. Most didn't, and left their secrets to those who did. The howl of apathy wound its way up the slopes and between the summits, and was joined with the deep moan that arose from the mist-drenched depths: the residual gasps of those that had tried, and failed, to reach the top.

It wasn't the chill that immediately grabbed her attention upon arrival, but the welcoming starkness that such a vista provided.

She felt like she could be herself this time. *No more performers and their tiresome clichés,* she thought, *this time I will face the danger. This time I will learn.* The curtain was an inconvenience; the Meaning she yearned for would have to be acquired through more direct means.

Her footing was sure and her eyes focused. Her muscles quivered with desire. The bow was clutched in one hand as the accustomed numbness spread through her bones and into her thoughts. She ground herself with her other hand, the sharpness of the rock underneath a mere inconvenience and not the hindrance it should have been. She would have shivered at the wind, felt the ice pierce her extremities and core alike, if she'd cared. Instead, she was focused on the little victims escaping from the tunnels of the mountains and into her sight. Ignoring the shadow-being that stood beside her, she steadied herself for the annihilation to follow. And yet the man who was her other would never let her have the first shot, or the last word.

Her antithesis pulled the bowstring taut and let loose an arrow that pierced a huddled creature, causing its ragged limbs to cascade across its rollicking body as it landed near the rest of its kind. She looked at the pile, sick with envy. He had killed so many; she so few. He was everything she despised, and yet everything she needed. The one character who could accomplish with actions, what the others had failed with words.

Her rival and companion noticed her disappointment, and immediately attempted to assuage her. "Coffee?" he asked, holding out a thermos.

"No, thank you," she had not earned it yet.

"Did you find anything of importance inside?" she asked as she replaced an arrow, her own shot wild and unwilling.

"Unfortunately, no," he replied with a hint of indifference as he hid away her caffeinated desire. "Empty like all the others. Well, of anything important anyway. I scoured the caves and tunnels, and this mountain is done for. Let's move on."

He stared at the creature-corpses that had rabidly pursed him out of the cave only a few moments prior, frenetically and franticly defending the secret writings and treasures that lay inside the mountain of their long-gone master. A fruitless endeavour, for most masters had abandoned their labyrinths a long time ago. Few cared to stay; even fewer cared to explore.

He cared though. For every being had a mountain: a gargantuan keep that enclosed their most precious thoughts and was guarded by their strongest desires. A beacon for a kleptomaniac like him, or a soul-seeker like her.

"This one has been sanitised," he concluded as he studied the scene. The mind was scoured, and the bad thoughts eradicated. He stretched, a glorious strain of sinews and symphonic cracking of synovial joints. He picked up his bow and quiver in one hand, and a small box of explosives in the other (which he saved for the most offensive facades) and motioned her to follow.

She did so dutifully.

And so they travelled, from mountain to mountain, peak to shining peak. She climbed and watched while he entered, excavated, studied and destroyed. They killed and ate and acted with mutual suspicion, as couples often do. They were perfectly unequal, and so their partnership lasted longer than any other. Resentment grew, however, as it inevitably does. She wasn't here to watch after all. She had already seen enough.

One day they came across a mountain jewel worthy of mention. She studied the glorious extravagance of a summit with an awe and intensity usually reserved for self-adulation. It *was* beautiful, mind you, brilliantly encrusted with stones of all cuts and colours, glazed with all precious materials (imagined and otherwise), and topped with platinum, for gold was too much of an understatement. The reflected sunlight was pleasantly blinding, and the opulence continued all the way down to its imagined depths. Such a mountain she had never seen, not in her wildest dreams. She found herself ogling the spectacle for what seemed like forever, unaware of the disappearance of her companion. She thought: *if this is what it looks like on the outside, I wonder what lies within.* She hoped it would last forever.

It was immediately destroyed.

"Sorry," her companion said panting, as he scrabbled up the slope, the detonator dangling from one hand.

"Forgot to get the rest of my stuff," he barely acknowledged her look of shocked indignation as he gathered his belongings for their departure.

"Oh don't worry," he soothed as he noticed her gaping mouth, "there was nothing inside. Too much effort had gone to the exterior."

"That's a shame," she replied solemnly. "It was nice to look at."

"Yes, the prettiest vessels are often the most vacuous," he stated with an unusual intensity, focused directly at her complaint. "Don't worry, I'll find another one just for you, perhaps even prettier and emptier."

He sneered as he studied the remaining explosives in his box, "Now let's go find something more real. Something with substance."

"Like yours?" she asked with an uncharacteristic bluntness.

"Mine? You wish!" he chuckled. "My mountain is easily the largest one here. You can see the whole world from the summit. In fact, such a view can't be seen from anywhere else. Such a perspective can't be replicated by anyone, not even if it was their only desire. And I have crammed the inside with so much knowledge, prophecy and treasure that it makes these hollow replicates," he waved his hands at the expanse around him, "nothing more than shallow facsimiles of what I have achieved. Do you think you have the intelligence to comprehend the nucleus of my being, or the determination to climb to the vantage point in which I reside?" he chuckled derisively as he led the way to the next path.

"Well, hurry up then," he shouted, "we have a job to do, and I don't know about you, but I take my work seriously."

She followed complacently.

They carefully lowered themselves to a craggy outcrop and made a small hop to the neighbouring peak. Again they climbed, and again she felt the cold rise up from the underworld that lie beneath that which people wished to present of themselves. The fog was ever present at these depths, permeating her clothes and stifling her breathing. They came across a small opening, and her companion immediately set himself to infiltrate while giving her the signal to wait for him near the top. She, however, was done playing the sidekick.

"I won't," she announced, as she followed him to the entrance.

He turned, squinting through the darkened orifice to her silhouette shrouded in gloom.

"I wish to study the caves with you," she said, less a command and more a plea.

"And why would you want that?" his voice echoed from inside the opening.

"I want to see what it is you do, and I want to know why you do it," she replied, confidence overtaking paralysis.

Immediately she felt that this was the right question and was glad that she was the one to ask it. She could hear him squeeze his way back. He slid out and landed by her side, his snarl of a mouth placed close to her ear.

"Let me tell you a secret," he murmured, as loud as the fog would allow, "I've spent a long time digging into mountains, and killing the little things that have popped up along the way. I've read many of the scribblings that are kept inside, and even encountered a fellow or two. Some had joined me. None had lasted, and none of what they write or say makes sense. Only my mountain does. I'm not here to learn, I'm here to make sure that there is no one like me. Because if there is, then that person is a threat. You are like me though, aren't you?" his voice purred into a monotonic key as his eyes became slits. "I was hoping you would've shown me your mountain by now. Show me. No delays!"

His sadistic snarl removed all security, as a chaotic cacophony of canines and claws erupted towards her now shrinking frame. Crouched effortlessly upon a precipice, the mountain lion roared! Its prey scrambled across rocks, scrabbled up slopes, and ran for wherever seemed like sanctuary. But all she could find across the range were the remains of prior companions and those that had stayed to defend their sanctums. Some had arrows embedded in their temples. Others had their thoughts removed with more primal means.

The peaks were nothing to the Hunter, but she was still learning. She could feel her own mountain calling, but it was difficult to follow a feeling, no matter how strong that feeling might be. She required a direction, but the only motivation she had was fear. *He* had purpose, and so caught up to her with little effort.

With a nimbleness achieved through practice, and a penetrative stare powered by malice, the beast cut short her getaway. She stumbled and split herself on rocks. A wretched pain poured down her spine and up her arm. The pain felt remarkably comprehensible, and she lost her sense of direction and purpose. Her vision lost focus, and the Hunter began to shift from cat to beast and back again. As she began to gather herself and try to flee, the man-lion lunged, but this time the pain was all too real.

* * *

She massaged her shoulder as the rain continued in an unending stream outside. The window was fogged and her dog was snoring, but she was ignoring everything except for her battle wound. She had twisted herself in her sleep, and her arm had paid the price. As she soothed her injury, and watched the clock hit 4 am, she simultaneously shivered and marinated in her own frustrations.

She was close that time. So close. The mountain had Meaning. The mountain had purpose. The mountain had a peak that could actually be climbed. All that remained now was the cold.

She switched on the heater and resumed the search.

Act 3: The Cosmic Engine

The sand should have been searing, the air baking, and the wind blistering in the arid landscape that she now found herself in. Instead it was quite warm and pleasant, enticing even. Flooded floorboards and misty mountains were now mere memories dissipating in the sweltering sun. She had a renewed desire to explore, to tread untouched ground, and rummage up the vast dunes in search of an oasis of knowledge. Desire was her compass, and instinct her motivator. The hike energised her, and the roasting radial rays of the scorching sun filled her with a vigour and vitality that could only mean one thing: optimism. When she saw the gargantuan beast and its many contradictory orifices presented against the wavering solar backdrop, she was not surprised. She was impressed, however, with its desire to remain recognisable, while simultaneously rejecting all concept of reality. A facility fabricated for the modern madwoman who spends her slumber searching for surety in the abstract. Easy on the eyes, difficult on the mind. Like an impressionist interpretation of a cubist blueprint of something so simple:

The Library of Meaning.

Finally, she made it. And what a journey it had been! What a long night of excruciating rest!

Outside, a swelling crowd had gathered and begun winding its way towards the Library. A great anticipation gripped the hearts of iron and marshmallow alike. She stood in line amongst the throngs of anonymity and watched the strange figures entering ahead:

A little mendicant man nibbling on what's left of his feelings. A rational woman attempting to examine her own mind (she had to pull it out of course, thereby killing herself). The figures of Urgency and Apathy endlessly straining at the tug-of-war rope, with Death watching calmly from the side. And of course, the silhouette that hid the many profiles of Dream and Reality. It turned to reveal multiple faces, one of which was clipped and proper and difficult to look at. She couldn't bear its gaze, and so turned to the figure beside her.

"And who might you be?" she asked.

"Me? Oh, I'm Nothing," he said, and disappeared.

Attempting an unperturbed air that such a situation did not merit (and that she did not really feel), she followed the meandering crowd to the cool awning that would hopefully be the end of her night-time quest. Inside, the custodians were showing their scripts and wares to all that entered. Outside her old friend Sanity had just arrived, but too late! By the time Sanity had called her name, she was already gone.

She picked up one of the books, and leafed through the pages to find a script that escaped her comprehension. Frustratingly, each book and item presented the same conundrum: the information was there, but she could not comprehend it. This is what had infuriated the Hunter, and motivated the Parasite, compelling them to scour the mind, body and soul of any and all they encountered for an iota of understanding. She approached a custodian with her hands full of texts and treasures, hoping for a less destructive method of information retrieval.

"I can't read these!" she distressed.

"Of course not," he replied. "If you could, you wouldn't need to be here."

To her dismay, many were already leaving, having barely sampled that which they could not understand. Those that had found Meaning were leaving under the symbols of the crescent, crucifix and wheel, or the coin, sword and hammer. Perhaps the brush, ball and screen if they were feeling adventurous. Some were already fighting, anxious to prove Meaning lest it leave them (they were strongly urged by the custodians to never return). Others meandered through the aisles, sampling, tasting, dissecting. They had created their own stitched-together reality, leading to the paths, loops, and dead-ends that such thoughts often do.

Such a cacophony under one roof was never bound to last.

It was becoming less an orderly repository and more a directionless assembly of ephemeral ideals and principles. Space and Time had no meaning, of course, but it was disappointing that Thought had lost its way as well. She sighed, and so drew the attention of the Curator.

"Anything I can help you with?"

"Oh, I just want to know the meaning of my existence," she replied casually.

He waved one hand, and from the sand emerged a schematic of desire: the ever present coffee cup that signalled the beginning of new adventures. Its warmth was felt, but its aroma and texture were far away. These seemed to be more difficult to grasp and frustratingly murky. How could she possibly understand something without all senses present?

"If only it were so simple," she sighed.

"For some people it is," the Curator replied.

She looked around at the endless corridors and infinite escalations, and all the dark pathways she had already traversed. "I don't want to glimpse the darkness anymore," she stated, "I want it all to be revealed."

"All of it?"

Multiple eyebrows were raised.

"I'll see what I can do."

A whiff of understanding had begun to emanate from the steaming cup, but before she could fully grasp its potential, she reverted back to obliviousness. The cup had returned to the sand which had made it. As had the book in her hand. All the books in fact, and the structures that contained them. They were replaced with a desert of beautiful bleakness that spread in all dimensions for at least an eternity. She dared not look too far, or too close and instead looked at her feet. Looking down was more than enough.

"I don't understand this."

"What don't you understand?" the Curator replied, his voice low and tone probing. "You wanted nothing hidden. There is nothing hidden here. Each sand grain contains a worldview, idea, memory, or piece of knowledge. You can view them all if you wish. What *I* don't understand," he continued in an irascible tone, "is why *I*, who have changed the entire nature of reality just for *you*, have not received a thank you!"

He stood back with a puffed chest and a look of self-assured anticipation.

"I want it changed back. I want the books. Just the books," she whispered.

The pufferfish deflated.

"Then crawl fast, little bookworm. Thought may be infinite, but you are not."

An unbearable hiss emanated from beneath her feet as the sand gathered, solidified, and replaced the bleak landscape with an unending latticework of possibility. A scaffolding of books stretched beyond imagination, rising above the dwindling dunes until it had eradicated the notion of spatial awareness. She elevated along with it, her nausea turning to vertigo as she made the mistake of looking around and attempting to comprehend the incomprehensible. Only when the structure was complete, and the air had settled, did she attempt to find her feet.

Standing on a bridge of books, connected to many others, it was all so overwhelming. *Nothing is greater than insignificance,* she thought. The structure inspired awe and terror, though the materials were commonplace. This beautiful, intermingled projection of fantasies and impossibilities, reduced to the solidified mass of the everyday mind. She shrugged. It was the best she could do.

She began to cross one bridge onto another, following the nagging thought that the right path would lead to the right answer. The books weren't categorised or classified in any way that made sense (this reality was sorely lacking a librarian), so emotion was all she had to go on. Each footstep was a test of her diligence, each instant of not looking down a test of her willpower. She could feel the end, however. A satisfaction within her grasp. All she needed was the right book, and everything would be okay. It was instinctive to believe, and even more so to seek proof of that belief. *She knew it was there,* and even more so, could rationalise her journey in searching for it. But the latticework of book-buildings stretched on forever, and despair began to mingle with blind hope. She could hear the dry chuckle of the Curator, a smug satisfaction that she did not share.

"Would you prefer a digital alternative?" said a raspy voice close to her ear.

The tome-tower in front of her began to envelop in on itself and then reach for her with a momentum uninhibited by her protests. Inside she could see packets of information in its rawest form, swimming and subducting over one another – a gaping pit of information overload. Yet her answer was inside, she could feel it stronger than ever. She reached in, but the information slipped and slithered away. Using both hands, and the might that only a full night of sleep can provide, she grasped what she desired and pulled it out struggling into the glow of understanding.

As the data began to unravel in her hands, her mind began to start organising it into something comprehensible. From the pit she could hear a rising hum, volume and pitch reaching a banshee's wail. In the time it took her to realise what was happening, the noise had already penetrated her mind and shattered her reality.

* * *

She thrashed around frantically, searching for the dreaded sonic intruder that had ruined her beautiful nightmare. It didn't take her long to find it. The music from the speakers made it abundantly clear who the culprit was. That dreaded harbinger that dashes all hopes for another day: the alarm clock.

Final Act: For a Cupful of Coffee

The sunlight had disseminated through the gaps in the blinds, a feeble attempt to keep the day away. She stared groggily at the dispersed light hitting all the unwanted corners of her room. This was no beautiful diffraction of colour, but dumb light attempting to illuminate that which was purposefully unfocused. She strained her eyes, and looked directly into the path of illumination.

"Ouch!" she exclaimed, shutting her eyes to reveal a detailed negative of her room. The final insult! Now she had to get up, lest she risk permanent blindness. Her ever present sentinel snored at the foot of her bed. He was not done with his search for Meaning. No doubt it involved a tennis ball. *Good luck, mighty Fenrir,* she transmitted, *may you find that which eludes you.*

Gingerly stepping over the frigid tiles of the hallway, she made her way towards the safety and comfort of the kitchen. One final trial, one last obstacle stood in her way. She swore as her foot came in contact with the tiles, a frosty aura shivering her ankles and swaying her legs as she walked (her slippers were long forgotten in the world of dream). Ahead the kettle awaited, and with it some solace from what she had just experienced. Weak light bathed the kitchen counter, and the remnants of rainfall provided the soundtrack to her early morning routine.

She switched on the kettle greedily. Her blind, probing fingers grasped a mug from the top shelf, as her mind struggled to retain what she had experienced, what she had learned. She knew in a few moments that the pressures of reality would eject that which mattered most. She studied the mug as the water boiled. On it was a crude cartoon of a confused man sitting in front of a computer, with the words "How To Think Properly, Stupid" displayed on the monitor. *Not funny,* she thought, as she put down the mug.

The boiling water submerged the coffee grains, turning the emulsified mixture to a deep, dark brown. The aroma permeated the kitchen and immediately piqued her senses to her surroundings. By the time the enticing warmth of the first sip had penetrated her base essence, and the bitter-sweet aftertaste had lingered as far as she would allow, she knew all had been forgotten. Yet there was a comfort to this feeling of loss. Within her, she knew, was a compass for finding her way back. Where it would lead her, she didn't know, but she knew she would get there eventually. She savoured these thoughts as she savoured her coffee; those moments of contemplation and escape that time so rarely affords.

She stared out of the kitchen blinds at the world beyond. The growing light was mingling with the raindrops on her window, casting little illusions upon her face and her own little world. She knew the day ahead consisted of formalities, pleasantries, duties, and other tasks fit for automatons. But she also knew she would return home and the real work would commence anew. She smiled at that thought; her first smile of the day.

Staring around her kitchen, she sighed, and drank the last of the warm gold.

This substitute will have to do. At least for now.

Sleep

Jannet Xie

isn't it amazing how no-one ever dies? between the moment you close your eyes for a night's sleep and the blossoming morning, some take their last breaths and new ones their firsts. perhaps you cannot whisper their names, but i am sure you could tell me the story of your great-grandma, or the tale of your young son's birth. oh, how the names, times and events have been imprinted into our minds; of the ones to live, of the ones who have lived. who will speak of you when you are gone?

Echoes of the Guslar

Dunja Dudic

Upon the hills of a distant Balkan land,
By an ancient river that flows at Nature's command,
An old traveller wanders round,
Towards a nearby town; his path is bound.

When he arrives, peasants welcome the musician,
They ask of him, as was the tradition,
To sit by the fire and sing them a story,
Of fallen heroes and tales of glory.

He speaks –

"Gather round,
I have an epic tale to tell,
Before the morning comes and I bid you farewell.
For centuries, I have been around,
Travelling from town to town,
Playing my instrument of one string.
I am a musician,
A singer of songs,
A teller of tales.

I tell the stories that are never told,
For all you Serbs, who have been silenced.
I sing of the lands you know and the people you are.

"I am a *guslar*.

"Let us roam the mountaintops,
And cross the winding rivers,
By the old watermills,
Let us wander through the green oak forests,
Passed the ancient castles and monasteries,
To your own village,
Where I am sure you know,
Lived the very first *vampir*.

"Born in 1662,
Died (the first time),
In the year 1725,
A dead man who was alive.

"House by house, one by one,
Villagers would awake in the morn,
To find their clothes all torn,
"And on their necks,
Were two red spots,
The cause of blood clots,
Scratching the painful itch,
Left by the bite of Blagojevich.

"Within a day,
Eight people became ill,
Throttled in the night they said,
By a creature who desired
To kill.

"His wife sat awake one night,
After his death, weaving cloth,
When he arrived at their doorstep,
Pale white skin, mouth full of froth,
'Where are my shoes?' he asks her,
Like he had in life,
And when his son refused to make him food,
He drained him of his blood.

"The Austrian official Provisor Ernst Frombald,
Listened to the locals, shocked by what was told,
He called for the town priest,
At the churchyard, they looked at the deceased.

"But when they opened the coffin,
Blagojevich was in there,
Looking like the day they buried him,
Beard grown, his eyes were closed,
Body undecomposed.
Holding a cross,
While chanting a prayer,
The priest staked the body through the chest,
Then burnt it, leaving his soul to rest.

"Many years later,
And to this day,
Nobody has been able to identify his grave.
So hang some garlic on your door,
Like our ancestors did before,
To prevent the coming of the dead,
At night while you lay in bed."

That is how my story ends.
The light of morning is here,
It's time for me to go on.
I must leave you now,
And you must return the way we came.

Besides fields of yellow daffodils,
That have lost their colour.
Past the ancient castles and monasteries,
Most of which have been destroyed.
Through the oak forests,
That aren't as green as they once were.
By the old watermills that stopped working long ago.
Across the winding rivers,
That now flow with the blood of men.
You will look out upon the hills and mountaintops,
Roamed by the travelling storyteller in past time,
Hearing the sound of church bells chime,
Returning home you will never be the same,
Since that fateful night the *guslar* came.

The Forgotten Guest

Alex Ma

I never expected an invitation to stay at Bonython Abbey. Although I went, the Master and Lady of the house seemed to disregard Me. They took their breakfast without me, left me alone while they travelled to the city, and did not even ask if I had slept well. I grew accustomed to their indifference. It seemed like the beginning of a sinister plot; I felt I was an unknowing heroine of a gothic novel. Certainly, the setting of a lone abbey in the country added to my unease.

The looming bell tower of the abbey pealed whenever the hour struck, so I was roused by the reverberating brassy tones every hour. Upon waking, I slipped on a fleece-lined dressing gown. The fireplace in my chamber crackled and puffed out sad embers. I then sat at the vanity observing the reflection. My skin was passably smooth, my hair somewhat dry, and the air had raised bumps on my arms. I brushed my waves into regular undulations.

Lady Daphne always appeared with impeccable presentation. Whereas I was obliged to don a scarf and overcoat, my dresses being far too thin. I did not care if my outfit looked unseasonal. I wondered if her outings were to a salon, where a beautician shaped her into perfection like a goldsmith hammering upon his metal. And despite being a mother, she had no maternal air; she reigned high above the toils of child-rearing.

At the stone staircase I found a servant, and inquired of my hosts' whereabouts. He said that Lady Daphne was asleep, and the Master was dressing. I thanked him for his trouble. I also observed that the servants were treated with an uncomfortable coldness. After all, they were the ones responsible for the upkeep of the abbey. The Master did not carry out the strenuous labour that polished the silverware or fixed the bathrooms or cleaned the windows.

I stood by the tall window of the drawing room, gazing into the brumous distance. A field of lawn surrounded the abbey, like an interminable green ocean. I thought it a waste, if there was such an expansive lawn, and nobody ever went riding. Not that I was a proficient equestrian – I could only go as fast as a canter, and always under the supervision of the groom. The abbey must have stables, for this upper class takes to riding and hunting. A cruel domestication that exemplifies their power over nature.

A log in the fireplace crackled. I warmed myself, pretending that I was in a more pleasant clime. The Master and Lady must be vampires if they inhabited such a freezing place. Was I their unsuspecting victim? I had never felt such chill. Everywhere they went they left a repelling chill. Then I thought of all the scary novels I read: the likes of *Dracula* and *The Woman in White*. A big manor like this must harbour some phantom. Yet I was still here, my stay extended day by day, no end in sight …

Soon I heard the click of heels on the floorboards, and whispers floating down the hall. It was certain; the Master and the Lady were having breakfast. They would sit at the table and have a domestic conversation. I asked for breakfast from the servant. He obliged, and soon came back with a silver tray.

I ate alone in the drawing room. The smell of burning fire placated my senses. I did not expect the Master and the Lady to join me. Being the weekend, they were probably going out to the city. If I was lucky, they would come in to inform me of their plans, and then bid goodbye. When they went out, they did not return until late.

The door opened – just as I suspected, the Master and the Lady were here, and they were taking the train. I nodded, wishing them a marvellous time.

Lady Daphne glanced at me. "Are you faring well here?"

"Oh yes, indeed."

Her eyes sparkled. "So well that you don't want to leave?"

I chuckled. "Yes, you could say that."

"Good." She said that final word with a strange emphasis, her dilated pupils seeming to pierce through my heart.

They left swiftly and soundlessly.

"Now what shall I do?" I shuddered.

Before I could despair, the servant came to inform me that someone was calling me.

"Valerie Smyth, milady."

The servant showed me to the study, its walls bordered by bookshelves full of old hardcovers. He handed me the receiver.

"Hullo dear, it's Valerie. What're you doing to-day?"

"Valerie, dear, I did not expect you to call. Is there an emergency? I'm stuck all alone; the Master and the Lady went out."

"Ah, chucked again?"

"No. They always just go out without even asking if I want to go."

"Sure, they sound like the owners of an old gothic manor."

"Anyway, what are you calling for?"

"Nothing, dear, only wanted to hear what was happening, what with you away for two weeks."

I sighed. "I'm afraid there's nothing to report. No salacious gossip for you to delight in."

"Aw, you really mean there's nothing? Not even between your congenial hosts?" Valerie whined.

"No, certainly not. They're rather middle-aged, despite being thirty. I suppose when you settle down in such a house, you're going to be committed to it."

"Boring!"

"You can't blame them. That's what they're born to do."

"Do they not go to parties or hunts or races or the opera or ...?"

"Not that I have heard of. This morning they went to the city but didn't specify anything."

"Come on, don't be so polite. The next time they do so, invite yourself. They can't stop you."

I shook my head, "Valerie, I'm still their guest. I can't impinge on their private outings. If they want to go out, they'll go out. I can entertain myself at the abbey."

"They sound like awful hosts. Why invite anyone if they won't even do something with the guests?"

I turned aside. "I can't tell ... but there is something about Lady Daphne."

"Why dear, what do you mean?"

"She sent the invitation for a week's visit. It's been two weeks, and still no talk of when I'm going back."

Valerie smacked her lips. "Lady Daphne must really dote on you."

"Yes! That's what I'm saying!"

"What? Can't she be partial?" Valerie rejoined.

"Listen to me. Lady Daphne dotes on me the same way that Miss Havisham dotes on Estella."

Valerie snorted. "Of course. I should have known. You and your big imagination and novel-reading."

"She wants to keep me here. I can feel it."

"Sure thing, dear. And the next thing you'll tell me is she has fangs."

"Oh, Valerie." I shook my head.

"Now, is there anything *real* and salacious?"

"No, I must go now. Goodbye."

"Goodbye, dearest. Next time you must take me to the abbey."

I set down the receiver. Intuition told me something malignant was afoot. They *intended* to keep me isolated. Books always appeared larger-than-life, until now. The image of Lady Daphne's uncanny, soulless gaze lingered in my thoughts.

Outside, I spied a child perched upon a pony. It must be their son, Christopher. I had rarely seen him except for a few moments passing by, where he'd greeted me coldly, and walked away with his nanny.

He leaped and trotted about the grass. A man guided him over the jumps. Christopher seemed to be very malleable to his instructor's words, only peering up at him with glistening, wide eyes. The man shouted and gesticulated with vigour. I thought it inadequate that the young boy should be left without his parents. He would grow up unconfident.

Later, I met Christopher with his nanny.

"Good morning, miss," he said. "Why are you all alone? Don't you have something to do?"

I was taken aback.

"Your mother and father went to the city, so I am staying in."

"Didn't they ask you to go with them?"

"No, I'm afraid."

"Then you must be very bored here."

The nanny ushered him away. "Come along, we're going back upstairs."

I heard the faint trails of Christopher's voice. "I don't like that lady staying with us. She doesn't do anything except for sitting all alone in the drawing room."

I shivered. When and why did he see me?

As I had no occupation for the day, I settled in the drawing room, flicking through glossy magazine pages. The ladies in fashionable dresses seemed to morph into Lady Daphne. I saw her in each advertisement – on a promenade, by the riviera sipping a cocktail, driving through the countryside in a motorcar. She was everywhere, and she belonged everywhere. And I swore that momentarily, Lady Daphne was one model holding an orange drink – and her cartoon lashes blinked.

Noon passed, and so did evening, all alone in the abbey. I took my meals in the company of oil paintings. The bell tower tolled its sombre tones each hour. I was a lost creature trapped in a labyrinth. I wanted to get out of the drawing-room, but where was I to go? The library or study perhaps, to peruse books that smelt of old dust. Or I could ask for some paper and write letters lamenting my inhospitable hosts. I needed respite. I needed escape. I could sense myself slowly growing mad from solitude.

Ultimately, I retreated to my chamber. I sprawled on the bed, staring at the ceiling in a reverie. Home was never an ideal place but compared to the abbey, it was placid. I never had a worry in my blue room. I finally realised, I should have never forsaken home for the vacuous glamour of Bonython Abbey. Lady Daphne had preyed on my weakness: my wandering mind, too fascinated by opulence to examine what ugliness hid underneath. But I would not let her win.

Echoes of chatter and footsteps alerted me. The master and lady had returned. I did not stir. A succession of quick steps came to my door.

"Evening, how did you get on while we were away?" It was Lady Daphne. She was leaning on the threshold, her cheeks tinged with pink rouge.

"I'm well, thank you, I had a cosy time reading by the fire."

"You sound just like Quentin," she quipped.

"I like to keep to myself more than I like to go out."

"Now's not the time," she came next to me. "I wanted to ask. Will you stay with us longer?"

I started "Longer?"

"Yes, I'm surprised too. But I thoroughly convinced Quentin to let you stay. You see, the emptiness of Bonython is so tiring. We keep a massive house, but nobody is here except for us two. I thought it was time that we used the house to its original purpose."

I hesitated, "I thought I should go home now. I've already stayed here for two weeks, I wouldn't want to infringe upon your hospitality any longer."

Lady Daphne's countenance distorted, "I suppose ... But I rather liked you staying at Bonython."

"Why's that?"

"Oh, you just seemed like the kind of person who would appreciate such a house." She peered through her curled lashes, "I think the house is awful, far too large and in need of constant improvement. And no company except for my husband. The boy only provides marginal affection."

"I do like Bonython Abbey, quite a lot."

Lady Daphne grinned, though her teeth appeared strangely sharp, "I knew I was right. You were exactly the right person to invite here."

"Of course. I'm glad, but – "

"But what?" Lady Daphne's tone became ominous. She leant into me, her red lips becoming redder.

"I ought to return home."

She clutched my hands, her varnished nails digging into my skin. I gulped. Lady Daphne's skin was as lifeless as it was white.

"Don't say that phrase," she sneered.

"Get away from me," I forced myself from her grip, she stumbled backwards.

"Return home," she gritted her teeth. "Return home, and leave me to suffer in this empty house? Leave me to waste away my precious youth? My husband and my son drain me. But you? You could – "

"I knew it!" I spat out my words, "You want something from me."

"Stay," she wailed, "Stay here as I command you to!" The points of her manicured nails lengthened into talons. She raised her deadly palm, ready to strike.

I lunged at Lady Daphne, exerting all my energy, and slammed her against the door. I restrained her by the neck. A trickle of blood glided down her collarbone and stained her diaphanous blouse.

"You ... you ..." she choked. "You humiliate me."

I knocked her temple harshly on the wood. She passed out – but not without an eerie, vampiric cackle. Her eyes rolled back to reveal bloodshot sclera.

I had to escape. Adrenaline dominated my senses, and before I realised, I rushed down the stone steps and grabbed the telephone. *Brr, ring, ring ... Brr, ring, ring ...* I couldn't wait. Not when time was working against me.

There was a click.

"Valerie! Valerie!" I rasped, unable to raise my voice, "Valerie!"

"Darling, what's the matter? You sound positively spooked."

"Valerie, drive here right now. Get me out of here. I need to get out."

"Darling, are you alright?"

"Valerie! Get me out now!" I shot a look behind me, "Lady Daphne could wake up any moment."

"Oh."

I slumped onto the marble floor. My muscles were dancing on their own, at once dynamic and immobile. The abbey descended into utter silence. I anticipated Lady Daphne's presence, her high heels striking the tiles, emphatic like a sword being unsheathed. But instead I heard the night wind whistling through the stygian air.

Minutes passed in what felt like an hour. My pulse raced, unrelenting, telling me to run from danger. Yet I held myself still. If I was truly trapped in a story where I didn't belong, there must be a resolution. *Please, Valerie, rescue me*, I thought. *This is not a tale I want to live. I depend on you.*

The screech of tires on the gravel alerted me. I shot up, running to the front entrance. I thought the solemn portraits on the wall reprimanded my escape. But I continued. They could not confine me here. I refuse to be an unfortunate heroine. The wind had forced the great double doors open, and

I ran out into the frigid night. Valerie was parked before the steps.

"Darling, there you are – "

I leapt into the passenger seat.

"Go! Quickly!"

The motor ignited, and we drove off. My head drooped. Valerie had a cigarette perched in her mouth.

"Dear? What happened? It seemed so unlike you to call me like this."

"Oh Valerie!" I tried to articulate, "You wouldn't believe it – "

"What?"

"It was a matter of life and death."

"Really?" she puffed out a perfectly circular tendril of smoke.

"Yes! Lady Daphne … she … well, she had bad intentions."

Valerie glanced at me, "Like what?"

"She wanted me to stay indefinitely in the abbey."

"Beastly!"

I tried explaining to Valerie, "No, I meant that she wanted to keep me there. For herself."

"Sounds just like something those toffs would do."

"No, not that …" but I checked myself, "I felt like I was dragged into the prologue of a grotesque story. They wanted me to stay, to play a character for their pleasure."

Valerie chuckled. "Why, yes, darling, those rich people are always entangled in some foolish conflict. They like to project it onto someone else."

She hit a bump on the dirt track, gave a conspicuous *whoop!* then carried on.

"I bet they're about to divorce. It always happens."

"Poor Lady Daphne," I remarked sardonically.
"Poor her," Valerie agreed, "but at least it ended here."
So, we sped off into the winding midnight.

To Story

Mabel G. Rytmeister

Betrayal by a long-time friend
Walk on, walk on

Slowness
Halting
Hoping
Heaving

Wheezing   Pleasing   Grieving   Leaving
YearningBurningLearning
Leaping
                    Into story
I feel my pulse returning

And I run
        I run
              I run
                    I run

And breathe
My own culpability

The loneliness beneath it all
I'm sorry, I'm sorry
All this is backstory

Breath
Spine
I bind pages
Through my rib cage
I strike through the heart
I am drawing this all
Into art

The End of Art?

Phil Nondum

There is a trivial sense in which a novel ends: you arrive at the last page, and there is no more to read. You set down the book, relieved and a tad weary. Perhaps still the echo of a phrase lingers like a pedal note, but that would fade too. In that its experience has a natural, conventional order, a novel is more like music than painting or sculpture. There is, however, a more philosophically interesting sense in which a novel ends. It involves seeing reading as a directed activity, aimed at some prescribed goal – the elucidation of some insight, perhaps, or the evocation of an emotion. To caricature a little, on this view reading is like ticking a box on a checklist: when I have got the message, experienced the emotion, and thus emerged a little wiser and more sophisticated, the book is just something I *have read* – the aesthetic experience has reached its apotheosis, that is to say it's terminus. The prevalence of such a view reveals something about the place of literature, if not art in general, in our society. (Put simply, we do not take it seriously enough.) In this piece, I wish to question this idea, and propose a way of viewing art in general, and reading literature in particular, that treats the experience as having no end – as an exploration with no destination in sight, where each step holds the promise of an unknown adventure.

I. Art and Messages

Like music, a novel physically terminates, but the affinity fades when we consider the second sense in which a novel could "end". Before a fine painting one lingers, savouring each brushstroke; we listen to the same song a thousand times – but only the most perfervid reader, it seems, would willingly read a novel more than once. Certainly, ploughing through a novel is arduous, and much of the joy of reading comes from the suspense. But this is also true of, say, listening to a symphony, if to a lesser extent. We are prone to see rereading as "a waste of time", the magic of a novel taken to be something that, upon contact, begins to evaporate immediately – it is telling that we never speak of "spoilers" in the case of a painting or a song.

We are inclined to think this way, I think, because a written work has a salient content that one easily mistakes for its essence. Because its vehicle is language, it is far easier to conceive of a work of literature as essentially an act of communication; of conveying a message, or telling a story. More than any other art form, literature seems transparent, democratic, practical – and hence especially in need of justification.

We are familiar with the usual justifications. Reading teaches critical thinking, eloquence, clarity of expression. It develops one's character. Literature is a mirror, it reveals deep, universal truths. Reading a novel for these putative benefits is like listening to Chopin to fall asleep – even if the use is legitimate, the work is not taken seriously as art. Indeed, the last item in the catalogue is the only one that at least pretends to accept literature as profound, but even so, one worries if it is not a false profundity rooted in obfuscation.

To take art seriously is to grapple with what makes it valuable. There are works of literature which we properly call "timeless": Shakespeare's plays, for example. They seem immune to not only "spoilers" but the most thorough analyses and interpretations. No matter how many times they are read, performed, and critiqued, there are always new gems to catch one's eye, new interpretive avenues to be unearthed. It would be absurd to say, I think, that it is their supernal messages which make the plays so great. Messages are simple, general, banal, whereas a work of literature is complex, sui generis, endlessly interesting. If one insists that *Hamlet* could be reduced to a set of messages, we should ask them to write it down. Keats wrote, "Beauty is truth, truth beauty", but to equate art with knowledge is not to vindicate it, but rather degrade it. Knowledge can be summarised, but art cannot; knowledge can be grasped, but art eludes. The observation here, self-evident but critical, is that the value of a work of literature has more to do with its fine details than any grand scheme or message that purports to encapsulate it. A great novel may have messages, but even in a case like *Animal Farm*, where one might say that the primary concern is political, it is not the messages which make it great as a work of literature.

From a young age, we are taught that a story needs a moral, and in high school English, reading is often presented as a "meaning-hunting" exercise: the writer has hidden it, the critical reader must pry it from the text. The training is no doubt vital – serious engagement with literature requires the intelligent interrogation of its content – but the student is easily misled into thinking that literature is nothing more than meaning obfuscated. To take literature seriously is to no longer view reading as a directed activity – it is no more directed than listening to music is. The novel is not a consumable that perishes once its message is gleaned, but something worth savouring and lingering over.

II. An Invitation to Art

The central thesis in this piece is that rather than thinking of reading as a journey with well-defined destinations, we should think of it as an exploration, and of the novel as a world that stands on its own. What I find apt in this analogy is that it captures both the quality of *depth* an artwork seems to possess, and the sense of exhilarating *freedom* the experience of it involves. To illustrate what I mean, let us consider this haiku written by the 17th-century Japanese poet Matsuo Bashō:

> *Clouds of cherry blossoms.*
> *Is the bell at Ueno*
> *Or Asakusa?*[1]

In interpreting this poem, the natural place to start is the metaphor equating the cherry blossoms with clouds. Perhaps it is meant to suggest that the writer is looking up, that the blossoms are so copious they fill the sky. The line then suggests a way in which flowers, that supreme symbol of sweetness and innocence, might begin to appear intimidating as an image of sublime nature.

But perhaps, rather, a sort of dreamy thinness is intended. The flowers, on branches or dancing through air, offer a

---

1   The original Japanese reads: 花の雲鐘は上野か浅草か. The translation is mine.

moment of heavenly bliss that, the next instant, is interrupted by the (temple) bell marking time, where the shift from the visual to the aural is also one from the unbound beauty of nature to the monotonies of daily life. The doubt and uncertainty suggested by the question about the bell's provenance, moreover, contrast with the confidence with which the author was ready to superimpose two elements of nature. We could thus read the haiku as the expression of this intense emotional transformation.

Yet another reading of the initial metaphor sees it as emphasising the frailty and transience of the flowers – rootless, at the mercy of wind – which we naturally project onto ourselves. Once we grasp the metaphor's existential implications, the subsequent question might even take on a tinge of irony: why does it matter where the bell comes from? We see now that the shift at the second line is not so abrupt after all. The emphasis on ephemerality is carried on in the sound of the bell, which marks *time*, and what we saw as the contrast between nature and culture also threatens to break down – the place names, *Ueno* and *Asakusa*, literally mean "upper field" and "faint grass", and their implicit reference back to nature is transparent when written in Kanji.

What I strove to show with the analysis is the astonishing extent to which "meaning" – if we must use that word – could be found in those three short lines. For me, the haiku is nothing less than a demonstration of the possibility of art, a world that draws us in and asks to be explored. We ponder over every word, guide our imagination through the endless hints and suggestions within them. We pause, backtrack and move forward again: it is impossible to read the haiku only once. A corollary of its complexity – whose twin is ambiguity – is that the poem cannot be reduced to any single interpretation. The wisdom in the familiar dictum, "show, don't tell", is that an artwork should suggest via subtle hints, and not ply the audience with definite understandings. For essential to art is the freedom to explore, and when a work foists an idea or response upon us, we call it vulgar, bathetic, manipulative. It is precisely this capacity for imaginative exploration which makes the great artworks immortal: there is always more to be said about them.

We thus arrive at a tentative definition of art: an artwork is something that sustains, if not amplifies, our interest as we engage ever more deeply with it, and it does so by inviting the viewer's free exploration. Many things could make an artwork interesting: the ideas it explores; the emotional journey it takes the audience on; or, simply, the grandeur of its technical or creative vision. What is essential, however, is that the artwork has the character of depth, which we discern by examining how the creative intention embeds itself in the fine details. What makes Chopin's nocturnes beautiful is not any particular emotion they evoke, but the infinitely fine shades of sadness, longing or hope one finds in attending carefully to each note. When confronted with a painting like Bosch's *The Garden of Earthly Delights*, or perhaps Jackson Pollock's *No.5*, what amazes us is not so much that it is complex, but that we could speculate endlessly about the painter's underlying vision and still hit upon new discoveries.

My definition is, in a sense, an exigent one. On the one hand, the somewhat oxymoronic category of "bad art" gets flattened. It still makes sense to speak of one artwork as being superior to another, but to call something "art", under this understanding, is already to affirm its value as something interesting and profound. On the other hand, as calling an object "art" becomes a normatively charged, significant gesture, one must be prepared to defend one's judgment with reasoned argument – crude appeals to conventions and authorities will not suffice. In another sense, however, the definition is decidedly a liberal one. It has no bias against popular art, or genre fiction, and admits any well-crafted object, from creatively designed furniture to fine samurai swords, to be potentially considered as art.

By characterising art as something profound we can begin to make sense of its special place in our lives, but it also begs the question of how to settle if an object is art when there are disputes.

III. Who's to Judge?

In 1913, Marcel Duchamp produced *Bicycle Wheel*. Consisting of a bicycle wheel mounted on a wooden kitchen stool, it was the first of a series of ordinary objects – "readymades" – that Duchamp chose to call art. The assumption behind it is a bold one: namely, that the artist has the ability to elevate an ordinary object to the status of an artwork, that merely by declaring something to be art they would make it art. We find a version of this view also in Arthur Danto, for whom any object could be art if there is an acceptable art-theoretical interpretation of what it means. According to Danto, the Brillo cartons one finds in the supermarket are not art, but physically indistinguishable facsimiles of them – Andy Warhol's *Brillo Boxes* – are artworks because they are made by an artist and justified by a theory.[2] The conclusion, Danto acknowledges, is a decidedly nihilist one: he saw art as coming to an end, consuming itself in self-conscious, increasingly abstract theorising.[3] Art has come to an end in the sense that anything could be art, and one has no way to distinguish the ordinary from the artistic apart from keeping up with the theory.

What is wrong with Danto's view, I think, is that he theorises without an adequate appreciation of why art matters. For him, art is essentially a message embodied in some medium – a criterion that seems too lax, doing scant justice to the depth and power we expect from an artwork. Even if they indeed "say something", Duchamps' "readymades" and Warhol's *Brillo Boxes* are simply too one-dimensional. On my view, they are better read as provocations and declarations that tug at the theoretical boundaries of art, rather than artworks in the true sense.

In a way, however, Danto's view is perfectly understandable. It is a concession to the perhaps commonsensical observation that almost anything can be wilfully seen as "art". Having scribbled some colourful lines, what prevents me (or others) from imputing all sorts of creative intentions upon it? With sufficient ingenuity, we could in our imagination reinvent the stalest cliché as novel, and discover a poetic lilt in the most commonplace utterance.

What should we conclude from this? Certainly not, I hope, that art is a matter of subjective taste ultimately unamenable to reason. To be sure, there is no scientific test for an artwork's value, and our characterisation of art makes it dependent on personal judgment. Yet if the aesthetic judgment is not "purely objective", neither is it "purely subjective". When asked why I do not like a widely enjoyed dish, I could simply say, "It does

---

2   Danto 1964, 580.
3   Danto 2005, 111. See note 1.

not suit my palate," and there would be no need to explain myself further. In such a case, one might say, it is merely a matter of preference, of psychology. We do not come to blows over whether a dish is delicious. In art, however, the situation is quite different. We take aesthetic judgments to be significant, and disagreements are met with great consternation.

Suppose you were to say, "I think Liszt's *Bénédiction de Dieu dans la solitude* is a soulless piece of music," then I would be shocked, and would not let you go until you have explained yourself. I will perhaps ask you, are you not seduced by the opening tenor melody, shining like a clear lake under moon over the undulating accompaniment? Do you not feel the trembling hope in the rising motion, the subtle doubt told in a modulation, the unfulfilled longing unleashed in a sweetly upreaching major sixth? To convince you that it really is a timeless masterpiece, I would trace for you, as it were, the very terrains of its musical world. I would do that with metaphors, with theory, with animated gestures. As in any aesthetic argument, the aim is ultimately to get you to see for yourself the beauty that I claim is there, to reproduce my judgement within you. You may put forward some arguments of your own – perhaps you find the melodies too predictable, the themes too underdeveloped – and we may go on arguing about it. But suppose you were to say, "I see what you mean, but I just don't like the piece," then we cannot help but feel that this is a feeble response. Whereas it may be acceptable in a conversation about what snacks one likes, it is grossly out of place in a discussion about art. Aesthetics is not reducible to psychology: one can and must justify one's judgments with reasons.

Aesthetic judgments, as Immanuel Kant once observed, are really subjective *and* universal: subjective in that one has to make the judgment oneself, yet universal in that the grounds for one's judgment should be valid for all.[4] In judging Liszt's *Bénédiction* as a masterpiece, I do not merely claim that it is a masterpiece for me. I speak on behalf of everyone, and my judgment demands, without presupposing, your agreement, by which you would also prove to me that you have taste.

Let us return to the claim that virtually anything that is written down, when one chooses to read it in a tendentious way, could be seen as literature. This may be true, but one does not expect others to agree with the judgment. A neutral observer would say, rightly, that the analysis is the indulgent projection of private feelings. They could point to the lack of creative organisation in the supposed literary work, or infelicities in its phrasing, but ultimately, what they are saying is that they fail to see in the work the proclaimed aesthetic value. Treating something as an artwork does not make it one, and the fact that no aesthetic argument can be proven does not entail that all arguments are equally sound.

Aesthetic judgments do not devolve into subjective preferences because they are subjected to a demanding standard. This standard is not one of deductive proof as in logic, or of empirical demonstration as in science. An aesthetic argument may of course make use of data and logic, but ultimately it is tested against whether other people, upon viewing the artwork, could see what I am claiming is in there, and reproduce my judgment. The situation here is similar to that of ethics, where one has to answer for one's actions with

---

4   See Kant 1987, 303.

publicly acceptable rationales that are, nevertheless, not provably right-making. Ethical justifications may draw on logic and facts, but ultimately, they appeal to sensibility and intuition. The extent to which our intuitions agree is frequently surprising, but they also clash often enough to cast doubt on any claim about universal human nature.

The dominance of scientism in our society means we are wont to draw a sharp line between the "objective" and the "subjective", as if these words signified well-defined poles. Yet, when someone says, "judgments in ethics (or aesthetics) all come down to subjective preferences", we must ask whether this is how they treat them in practice. When they say, "Murder is wrong," are they voicing a personal opinion and not positing a universal law? The intersubjective character in the way we perform and react to judgments in ethics and aesthetics is a datum that we should take seriously.

Even though an aesthetic judgment, like an ethical one, can often feel incontrovertible when uttered, persistent disagreement is more than possible. While empirical disputes could, at least in principle, be settled by data, when sensibilities clash there is no higher court of appeal. The fact that arguments in aesthetics do not compel but merely invite the conclusion, however, should be seen as a strength and not a fault. It means that one's judgment is free and entirely their own – to declare an object as art is to take a personal stand. Just as a courageous act is commendable only insofar as one could have remained cowardly, an aesthetic judgment shows "good taste" only insofar as it was not compulsory. And here we hit upon another hint of why art is so important to us: the sort of judgments we make about art, the artworks which we regard as significant, reveal something about the sort of human beings we essentially are – they unite and divide us.

The answer to the question "Who is to judge if an object is art?" is that it is each and every one of us. This does not mean that all opinions are equal, or that art is a matter of mere preference. Rather, the judgment of an object as art demands our intersubjective agreement, by which we would prove our sensibility and taste.

IV. Whose intention?

While an argument in aesthetics and ethics demands others' endorsement, it does not automatically fail when others disagree. If I were the last person on Earth to believe that slavery is immoral, or that Beethoven is sublime, this may be more evidence that the world has gone to seed than evidence that I am wrong. Aesthetics, like ethics, does not reduce to anthropology. There is, however, a particularly interesting case which merits special attention: what if the person who disagrees with you is the author of the work you are critiquing?

Reading Kawabata Yasunari's *Snow Country*, the critic Nakamura Mitsuo saw in it the influence of traditional Japanese Noh drama.[5] In Noh, a supporting player (*waki*) sits with profile toward the audience, and their primary function is to draw out the inner thoughts and emotions of the protagonist (*shite*). The same dynamic, Nakamura argues, can be seen in *Snow Country*, where the impassivity of Shimamura, the character through whose eyes we see the narrative unfold, is a foil to the rich inner world of Komako, the geisha who falls in love with him. Indeed, Shimamura's experience seems to align too perfectly with the common Noh trope of a dreaming

---

5   Araki 1969, 334.

traveller, who encounters in a foreign place someone with an (at first) inexplicable alluring quality. Nakamura's analysis is, no doubt, a fruitful contribution to our understanding of the novel, but what is particularly interesting in this case is that Kawabata apparently replied, publicly, that Noh had not occurred to him when he wrote the novel.[6]

Despite Kawabata's denial, it seems too quick to decide that the interpretation had been a "wrong" one. Perhaps Kawabata had thought about Noh but forgot about it afterwards. Perhaps his debt to the traditional drama is a subconscious one. Just as an experienced pianist might, intending to deliver a softer sound, collapse their fingers without knowing precisely what they did, a novelist might shape the narrative intentionally but unconsciously towards some dimly revelated vision.

The analysis of an artwork is necessarily teleological – it postulates a creative intention which undergirds it – but this intention in question has less to do with what the author was thinking than what one discerns from the artwork. In many cases, an artwork (say a movie, or a song) is the product of many people working together, yet we speak as if a unified intention had been behind it (and sometimes we do not, as when we use the documentary hypothesis to study the Torah). We say, the director intended such and such – but could this not be a mistake? Perhaps an actor decided it on a whim. The answer is of course it could have been like that, but that would make no difference. In art criticism, the author is really an imagined, postulated being, constructed from what the artwork seems to reveal. We are concerned primarily with the artwork, and only secondarily with the author. What an

---

6   Araki 1969, 335.

author says about their work is valuable only insofar as it can be confirmed in the artwork itself. If Barthes is right that the author should be stripped of their godlike status, there is a sense in which the god-author analogy surely makes sense. The author is the creator of a world, and thus responsible for every feature within it and every reasonable interpretation that arises. The hypothesis that Kawabata owed an unconscious debt to Noh is a plausible one, because one expects him to acknowledge the affinities when they are pointed out to him. Denying compelling interpretations (not as "true", but as reasonable, as valid), that it is already suggested within the artwork, counts more against the author than against the artwork or the critic – it suggests that the author does not know their own work. "That was an accident" is, of course, never a defence available to the author.

In art criticism, there is no such thing as a "wrong" interpretation in the sense of being empirically false: criticism does not aim at truth in this way. Rather, what a good piece of criticism does is enrich our understanding of the artwork's landscapes, to illuminate its paths for the traveller. There are, however, "bad" interpretations in the sense of being unreasonable. It is not far-fetched to posit that the structure of Noh had been unconsciously woven into *Snow Country*, because Kawabata is Japanese and well versed in the traditional drama; but if he had been a European who had never heard of Noh, then the claim could not be taken seriously.

V. Epilogue: The End of Art?

In this piece, I have criticised two theses about art. The first seeks to reduce art to a utilitarian function, and the second holds that since anything could be art, art has come to an end. Too fixated on understanding art in tangible, "objective" terms, they lose sight of an artwork's depth and power. But when we recall our subjective encounters with art, and the important role it plays in our lives, we realise that there cannot be an "end" to art. To really understand its value, we must reclaim art as a site of imagination and creativity, and appreciate the artwork as a world that charms and seduces.

Acknowledgement

I am heavily indebted to Professor David Macarthur, whose course *Aesthetics and Art* PHIL2618/3681 is the origin of many ideas explored in this piece.

Bibliography

Araki, James. "Kawabata and His Snow Country." *Centennial Review* (1969): 331-349.
Danto, Arthur C. *The Philosophical Disenfranchisement of Art*. New York Chichester, West Sussex: Columbia University Press, 2005. https://doi.org/10.7312/dant92294
Danto, Arthur. "The Artworld." *The Journal of Philosophy* 61, no. 19 (1964): 571-584.
Kant, Immanuel. *Critique of Judgment*. Hackett Publishing, 1987.

Sometimes I Worry...

Kate Leckie

I am not a natural poet,
Which is a silly thing to worry about
because writing is not natural.
Silly, also, because it is definitely true.
It is silly to worry about things that are true,
even more than it is silly to worry about things that are not.

Sometimes I worry
I will write something, and everyone will think:
What the fuck is she talking about?
Another silly thing to worry about
because that is how poetry is read.
It is silly to worry about how things must be,
even more than it is silly to worry about how they may not.
It is silly to worry about poetry *at all,*
which is already so silly to begin with.

I know I am not a natural poet,
because I struggle so much not to explain:
"The dog is a metaphor for childhood trauma" or

"The twin is a symbol for reflecting on the self" and
"Water is nearly always a metaphor for mental illness"
(*all* true, in case you were wondering
though I imagine you likely were not),
because you are reading a poem
and are therefore fully aware,
when a thing is not what it is pretending to be –
like a poem about poetry that is not about that at all.

How did you become so secure in your ability
to drift through poetic turbulence
and land safely at intended meaning?
As though reading every word in order
means you have read a story.
I bet you would read a poem that is just sequential Scrabble
    turns
and discover the fourth dimension …

Sometimes I worry about the fourth dimension.

"This poem is about anxiety"
(in case you were wondering).

Les cendres de l'auteur

Maxwell K. Han

The Ashes of the Author

> The war was hard-won and long-fought. The
> country was cleaved in two; brother clashed
> violently with brother; and the ways of human
> life were defended with these very same human
> lives. Yet one day blossoms might bloom from
> the blood-imbued loam.

— Chapter One, *The War That Was*, J.L. Carter

What a lovely day for a funeral, Vignesh thinks. With his
friends on either side of him, his eyes scan the cultivated yard
that hugs the Carter mansion. Sunlight spills on rows of white
chairs and their occupants, mostly older men he has never met
but knows by reputation. James arranged for them to sit in the
very front seats, and Vignesh can spy every detail of the casket,
an ornate thing of wooden beauty.

"Are you feeling nervous?" whispers Mia.

"A little," Vignesh confides. And he is. To speak at the
funeral of someone you hardly ever knew is going to be
daunting for anyone – but James had asked him, and he can
never refuse James. But there's also a thrill echoing in the
chasm of his stomach. It's shameful to admit, but he's delighted

to have the opportunity to talk about his favourite novel before an audience of such literary calibre. Already he's spotted J.L. Carter's agent Tracey, a science-fiction author who's written multiple bestsellers, and even a handful of English literature scholars.

"I know him," Chloe, a Caucasian friend of his, said earlier. She pointed at one of the professors, a white man with whom J.L. Carter had presumably been friendly. "He was caught having an affair with his teaching assistant."

"Chloe," hissed Mia. "Not the time."

Vignesh's exhilaration escalates when his best friend James takes the stage. He gives some brief words about his grandfather J.L. Carter, who died from head trauma last week after falling off his chair. James' expression, usually handsomely crinkled with laughter, remains solemn as he finishes his address, adjusts the microphone and clears his throat.

"Now, I would like to summon a handful of speakers to share some words about my grandfather. This might seem unusual, but my grandfather was an unusual man, and he would have loved us all discussing him."

If anyone else notices any bitterness in James's tone, Vignesh cannot tell.

"First, I would like to call to the stage a classmate, my dear friend Vignesh," James says, and they finally make gentle eye contact, "who is also a huge fan of my grandfather's seminal novel *The War That Was*. I know my grandfather would have appreciated Vignesh speaking about him and his contributions to the literary world."

This, he knows, is a lie. James has invited Vignesh many times to stay at the Carter mansion, something which used to inspire excitement in him. Vignesh, invited to the very home in which J.L. Carter penned his magnum opus? A dream come true. But after several stinging rejections and dismissive silences from the old man, Vignesh mostly stopped trying to speak to him.

Chloe says nothing, but Mia smiles at him. "You've got this," she says.

He stands, taking shaky steps until he is onstage. The palm cards in his hands feel heavy. The casket looms before him, which he finds unsettling; in his culture, they cremate bodies instead of letting them rot away to nothing. He turns away but a more menacing sight materialises before him – a hundred strangers he has never met, all of whom were closer friends with the corpse behind him than he ever was.

As he readies the microphone, he is reminded strangely of his favourite moment in the last chapters of *The War That Was*. The novel's protagonist Hal rallies his knights just before the Battle of Sharktooth, crying to them: "You are bedfellows of anguish, intimate lovers of loss, and strangers to respite. Yet above all, you are friends of mine, and even beyond that, enemies of the Northfolk!"

Vignesh loses himself then. He imagines that he is the hero Hal. He is standing on a precipice at the end of the world, the open ocean churning beneath him. In his hands is a broadsword, raised in the air so high it catches the fiery sunlight. Before him are his one thousand knights, gathered in raptured silence to follow in his holy words.

He takes in a breath of the salty sea air, and then begins to speak.

* * *

"Where does the author go, once he dies?" their tutor, a white man named Franklin, asked once. "Is there, say, an 'epilogue' to his 'final chapter'?"

Class had just started. James and Vignesh were barely in their seats yet, and the question caught them all off-guard.

"Sorry?" said Mia. "What do you mean?"

Franklin flashed a velveteen smile. He liked to do this, lord knowledge over them like suspending a toy in a cat's face. "Well, Miyoung – "

"Just Mia, please," she said with a pained smile.

"Mia. Well, Roland Barthes famously called for the death of the author," he said. "*La mort de l'auteur.*"

Chloe raised her hand but did not wait for Franklin to call on her.

"Wasn't Barthes one of those French intellectuals who petitioned for the age of consent to be lowered?" she asked.

Vignesh and James exchanged eye-rolls.

Franklin pinched the bridge of his nose. "I'm not sure if that's relevant, Chloe."

"To answer your question, Franklin," said James, turning to the class and straightening his back, "I believe that's the entire point of Barthes' essay. The author isn't merely dead; he disappears once he's published his work. Or did he even exist in the first place? The author's intent or history doesn't matter. He doesn't matter."

"Or she," said Chloe.

"Or she," James amended, shooting a smile in her direction. "The reader's interpretation of a text is what has primacy."

"Fantastic," said Franklin. He tried to pace around but there was little space in their small classroom. "Do the rest of you agree? Vignesh?"

Vignesh scratched his neck idly. "Didn't Foucault say something about that as well?"

(They all ignored Chloe, who muttered, "Didn't Foucault sign that petition too ...?")

Franklin's smile widened. "He did! A couple of years after Barthes' essay, Foucault gave a lecture: Qu'est-ce qu'un auteur? What is an author? Do you remember what it entailed?"

"Foucault mostly agreed with Barthes," said Vignesh, "but he seemed to think abandoning 'the author' was a touch more difficult than Barthes proposed."

"Indeed," said Franklin. "He did not think, like Barthes, that the author blinked out of existence once he 'died.' Instead, he believed that there was baggage to 'the author' – that his ghost haunts us. How do bookstores organise their novels? By author's names. What do we do when we uncover a lost text? Why, we try to find who penned it. Why else do academics kill themselves investigating if a new poem fragment is a Sappho, or if it is merely an imitation of her? If we were to suddenly discover that Forster was not, in fact, the author of Maurice, wouldn't we have to reclassify each copy on our bookshelves?"

"He wanted us to abandon the absurd idea that authorship means a lot, or anything at all," said Mia, always happy to contribute.

Franklin clasped his hands together. "But do we agree?"

"Cautiously," said Mia. "A book shouldn't have to carry the baggage of whoever wrote it. However, I still think it's valuable to research an author's background."

"Fun, even," added James. "Isn't it a bit like detective work, figuring out why an author said something he said?"

"Right, but what happens when you find out your favourite author's a bigot who named his cat a slur?" said

Vignesh, and his heart leapt when James grinned at his Lovecraftian reference.

"That's funny coming from you," said Chloe with a frown, "when your favourite author is a well-known bigot."

Vignesh's smile fell.

"Are you talking about J.L. Carter?"

"Yes," she said, and James laughed. "Sorry, Jamie, I know he's your grandfather, but it's abundantly clear that his novel promotes all sorts of horrible stereotypes about racial minorities and women – and it defends slavery, to top it all off."

Vignesh felt his scowl deepen. He had seen these criticisms a million times online.

"That's not true. The novel lacks ideology. The opening passage describes that arbitrary differences in lifestyles often lead to unnecessary conflict. The novel becomes the perfect war novel: one fully and freely about war."

"It has slavery in it!"

"The bondmen aren't slaves," he insisted. He heard his own voice become louder. "They're a species of magical creatures that are naturally subservient. They aren't real."

"That doesn't mean Carter wasn't thinking of real life when he wrote it," she said, leaning forward on her desk. "Plus, you've met him. Many times! And he doesn't like you one bit, Vignesh! Why do you think that is?"

"Chloe," said James, no longer laughing.

Vignesh had no response. For a moment, he imagined he and Chloe were on opposing sides of a war, and it was his divine duty to swing down his blade in an arc to fell her.

Franklin used this lull in the discussion to intervene. "Let's return to Foucault and Barthes, yes?"

Chloe sniffed. "Disturbing petition aside, I don't really think those men's ideas are all that relevant in today's literary landscape."

"Why not?"

"It's implausible to try to ignore 'the author' when authorship is even more of a personality cult than it was Foucault's day," said Chloe. "Authors do interviews now and tell fans what happens after the book's ending, or an author might get exposed as a raging transphobe. There's an overload of information nowadays ... ultimately colouring the way we consume media."

"But that's exactly the point," insisted Franklin. "Barthes and Foucault want literary criticism to dismantle the idea that some 'divine' authority wishes to communicate some 'true' meaning of a text. Foucault finishes his lecture beautifully: What difference does it make who is speaking?"

Franklin's eyes were glimmering with conviction. He had clearly rehearsed this – and Vignesh relished it.

Chloe looked unimpressed. "For certain groups of people, it makes all the difference in the world."

Franklin sighed. "I think you're wilfully misunderstanding them."

"Yes, well, I think," said Chloe in a tone that Vignesh knew meant she was about to say something irritating, "that if Barthes and Foucault really cared about all that, they'd have published their works anonymously."

* * *

After the funeral, James asks them to stay for a few days. His mum has returned to her new husband's house, so James will be all alone in the enormous Carter mansion until Monday, when classes start again. Of course Vignesh stays.

After a quiet dinner they traipse to the sitting room and make themselves comfortable. Vignesh thinks the idea of a sitting room is hilarious – his house certainly does not have one – yet this one is special. It boasts a collection of *The War That Was* memorabilia, from glass cases containing manuscripts, or the typewriter on which J.L. Carter famously wrote the first draft back in the late sixties, or even a prop of Hal's sword from the film adaptations. A fireplace – yes, a fireplace – crackles in the centre of it all.

"That was a lovely speech today," says Mia.

"It was." From the next sofa over, James grins, black tie loose around his neck.

"Really?" Vignesh scratches the back of his neck. "I only focused on one part of the book, not even my favourite section, and you know I had so much more to talk about –"

James leans over and squeezes Vignesh's shoulder. "Really. My granddad would've loved it."

Again, this is a blatant lie. But it is a nice one, and Vignesh lets the lie linger.

Chloe, however, can remain silent for only so long. "It was impressive on a technical level …"

"But?" Vignesh readies himself for a brawl.

"But I disagree with you. It actually made me uncomfortable to see you glorify such a problematic text and author."

"Didn't you learn a thing from Franklin? Separate the art from the artist, Chloe!"

"That just makes you morally lazy," she bites back. "I'd hate to think you're just as awful as the authors you read."

Vignesh feels his temper rise once more, but it is James that stops her before she is ahead.

"Chloe, that's enough," he says, and there is a coldness to his voice none of them have heard before. "You might have your opinions about his writings but that's my dead grandfather you're speaking about. I cared about him very much."

Chloe, for once, looks startled into silence. "Of course. I'm sorry."

Nobody feels much like speaking after that and so they retire to their rooms. The Carter mansion, of course, has enough guest bedrooms for them all.

Vignesh is leafing through his readings when someone knocks at his door. It is James, who has changed into pyjamas with his initials monogrammed on the breast pocket.

"You're wearing those again!" They have all made fun of James' pyjamas before, gifted by his late grandmother and pretentiously adorned with their family name.

"I was feeling sentimental," says James, closing the door behind him.

Vignesh moves his laptop so James can sit on the bed with him. "How are you? Did you want to talk?"

"Actually," says James, eyes lighting up, "I have something to show you. My mum asked me to find something that belonged to my grandfather – whatever, it's not important – so I was in his study – "

"The one nobody's allowed in."

"The very same," he says with an even grin. "Look what I found."

From his pocket he fishes out yellowed pages, which crinkle as he unfolds them.

Vignesh's heart skips a beat. "What's that?"

"You won't believe me," says James. "It's the unpublished prologue of *The War That Was*."

A momentary silence.

James attempts to pass the papers to him. "Read it!"

"I don't believe you," says Vignesh, half-laughingly. "Don't tease me. You know how exciting that would be."

"It's true!" James insists, taking him by the shoulder and shoving the papers into his hands. "I looked through old files and letters, and I figured out that my grandfather's editor disliked the original prologue and epilogue so much that she had them cut. They were boring, apparently. They undercut the rest of the novel."

Vignesh stares at the pages in his hands.

"I think I'll go looking for the epilogue pages tomorrow," muses James. "Join me, will you?"

All Vignesh does is nod idly.

"I know how much you love the book. I thought it was only right you got to read this." James' eyes crease at their corners. "So, what do you think? You'll give it a read?"

"Yes," whispers Vignesh. "I'll give it a go."

James leaves him alone with nothing but the ghost of J.L. Carter for company.

* * *

Prologue

'Twas a strange sight to see a knight in the town tavern, at noon on a midsummer's day. Yet this was no ordinary knight, and this was no ordinary day. For what knight wore armour so fresh a squire had not yet oiled each plate and tendril of mail, that not a hint of rust had gathered? For what day tormented mothers into keeping sons indoors, until the streets were emptier than the hollow void of a helmet?

This particular knight, beer-drunk and bleary-eyed, was slumped against the wooden table. Yet it was not for reasons of inebriation. He was startled awake when he felt the heated touch of a hand on his neck. Swiftly he turned, his new armour clanking with the great movement.

"It is you," he marvelled. He peered at his friend, the farmer.

"It is me," cried the farmer with a cheerful smile, pulling out the seat opposite him. He craned his neck to bother the bartender. "Two of your best, please."

"Oh, please, no more," groaned the knight. "I have imbibed enough to kill a horse."

The farmer raised an eyebrow. "You will kill much more than horses, the places you're going."

This sobered the knight up. He sat up in his wooden seat, the armour clanking loudly once more. The bartender passed by and placed their two beers on the table.

Sighing, the knight took a swig then slammed the tankard down with a grimace.

"What brings you here? Do you not have a farm to look after?"

The farmer smiled.

"I have come to see your new armour."

"Well, what do you think?"

The farmer stared at him for a long moment, as if Time herself had ceased her endless passage. Sweat beaded the knight's forehead, yet it was not from the heat of day. His eye twitched every so often; it had never done that before. Yet the farmer merely said, "It is too large for you."

They both chuckled. As the hours strolled by, they eased into the chatter of their childhood. They talked of nothing significant, of the farmer's crops and the knight's sisters, of the construction of the new school, of the way the sunlight glanced off that wineglass through that window over there.

And yet the conversation circled back to the most pressing topic: the reason the knight was clad in such newly fashioned armour, the reason the streets were vacant.

"Must you go tomorrow?" asked the farmer.

"I was one of the first to volunteer," answered his knight friend. "I must go."

"But why?"

"We are defending our way of life. Those Northfolk are coming onto our Southland and expecting us to listen to their way."

The farmer shook his sorrowful head. "They think what we do in our country is wrong. I, for one, agree."

The knight frowned. "I refuse to argue with you about this. Our leader Hal claimed that dissenters will try to turn the blame back onto us. You know that the war is not about that race of people, the bondmen, at all – it is about our ability to exercise our rights!"

"What about the bondmen's rights?" the farmer asked, his eyes imploring.

The knight grunted and rose to his feet. Again, his armour clanked harshly. "If you came to scold me, it will have been for nothing. I am fighting for my land, for the hero Hal."

The farmer stood too, reaching out to gently cup the knight's elbow. Yet all he could feel was cool steel. "I apologise. Stay."

The knight glanced at the farmer's hand. "Just a little longer, perhaps." Yet something unusual stole the knight's attention and he darted to the window through which the dying sun glowed.

"Do you hear that?" he asked with a desperate gasp.

The farmer looked curiously at his longtime friend.

"I hear nothing."

"I hear the bells of war."

"I hear nothing," said the farmer.

A tear formed in the corner of the knight's eye. "Listen closer," he said.

— Unpublished Prologue, *The War That Was*, J.L. Carter

* * *

When you love someone, you do so one detail at a time. Each new little love-detail is like its own pickaxe chipping away at some formless stone, until suddenly one day you wake up and realise you are gazing at a full-figured marble statue. Vignesh knows plenty of details about James, like his favourite order at his favourite café or the complex push-and-pull of his relationship with his late grandfather. Vignesh is especially intimate with James' sleeping habits. He knows that James snores, a guttural, unhealthy sound; that James is not a morning person; and most of all that James is a deep sleeper.

And so, when a yawning James stumbles into the dining room at high noon, Vignesh smiles.

"I made breakfast," he says, sliding the plate of eggs and toast over, "though it's possibly cold by now."

"You're a legend," says James, dropping into his place at the table, which is far too large for just the two of them. "Where are the other two?"

"Oh, about that ..."

Vignesh tells James what transpired whilst he was sound asleep in his master bed. The topic of *The War That Was* had naturally come up, and even Mia was unable to keep Vignesh and Chloe from warring. Chloe claimed that Vignesh, a man of colour, should see the ethical problems with consuming racist literature. He dismissed her; didn't Barthes declare that we needed to free ourselves from interpretive tyranny, from the limitations of "the author"? Chloe said that it was ironic to talk about freedom when his favourite book was slave apologia. He called her a white feminist, she called him a non-critical consumer of literature, and, with Mia in tow, stormed out of the house.

"Viggy," says James while chewing on his piece of toast, "I've told you before. You need to let her win arguments, otherwise she'll never shut up."

He scoffed, tracing his finger on the fine tablecloth. "She's going to be a pain in the ass on Monday."

"Isn't she always?" James sets down his cutlery and suddenly leans forward. "Hey, on the topic of *The War That Was*, how did you feel about the prologue I found?"

Vignesh has prepared an answer for this.

"I ... don't know how to feel. It's so different from the rest of the novel, no? It's dialogue-driven and it's about some side characters that never appear again. I'm not quite sure why it even exists. I completely understand why the publisher cut it."

James' face falls.

"Well, then," he says, standing and leaving his empty plate on the table. "Hopefully when we find the epilogue, we'll have a better understanding of my grandfather's intentions, right?"

Vignesh has the half-urge to say something like That's not very Barthesian of you. Instead, he says, "Yes, I'll help. Why don't you go on ahead? I'll catch up."

There is surprise on his face, but James cannot refuse Vignesh as much as Vignesh cannot refuse James.

"You know, I was hoping you might have an interpretation for me, since you love the book so dearly. I think my grandpa wished I liked it just as much as you did." James' voice sounds wistful.

Suddenly Vignesh feels guilty for raining on James's parade. This is clearly part of his grieving process, his clinging onto the last of his grandfather's writings. Of course Vignesh knew James often oscillated between affection and vitriol for the legendary J.L. Carter; but he's genuinely surprised at the fervour with which James is chasing his grandfather's ghost. Maybe he doesn't know James as well as he thinks he does.

"At least he liked you," is all Vignesh can say.

James, his body made of misshapen marble, exits the room. He leaves white dust in his wake.

Once he's sure James is gone, Vignesh reaches into his pocket. From there, he extracts J.L. Carter's unpublished epilogue, pages which he has already read through several times before.

* * *

Epilogue

'Twas a strange sight to see a knight in the town tavern, late in the evening during the coldest winter in years. Yet this was no ordinary night or knight. For what night was filled with the victorious processions of mothers and wives celebrating the returns of their men from war, or mourning their honourable deaths in the name of Southland? For what knight, shivering despite the layers he covered himself with, crouched in the corner of the room, the only one in a lonely tavern?

In the quiet of the night, one became two.

"It is you," croaked the knight, looking up at his friend with bloodshot eyes.

"It is me," the farmer said. Again, he placed himself in the seat opposite the knight, but now he made no move to touch the knight's neck with a gentle hand or give an affectionate smile. It had been too long. Time had placed herself firmly between them. The lines on the knight's face were more deeply wrought than a trench.

"I cannot sleep," the knight confessed. "When I lie in bed and close my eyes, I expect to see the black of my eyelids but instead I see myself crawling through blood and mud, striving to retrieve my lost sword. But I cannot find it, so I must instead hold down my comrade's fresh corpse and extract the weapon that had slain him."

The farmer reached out, but the knight retracted violently. "You won the war for us," the farmer said. "You fought valiantly, and you lived."

"I won the war, yes," said the knight, "but for whom?"

"For your land," the farmer tried. "For your people."

The knight ignored him. "We had bondmen fighting alongside us, you see, even though our side fought to keep their race enslaved. Those bondmen thought they might receive special treatment when we won – but Hal had them in shackles as soon as the enemy surrendered."

"The fault is not yours."

The knight rose to his feet. "I cannot even cry for those bondmen. What right do I have?"

"But what can you do now?"

The knight had no answer. Suddenly he took a sharp breath. "Do you hear that? The bells of war – they are back!"

And then the knight began to cry his undeserving tears, his body shaking with every wretched weep. The knight had long since shed his armour – so why could the farmer still hear the rancorous clanking of metal?

"I hear them," said the farmer. "I'm listening."

— Unpublished Epilogue, *The War That Was*, J.L. Carter

* * *

Vignesh remembers the first time he read this epilogue, in the dark quiet of J.L. Carter's study. The towering walls doubled as shelves, and everywhere he looked there were broken ballpoints and crumpled papers. Amid the disorganised filth sat Carter himself, like an ancient king sunk into his decaying throne.

"This is the epilogue?" Vignesh said hollowly. The pages in his hands felt brittle.

"Yes," Carter said in his haggard voice, "my unpublished epilogue. Does that answer your question of what happens after the story?"

"I don't understand," said Vignesh. "The last chapter in *The War That Was* is triumphant; this epilogue is tragic."

"Well, it's supposed to be," Carter snapped. "Give it back here, boy."

Vignesh returned the pages too willingly, as if they were on fire. "I thought the novel was sans ideology, that the bondmen were just an element of world-building."

Carter sneered, shoving the epilogue into his drawers with a slam. "I knew this would happen. My editor back then was some bimbo who couldn't understand that my readers might be just as air-headed as she."

All those quarrels with Chloe about authorship and *The War That Was*, and they had both been wrong. J.L. Carter's novel was intentionally imbued with the iconography of racism and slavery, but only insofar it was a veiled critique of said notions.

"So, we're not supposed to side with Hal?" Hal, the hero standing before his knights, above the place where the land meets the sea, his sky-bound sword glinting with godly light.

Carter laughed; it was a horrible, choking noise. "Not at all. Now, are you satisfied, boy? Will you stop bothering me – and my grandson?"

Vignesh had lost his patience.

"Why? Because I'm Indian?"

Of all things, this made Carter grimace. "Don't be so crass. It's bad enough that my grandson chooses to spend time with boys. I'd rather he keeps it within his people too."

He might as well have slapped Vignesh across the face or stabbed him in the heart.

"How can you claim to write an anti-slavery narrative and still be racist?" He had not meant to shout.

"Forgive me if I simultaneously believe that slavery is an immoral institution, and also that my grandson should stop affiliating with you," Carter croaked. You, he said, like Vignesh was of a different species.

"I believed in you," he said incredulously. "I believed that your novel was untouchable, that it was the greatest entry in the Western canon."

His memories of defending Carter made Vignesh feel ill.

"Well, then you shouldn't have asked about it," said Carter in between coughs. "But a deal's a deal. I expect to see you out of my house by tomorrow, and out of any classes you share with James soon after that."

But Vignesh pushed down the nausea, and he grounded himself by walking around the desk. He approached Carter, who was bound to his throne.

"I shouldn't have asked," he said slowly. "But you shouldn't have answered."

Carter shrank back, eyebrow raised. "What do you think you're doing?"

Vignesh did not bother with slapping or stabbing him. All he had to do was give a kick to Carter's chair – next came the loud thud and the sick crack of bone. Vignesh panicked at the time, but he needn't have worried; Carter was an old man, and James could sleep through anything.

And though now he regrets running away, he knows it is time to finish the job. He has made sure that he is all alone. James is in the study, and the girls are long gone.

While he walks towards the sitting room with its *The War That Was* keepsakes, he cannot help but think of Franklin's mysterious question. Had Barthes or Foucault been correct about "the author" post-mortem? Does he cease to be, like a number subtracted from itself, like a memory forgotten into inexistence? Or does he haunt the earth, like a ghost clinging onto lost life, like the oxygen that we cannot help but breathe?

Vignesh kneels on the floor as if he is praying. He shuffles closer to the fireplace. His actions are that of a paranoid man; he doesn't know whether the police even suspect foul play, and this epilogue is an important artefact in literary history, is it not?

But then he concludes that it does not matter what happens to the author's soul once he dies; what matters is what happens to the body. And, after all, in Vignesh's culture they cremate bodies.

He tosses the papers into the flames and watches them blacken and curl into nothing.

"What," says James' voice, "are you doing?"

Vignesh swivels around to see James standing at the doorway. His marble stone face.

For a moment Vignesh feels, not like the hero Hal, but instead like that nameless knight – hunched over miserably, invisible blood dripping from hands, forced to listen to the impossible cacophony of culpability. But that knight doesn't exist anymore, does he? He is turning to ashes at this very moment, Vignesh thinks.

He takes in a breath of the salty sea air, and then begins to speak.

The Good Samaritan

Tom Evans

Before

The morning commute. A station just down the road from the warmth of my inner-city terrace, but a pain all the same. It's a struggle not to touch anything or be sneezed on, but today I have the pleasure of being squished against a sniffling man who doesn't know what deodorant is.

"Arriving at Town Hall Station." The monotonous announcement brings a sigh of relief and I make sure I'm first off the train to make an exit out of the overcrowded station, heavy with stale air and lack of air conditioning.

Outside the building, the cold winter sun warms my moisturised face and brightens my new charcoal suit, tailored by the best and with the finest material.

With chin tucked in and chest out, I walk with intent to my office only a block away, each step thudding on the pavement with a soft squeak of my new designer loafers.

A brief respite from the suffocating train and station is short-lived, as a deafening scream bellows down the street from a homeless man on the corner ahead. In a mass exodus, fellow commuters in front of and behind me cross over to the other side of the road, some leisurely, but others quickly with fear.

There are, however, two people that remain on their determined path ahead of me. I slow down, cautiously waiting to see what unfolds, but also to fulfil the guilty pleasure of seeing such a lowly person interact with people with actual purpose in their lives.

The first to pass the rambling homeless man on the corner is a woman in an elegant pantsuit. She's wearing Prada sunglasses and carries a Louis Vuitton handbag as she quickly approaches him with an air of ambivalence.

He stops his wailing momentarily, standing up from his hovel and pleading with the woman, his hand clasped in front of him as if in prayer.

"Please, Miss," he says. "Please help me, I'm starving and need some money for food."

On his knees now, choking back tears as his whole body shudders. What a sorry sight of a man; face covered in dirt, browned clothing and no shoes revealing crusty socks and open wounds along his legs. Pathetic.

For a moment, the woman stops. Taking off her Prada sunglasses, she inspects the man and his mobile home – a shopping trolley full of plastic bags containing assorted goods.

She tightens her grip on her handbag before letting out a brief sigh and putting her sunglasses on to walk away.

The homeless man hangs his head, a nest of matted hair from his head and peppered beard obscuring his face as he turns to lie back down on the ripped piece of cardboard one could only assume is his bed.

"Sir, excuse me, sir?"

He's now approached by the second person in front of me, a man casually dressed in a jumper, jeans and sneakers. A grunt is emitted from the homeless man as he slowly gets up to plead with another member of the public.

"I came over here to request something," the man says. I now notice his hiking bag and New York Yankees hat in the telltale outfit of an American Dad.

"A request?" the homeless man says.

"Yes, a simple request!" the tourist replies. I'm etching ever closer to them now, finally able to hear the twang of his accent.

"Now, I'm sorry you're in this position right now, it truly breaks my heart." The homeless man's eyes widen to the size of dinner plates as he pictures his next delicious fast-food meal.

"But ..." he pauses, scratching his head and kicking his foot into the air, "you see over there?" pointing across the road to a café where a woman and young girl are staring back at them. "That there's my wife and beautiful daughter, trying to enjoy a nice brunch." The homeless man looks at the wife and daughter, then back to the man in disbelief, stretching out his hand and resting it on the tourist's shoulder.

"So, you're kind of scaring my daughter with all your hootin' and hollerin' and it would be great if you could maybe pack up shop and take your begging elsewhere? This is a special holiday for the family and I'd hate to ruin a moment like this."

A pause, then the homeless man begins tapping the tourist's shoulder.

"Ruining your holiday?" he mumbles. "Well I'm sorry for disturbing you, my good man! And my condolences to your family!"

He lets out a deep and maniacal laugh, pointing his tongue out at the daughter in between laughter and coughing fits as the tourist hurries back to his family and ushers them inside the café to another table.

I regret my curiosity as I now realise that I'm the next person to approach the sorry state of this homeless man who I don't want anywhere near my new suit.

Trying to avert eye contact, I walk cautiously past him as he tries to beckon me closer.

"Hey, mister. Yeah, you over there," he says, shuffling up beside me and forcing me to hold my breath and tilt my body away from him.

"Spare some change, mister business man?"

I scrunch up my face in disgust, but it seems like this homeless man won't let up and he starts to follow me to the pedestrian crossing.

"Anything you have, I'm just looking for something to eat, is all." I pause, turning around to face him before peering into my leather tote bag. He follows my gaze, watching intently as I rummage through my bag and pull out a wallet pouch.

Opening it up, I retrieve not a crisp note or shiny gold coin, but rather my AirPods case. Slowly, I open the lid before putting each one into my ears and put the case back into my wallet pouch and back into my bag.

I wait for the homeless man to break down, to throw a fit, screaming and crying and embarrassing himself in his futile begging, but he just stands there. Staring blankly at me, he tenses his gaze as if deep in thought.

The light finally turns green and I turn to leave.

"Wait a second," he says in complete disbelief. "I think I know you ..."

After

It wasn't always like this.

I used to work in that high-rise building just around the corner, climbing the corporate ladder and really making a name for myself.

Designer suits, weekend trips on my yacht, all the flashy cars and watches a man could dream of were part of my reality. Back then, I was really someone.

Then, it all went wrong.

First, the whispers at client lunches. Jokes about an easy way to make serious money. I say "jokes" because I would laugh at how simple it all sounded, and that's because it was. The only problem was that it wasn't technically legal. But, they told me, no one had been caught.

We all know the story: I got too greedy, flew too close to the sun. I hedged my bets, gambled my money and in the end, I was the one to take the fall.

By the time I'd reached this stage, I was already losing friends and family, even as the money came pouring in. But now, I had really lost everything.

Millionaire financial broker with the corner office at the top floor of a Sydney CBD office to homeless man on the streets of the same city.

Nothing could prepare you for something like this. The constant feeling of hunger and hopelessness. Always too cold or too hot, filthy in tattered clothing and maggots literally eating at the open wounds on your feet. The one pair of socks you have worn for so long without removing that the fibres have literally fused with the skin of your feet.

Moving around constantly, police barking insults at you to remind you of how pathetic your life was as you hurriedly push your shopping trolley filled with all that's left against your name to another temporary home.

Always sick, always sad, but worst of all, always hungry.

Each day is now spent clutching at my stomach in pain. My brain can't think straight most of the time now. My speech slurred and reduced to grunts as my life now revolved around finding and eating any food I could get my hands on.

Today is one of the bad days. No food scraps to be found in the nearby bins, and I slept through the short window to get something from the food truck at the homeless shelter.

Which leaves me on the corner of Queen Victoria Building in the city, a busy thoroughfare for the morning commuters travelling to work and my best chance for food.

I can barely make an hour of holding up a cardboard sign that respectfully asks for some money for food before the smell of takeaway coffee and pastries sends pains through my stomach and gives me a pounding headache.

The wailing comes out of me now in desperation. I'm deeply embarrassed as men fasten their backpacks and women's knuckles turn white as they clutch their bags. People begin to cross to the other side of the road in droves, some walking and others basically running away.

Only a few people are left that are still walking towards me.

A businesswoman approaches with a real presence about her, a long, sharp black dress and a trendy grey suit jacket complementing her Gucci sunglasses and Yves Saint Laurent bag.

The bright summer sun shines on her, almost illuminating her as she approaches me and I begin to bargain with her for food.

She stops for a moment to take her sunglasses off. Her big, dark brown eyes soften as she looks at me, then my shameful excuse for a home. I start to feel embarrassed as I realise this woman must only be in her late twenties – I couldn't imagine how uncomfortable she must feel.

I don't even realise that I'm on my knees now, begging her for anything she can spare. In reply, she lets out a deep sigh before putting her sunglasses back on and walking away.

Deflated, I retreat back to my cardboard bed and begin to pull garbage bags over me before hearing the unmistakable sound of an Irish accent close by.

A man stands over me now, clearly a man on a holiday with his baseball hat, white T-shirt, cargo shorts and white New Balance shoes with fresh knee-length Nike socks. He gives me the standard line of apology, saying he feels sorry for me and wishes he could do more to help me.

My eyes glaze over, only thinking about food, as is often the case these days, as I wait for him to say "this is all I can spare" before handing me a five-dollar note. Instead, he starts to point toward a woman and young boy across the road at a café and tells me that they're his wife and son.

My brief smile at them quickly vanishes as he tells me to move elsewhere because my shouting is scaring his son and ruining their holiday.

I can't help but laugh, so blinded by my hunger now that I start to yell at him and his family as he quickly returns to his wife and son before ushering them inside the café.

As they do so, I watch the boy staring innocently at me and a wave of guilt washes over me. I had reached rock bottom, reduced to frightening children and making adults feel uncomfortable. The worst part is that my hunger and helplessness often mean that at times like this, I don't stop and think about this reality.

Was it wrong for the father to want to protect his son? My dad was never really there for me growing up, but I wonder if I ever had my own son, if I would do the same.

I dwell on this thought as I see another man approach. This time, an assured businessman. I admire his expensive suit and slicked-back hair as he walks towards me, his shiny black boots clicking against the footpath with authority.

Ready to give up hope, I decide to follow this businessman to the pedestrian crossing in one last effort to get some form of sustenance. I ask in the politest way possible, that my foggy brain could allow, if he would be able to spare any money for me.

Turning his nose up in my direction, he instead averts his gaze. I get a whiff of his expensive cologne and can't imagine how horrible I must smell in comparison. We're at the crossing now, and to my surprise the businessman turns towards me and begins to rifle through his bag. My eyes follow his hands as he begins to retrieve a wallet pouch from his bag.

I realise that this complete stranger is wearing the same brand of suit I used to wear, and that the bag he is rifling through was one of the bags in my collection that I was fond of. Even the boots he wore were the same colour and style as a pair I once owned.

Would I ever have stopped to give a homeless man money?

There is no note or coin retrieved from his wallet pouch as he instead retrieves an AirPods case and begins to put each piece into his ears. The buzz of the green signal on the pedestrian crossing brings me back into focus as the businessman turns to walk away for the last time.

Standing there, watching him walk into the distance and be swallowed up by the men and women that all look exactly the same, I accept defeat like I so often do in this new life.

I look down at my blackened toes then up to the deep blue sky, an odd feeling sitting in the back of my throat as this businessman that has just eluded me causes me to whisper under my breath.

"I think I know you."

Of Course I Have Known Pain!

Zoe Morris

The pink roses are blooming,
the pink camellias
are dusting themselves onto the floor.

The sea washes over me like fingers,
the sky leaping in her satin gown;
there, the blinking of the stars and their long eyelashes, there,
    the touch of a hand to another,
though blood glistens on top.

Still, the bay opens herself up
to every sunset, sighing,
and still, the rain laughs as it tickles my nose,
the sunshine running through the wind in her yellow coat
to plant a kiss on my cheek.

I have been so down –
of course, I will have more!

Scars of the Wayfarer

Gil Kerr

De-abilified

Saturday 17 June 2023

Today is fifteen days since coming off Abilify, a mood stabiliser commonly used to treat mental conditions such as bipolar disorder, major depressive disorder and schizophrenia.

The last four or five days have been a battle. Words can't exactly capture the overwhelming rush of thoughts, feelings and emotions flooding my mind. But I'll do my best.

Abilify is like listening to a band, except the guitar and bass only have one string. The percussionist is playing a single drum. You can quite literally feel the colour slowly fade from your mind.

Coming off is worse. But,

don't you want to take a leap of faith? Or become an old man, filled with regret, waiting to die alone.

Let's start here. Right now, you're a blank piece of paper. Until one morning you hide the tiny little pills at the back of your bathroom shelf. And then the work begins.

And for a while, everything is fine. Until, well, it isn't.

You start off being creased.

Then, flipped over.
Punctured and mended.
Slammed between a palm and a desk.
Torn apart.
Who knows? Maybe you'll be crushed up into a ball and thrown into the trash, unwanted.
Until an idea comes to mind. A direction.
Transformed and reimagined.
A glimmer of hope.
This faith is all you have.
And then, it starts to make sense.
The creases tell you where to fold.
The folds tell you where to go.
Until finally you're turned inside out, maybe once, twice, or twenty times.
And it hurts.
But who knows? Maybe, on the other side, you'll be an elephant? A boat? Or maybe even a crane?
With wings strong enough to fly away.
Far and wide.
And leave this time behind as nothing but a distant memory.

Re-abilified

Friday 18 August 2023

At first, I'm shrugged.
When I have more holes to fill.
I'm tired of the plugs,
in the food, drugs, or pills.

So I move one way,
with no need to pretend,
so on another day,
this loop has found its end.

At the beach with no flags,
you watched from afar.
In the sand is my bag,
in the waves I found my spar.

And at last,
for nothing is yet scarier,
fading will be the past,
Cry Scars of the Wayfarer.

Quiet the Racket, Sport

Gautam Mishra

"We're just different people" he said, pausing for a break in conversation.

My father sat less than a metre in front of me, on the fold-out bed in a cramped Bali hotel room. Our previous hotel in Seminyak had two separate rooms, one for myself and another for both of my parents, but Nusa Dua was more exclusive (meaning: expensive), and two rooms would've been notably pricier. My parent's signature Indian (inherited) frugality wanted no part.

He dropped his glasses over his nose slightly, allowing him to hawk me over the top of them. He continued, "I know people in my office that are very different from their parents, some of them hate their parents, you know, some of them make it work."

His voice was slightly more monotonous than usual, wielding practically perfect English, though you might be able to find a mispronunciation or incorrectly used word if you spoke to him long enough, but it was still a remarkable feat given he was largely self-taught. Still, those errors bothered me, as trivial as they were.

My mind wandered in these conversations.

Yelling was a common-place sport in the Mishra household, and (not to brag) but I was able to play along without much conscious thought. Although participated by all in the three-person household, my mother would often step aside to let my father and I go at it. Accusations, arguments, evidence, all hurled at each other over our own pathetic net. Although individual matches would have distinctive beginnings and endings, they often ended with some half-hearted resolution on my part after a handful of tears, because I wanted out. My father could go on longer. He would never slip up, he was better. Hours, not minutes, measured how long we could go on for, usually towards the night especially in situations like these, after being forced together for more than a couple of days.

Despite winning most of these things, I think even my father would probably agree that we both lost at the end of the day. No one changed. I would always be the anxious son that always found a way to be self-centred while struggling to meet expectations, and he would remain the over-protective, neurotic, angry father that he always has been.

I thought I would die with our relationship like that. With the games being like that.

* * *

My relationship with my father has always been complex. He's a logical, neurotic, detail-oriented man, the kind who plans for guests a month in advance. Not just where they would sleep, but the type of curtains in their room – where they would put their laundry, how far it was to the nearest sink, managing the perfect laundry cycle so they could get the best set of sheets in the house. In such social situations, he seemed to operate well. I get the butt of those situations. Anger is what I get, actual anger. Probably something from the childhood, he was dealt with; a come-from-the-mud kind of story.

His father before him, my grandfather, was the first in his family to abandon generations of farming for academia, becoming a professor of physics at a notable Indian university. His son, my father, Rajesh Mishra, was born and raised in the seventies and eighties in a quiet middle-income area of Varanasi, India, when it wasn't quite the bustling city of a million-ish that it is now. My father was socially disciplined and academically inclined, so he flew through high school with good grades. He studied for his university entrance examination for three consecutive years and breezed through his admissions exam because he had memorised the structures of every possible question. He attended an Indian Institute of Technology, one of the best universities in the country with a sub one-percent acceptance rate, to study Electrical Engineering. Four years later, in the mid-nineties, he worked at a company now a part of HP at what I am sure was an auspicious role at the time: designing and manufacturing circuit boards for computers. It was then when he had an arranged marriage to my mother, and they decided to move out of India to allow for a better life for their children – first to Singapore, but finally to Australia after learning of the mandatory conscription requirements in Singapore if they gave birth to a male. They had their first and only child (that would be me) in Perth, Western Australia in 2003 but moved to Canberra when a work opportunity arose. They settled there.

We lived in a distinctly middle-class neighbourhood in Tuggeranong, but after ten years of comfortable dual-income employment, both in the Australian Public Service (what else in Canberra?) we moved out to an upper-middle class house in Woden. Over that time, my education went through some significant changes. From preschool in the middle of the Tuggeranong mall, to a public primary school in Isabella Plains, then another in Bonython, and finally in Torrens, all within a period of three years in pursuit of a higher academic ranking on myschool.edu.au. We finished by interviewing for admission at a top-ranked private school, where I would attend from Year Six to the end of high school, much to my dismay – I wanted to go to the local public high school where my friends at the time were going. Not like I had a choice in any of these decisions. Where there was an opportunity for a higher academic ranking, academic prestige, trust my parents to be there. I had to oblige, but not without arguments – a lot of them.

My father is very much a product of his childhood. Utilitarian to a point of fault, he doesn't watch non-fiction movies because they "aren't like real life". His favourite superhero movies, and the only ones that he has and will ever watch, are the Christopher Nolan's Batman trilogy, because they're "realistic, at least". Documentaries, otherwise. And we watched a lot of documentaries. He buys his clothing from Target because he refuses to spend more than ten dollars on a single item – "it's just clothes" he would say, proud of the two-dollar bargain on a belt.

Emotionally, he never quite understood my mother or me when talking to us. I would cry sitting on my childhood couch after being berated for what was certainly nothing major – maybe I had lost my hat at school that day. "First of all, stop crying" he'd say in a botched attempt to rectify things after being backed into a debate's corner. Academically, each day of each school year my father would sit me down to complete maths problems from exercise books he would get at Aldi or Dymocks. We sat every day for some ten years, completing maths questions. Such days often ended in yelling over tear-drenched notebook pages. Once after receiving my grades in Year Five, where I had received a record high four A's (B's in everything that didn't matter like history and art – and a C in PE), I was ecstatic. My father on the other hand: "That's good," he said, "do better next time."

Once, on the way to a family friend's house, he asked me a question about cross-multiplying fractions. I must have been in Year Two around that time, so he was asking about content one year above what I should have been learning, from Year Three.

"WHAT DON'T YOU UNDERSTAND ABOUT IT? WE HAVE DONE THIS AT LEAST TEN TIMES!" he screamed, driving down Tuggeranong Parkway. The car sped up a touch. "IF I HAVE THREE QUARTERS AND ONE HALF, WHAT DO YOU DO TO – tsk, STOP!" he added for my mother who was trying to stop him.

My answer was unintelligible behind the dam of tears he had just burst. We still made it in time to the friend's house, forcefully wiping the tears and snot from my face, hopefully appearing as if nothing ever happened.

"You know, I can even tell when someone has had an argument in the car on the way here." My piano teacher had once commented, on a suspiciously-well timed, miserable, Sunday morning lesson.

But can I really fault how it ended? In Year One, I could explain what a NAPLAN test was two years before anyone else my age could. In Year Two, I taught our class long division and was the first to get my pen license for flawless handwriting and spelling. And from Year Three until the end of my schooling, I was in the most advanced classes for Maths and English. I completed National Assessment Program tests, International

Competition and Assessment tests, the Australian Mathematics Competition – alongside basketball, cross-country, taekwondo, trombone (for the highest concert and jazz bands in school), piano (outside of school), and debated. This gauntlet of activities on top of the academic pressure was nothing out of the ordinary for the children of Asian immigrants I grew up around. Despite being forced into it, or forced to like it, I saw them all as exceptional, high achieving people.

"It's like the lamest version of Stockholm Syndrome," I half-jokingly said to a friend a couple of weeks ago when he brought the conversation up. He thought that his similar experience was his parents' way of showing love – the overambitious high standards, the strictness, the yelling. I didn't believe that. There was no man I hated more than my father. I was ashamed to admit it in public, but it wasn't wrong.

"You grew up in an easy environment," my father had once told me, sitting at the dining table.

"So, we had to make it harder."

Tears rolled down my face. He meant it.

* * *

2019 and 2020 were my final two years of high school. At least in Indian and other Asian-Australian households, that translated into putting in your blood, sweat, and tears for your ATAR, a number that doesn't mean very much all but a month after you get it. Of course, I'm still sore about it.

Each day I would wake up to a new trial. 4.30 am, grab a coffee: two subjects to study before school starts. English and Spanish on Mondays, Economics and Mathematics on Tuesdays, Sports Science and Computer Science on

Wednesdays, in a cycle. If I had band or basketball training, we would leave the house at 7.15 am, which gave me two hours of work. If not, I could fit in another subject. Get to school at 8.15 am, attend five classes until 3.25 pm. I would structure my day around the most anxiety-inducing presentation, test, or speech. Back home, I had an hour of rest before working on two more subjects, usually the ones I couldn't get to in the morning. Then, dinner at my desk and sleep at 8.30 pm. And do it all over again, the next day.

My entire life was structured around the amount of time I had until exams. Fifty-two weeks out, then forty-two, thirty-six, thirty, twenty-four, eighteen, fourteen, ten, eight.

One weekday morning six weeks out, I was making my bed and avoiding eye contact with my father as he stood behind me saying something, when it slipped. Suicidal thoughts, I told him, had been on my mind for the past couple of weeks. Retrospectively, given my schedule, it seemed inevitable. I added, "nothing new, nothing out of the ordinary". Having let my father in for the first time, a chuckle dressed the anxiety of my words. It was a desperate attempt by my brain to cover myself up, now naked. A glance back and I could see his eyes almost comically stretched open, pried back by reality itself. He stammered, "This is … serious."

Then with four weeks to exams, I finally collapsed. I lay face down on my bed, curled in as tight as I could, weeping and screaming. I couldn't stand the overload of information, the pressure, the people, the expectations, myself. I wasn't going to pass high school. I wasn't going to do my exams. I wasn't going to do … anything. I thought this was over, that this was the end. My parents crowded around me, confused – trying to understand. They hadn't seen anything like this before.

I couldn't move. I wept and wept and wept. My father, not knowing what to do, ended up taking a month off work. He sat with me every day for almost a month, watching and helping me study. I started seeing a psychologist, the closest that was available. And slowly, very slowly, I was able to sit those exams. I survived.

After my exams, I went to my first psychiatrist, one of the many that would follow. Being a child psychiatrist and acquaintance of my father, she allowed me to skip her six-month long waiting time. My father was at the sessions too, trying to ad lib in his experience to every word that I said, providing his side of the story. He was the same person as before, I was reminded. Nothing had changed. My father asked why I was putting too much pressure on myself, why I avoided talking to my parents, why I was the wreck I was.

Depression, she announced, siding with my father so often I thought it was a miracle she didn't tell me to just "stop being so sensitive". I was prescribed my first of many ineffectual antidepressants in that room. One 50 milligram tablet of Sertraline daily would evolve into a 75 milligram tablet, then to 100 milligrams. Then, the mood stabiliser Lamotrigine on top of it, equally as ineffectual. 25 milligrams, 50 milligrams, 100 milligrams, 200 milligrams. Closer to severe than mild. Beta blockers called Propranolol came as a complimentary extra for the anxiety.

And so began, as one of my friends called it, the research phase. Every day my father would text me some advice, some article, some spice to eat, some supplement to take. Lithium Oxidate pills one week, turmeric in my tea the next. Self-help books and YouTube videos that I never opened. Distrust turned into wilful ignorance towards anything my father advised – most of which probably could have helped.

My depression was (and is) a horrible, horrible sensation. Indescribable in its anguish, it compounds its horrors with persistent internal anxiety questioning if anyone is noticing, or even if anything is happening at all.

I had a silver lining at the end of this year, however. I left Canberra for Sydney to get away from my parents in 2021, from my high school past, from the issues, to university. Still, I was unable to get away from myself. I was doing a degree I picked for the prestige alone, surrounded by a group of "friends" that remained impartial towards me as I begged for their validation. I woke up for the sake of social obligations to maintain a facade of normalcy. After our scheduled meals, it ended with me crashing asleep on my floor.

Anxiety continued to control my life. On the day of my first tutorial, I was so anxious that I skipped it, creating a self-defeating cycle where I wouldn't go to the following tutorial because I was anxious of having not attended the one prior. I fretted over every text I received: sometimes refreshing my phone for hours consecutively, clinging onto the validation of each minor interaction, or other times being too anxious to open text messages for weeks on end in anticipation of a half-hearted reply, failure. This repeated for an entire semester, I might have attended three of the total fifty plus lectures and tutorials that I should have.

So, it wasn't a surprise, that when I sat my online exams, I knew nothing. From maintaining top standards in high school, to failing my entire first semester (and later the entire year) – oh how far I had fallen. I thought a change to another, less quantitative and probably easier set of electives in the Arts might improve things, give me the variety that I had back in high school. It ended the same. Every time someone brought up academics, I averted the question, fumbling in a self-made net of lies trying to hide from reality.

I checked myself in at a hospital for suicidal ideation one day. But still the days kept coming.

The accommodation I was staying at required all students to maintain a full-time course load and pass average, leaving me with little choice but to stop studying at the end of the year. Of this fact I was too aware, staring at the residential website, getting sick with anxiety from seeing the unread emails in my inbox. I hardly touched them, or the many text messages that remained unread, for the entire year. Not looking at my texts or emails had become an exercise of evading the consequences of being myself. At last, I decided to take a gap year – or at least that's what I told my friends at the time, that I wanted to travel and "reconsolidate what I was doing at university" – all the usual garbage.

If I told them the truth, I was convinced my friends would neither understand nor sympathise with my situation, all the while getting further ahead of me, graduating faster and making something of themselves. Far ahead of me. When I got home, I repeated much of the routine that I did at university the year prior, although with the additional pressure from my parents to get up and do something. In the few calls that I did end up having with friends in Sydney, I would lie that I had found work, or that I had an internship with a start-up in the US to justify to them, and to myself, that I was doing something with my time.

Since I had the time, I ended up taking a month and a half long trip to the US to stay with some extended family. They welcomed me, but after the first week, routines started to settle in, and I felt lonelier than I had ever before. I had two cousins my age, both being the sociable, academic, well-presented medical-students-to-be-types (the kind that parents dreamed of having). Both were lovely but had things going on in their own lives that I had now somehow whirled my way into. They had duties to perform, places to be, and things to do with their lives while I was there. Actually, one of them got into medical school while I was there to witness it: from sitting her exams to receiving her admission on the last day of my trip. That made me feel real good about myself. I returned the same person.

Later, my parents decided to use my "gap year" as an excuse to have their first international holiday post-COVID, so I finished out the year with a three-week trip to New Zealand. Yet, our relationship didn't change; the holiday was riddled with the usual suspects: anxiety, yelling, arguments, and the like. Our personalities clashed as they always were exacerbated by constantly being under the same roof in an unfamiliar space. A saving grace came in escapism, that I was desperately searching for. From what though? I didn't really know.

This entire year, I had set a date: the 15January 2023. The number came to me as I was staring out across the psychiatrist's carpark and saw the address of the building opposite me: Number 15. I knew nothing was going to change this appointment. Perhaps I would get a half-hearted dose increase, or maybe something else that was unhelpful. The target I set acted as a solution – if nothing changed this appointment, I would bear it out and just stick around for another day, another month, and then on the 15 of January, I could kill myself. I could end it, escape it.

Yet three months before the decided date, I was invited to a friend's twenty-first party on the 12 January 2023.

Then another one on the 22 of January. "Suppose I'll miss that one," I thought.

And then I was invited to a trip to the coast, from the 18 to the 21 January.

I could not have written a better script.

To my friends' faces, I said yes, RSVP'd and paid my share of the Airbnb deposit. I clawed my way through life, another day, another month, until it was the 12 January 2023. The first of the birthday parties.

Surprisingly, I enjoyed it.

I only had three days left, which came and went easily. Nothing to lose now.

Then, the fifteenth arrived. I stared at the calendar on my phone. "I should be dead by now," I thought.

I lived through the day, ate food, went on a walk, and talked to friends.

Uneventful.

I rested my head on the pillow in my bed, feeling suspiciously light.

The sixteenth came. And passed.

Then the eighteenth came, the day of our trip. I enjoyed it. It passed.

I hadn't conquered my depression – in fact, conquered wasn't the right term at all. In trying to conquer depression, in trying to conquer myself, I lost oversight of the tools I had developed just to bear with it. Not just bearing with it either, but living with it – learning to hit back at whatever it gave me. After waiting for that decided date to arrive, anticipating it as the only solution to my problems, like everything else it passed.

The realisation was a moment of quiet euphoria. It had hit back, and I had hit forth. Back and forth. Back and forth. Back and forth.

I started to see a new psychologist in 2023. This time, I was without the veil of either parent. The psychologist said that my dosage history given my symptoms was … off. He switched my medication instantly, another antidepressant in the form of Escitalopram took the reins from the others.

I made another major switch, in moving back to Sydney. I found myself amongst a new group of friends, one that I found a bit more comforting, and more accepting. This step away from my parents was much more manageable. At an arm's distance, a bad interaction could easily be avoided by a single tap on the "decline call" button. Yet even those dreaded interactions decreased in tension. Maybe I was just more active than I had been under their gaze? Maybe it was me?

I found myself wanting to focus on goals. On playing basketball, on running. On writing.

A few times I'd noticed the change in my mentality had been, almost comically drastic, but that's genuinely how I've experienced things. The excuses that held me over, the hodgepodge mix of strategies I had for getting to the next day, well they did get me to the next day. They held me over. The things I was doing, they seemed to be working.

They were working.

* * *

"Blue car," my father answered, anticipating my question. He added, "Do you need water?"

"Mmm …" I murmured offhandedly, "no, it's only three and a half hours." My words lingered, empty handed without a response in Canberra's cold air.

I had come down for the weekend – in what turned out to be a fully packed two days. One of my friends in Canberra had come to Sydney for a housewarming, after leaving the housewarming early, we drove to another friend's twenty-first party in Canberra, all while keeping tabs on our (fantastic!) Matildas playing against France – within an eight-hour span.

My bus to Sydney left the next day at 3.00 pm, so we would be leaving at 2.15 pm sharp from our house – forgetting that the fifteen-minute drive would leave me at the bus station with thiry minutes to spare. Our conversation that morning had been a lengthy one, with repeated questions and repeated answers. But I didn't hate it. I told my father that I didn't want to pursue the career I was looking down the barrel of, and that even with the degree change I had in mind, I was still uncertain about the whole thing. He considered it progress – my not continuing to bumble around, wasting time at university. That was cool.

When it was time, my father emerged from the house, sporting a chequered beanie, a black puffer jacket, and grey track-pants. In his right hand, he had a minuscule disposable water bottle, the kind you get on planes. For some reason my parents always kept one around. It might've had one hundred millilitres of water in it. I took the water bottle from his hand without a word and sat in the car.

Our trip to the bus station was as usual. We don't talk much during these trips. By now everything that needed to be said had been said. We had done this exact commute dozens of times, so it was nothing new. My father would usually bring up something small to talk about, this time it was one of my American cousin's new electric car. He thought it was a reasonable price. I agreed to keep the conversation moving, asking him about the car's milage. Still, it only lasted three minutes into the drive. Silence took the wheel otherwise.

Nearing Jolimont Bus Station, traffic increased, and the drop-off parking was packed back-to-back with taxis. "They think they can just make up their own rules," my father said, frustrated. He turned around at the next corner to find an empty – and maybe illegal – section of the sidewalk that intersected the bus section just long enough to accommodate a car for a moment before heading off. He turned in.

At seven years old, I was enrolled in weekly tennis lessons. It fit the singular requirement my dad had for a sport: something indoors, so I wouldn't get muddy, or a cold from the rain.

Although I enjoyed it, I was never particularly good at tennis. I had flicked my wrist too much on shots, had a weak backhand, and never learnt to serve properly. To start and continue games, I would just lob an easy forehand barely over the net, trying not to get caught avoiding a serve.

With how you're meant to play tennis, a serve lets both players begin afresh, regardless of who faulted. Where their old self ends, a new one begins. With my father, with ourselves, that relationship with beginnings and endings feels different. We work like I played tennis, ebbing and flowing with the mistakes and realisations about one another. We've never begun afresh with each other. And just like after one of my stupid forehands, when one player messes something up, the rally continues. Eventually it gets back to normal: back and forth, back and forth. Back and forth.

I don't think I ever learned how to serve, to change. And neither did he. But maybe we're just perpetually getting marginally better at understanding each other, letting each other breathe, lobbing each other's forehands.

Perpetually involved in a practice rally, a friendly.

"You can blame it on your father, I can blame it on mine," he had once said in one of our reformed-age conversations.

My father pulled the handbrake, and the nostalgia jerked to a stop. I unbuckled my seatbelt and got out without much sound. As usual, my father remained buckled in the front seat. I picked my bags up from the back, at which point he said, "Stay safe, and have fun!" elevating the tone and stressing the last two words. He's been trying some new positivity bullshit recently. He's decent enough at it.

"Bye," I responded flatly, like I normally did. But loud enough for him to hear it, and for me to mean it.

I even thought about waving.

Deucalion and Pyrrha

Zara Hussain

Did they tell you?
The oldest story –
flood and fear,
flesh-fed temper,
rage in bolts of silver.

Not long now,
till sun-softened marble
drips off statues; trees lose spines,
and water earns shape.

The eagles will stay –
they know how to feast
on bloated flesh.
Soft pink lungs,
briny pitchers.

Wake up and
fear the flood, Pyrrha.

The bones of your mother –
proof of life –
tossed into the wind;
and so it begins
again.

The oldest story –
did they tell you?

The Fisherman's Son

Vanessa Vu

Once in a dream, the Moon was my mother and She told me a story. It went something like this. On a night when she was softly lit, the fisherman's son pushed his basket boat onto the lake to catch his wishes. The gobies had been his playmates when he could barely lift a paddle, and the basa had tormented him for weeks when he was learning the rhythm of the nets, which he tossed out like limp jellyfish. Now, he could swiftly single out the carp: amidst the dull blues and murky metallics rose flashes of orange gold. *For every carp you catch, you can make a wish. But you must always release it. Let it go, and all will be well.* The legend was whispered across bedtimes from the sleepy village to the murmuring harbours. Even the fisherman's son, who lived beyond the stilted huts, behind the second hump of the island in a hut nestled by bamboo, had heard it.

He had heard it during the rainy season when he was practising weaving baskets. No cheaper way to make a living, the fisherman would tell his son. The baskets took them several days to make. They would gather the supple bamboo, leave it out to dry, and whittle the pieces down to exact lengths. Then came the weaving: strips of bamboo were interlocked to form a square, then a larger square, and somewhere in between the larger square and peripheral weaves the squares would curve.

When the fisherman's son skimmed the glassy surface for his wishes, he thought of the bamboo smiling benevolently over the sun-dried frames, and that made him smile too. After the frame was complete, the brushes would be taken out, and father and son would dip the wide bristles into pots of resin. Sometimes they talked whilst painting, other times they told each other stories. The fisherman's son collected these stories like his shells along the shore. If the fisherman's son told a good story, he got to play with the tides while his father finished the basket with sap. Fortunately, the fisherman's son forged his stories from truth, so he never had to finish the basket boats. Except when he made his own: the one he sits in now, hauling up wishes.

Never had he seen so many carp at once. They kept surfacing from the depths, materialising as quick as sand. The fisherman's son thought it might have been the Moon that brought them to the surface – she was brighter now, and this made him glad. He needed a moon-bright night with nothing left to Chance. Chance was dangerous: it did not care for "should-haves" or "would-have-beens". One by one the carp formed a carpet at the bottom of the boat, and the fisherman's son did his best to keep them from falling out. The round-bottomed boat would never capsize – he had found this out one indigo afternoon, when the monsoon swallowed the river whole – but the wishes were slippery. He had nine wishes, all of them the same but spoken differently, just in case. In case Chance decided to whisk them away, alter the sentiments, tumble the words inside out until they could hardly be recognised. They sent ripples across the water and the Moon caught hold of each one, a watery crease for a secret plea. She lifted them up with her slender fingers, trailing wishes like threads of spider-silk across the night. She brought them slowly to her lips. They tasted like salt air and being lost. The Moon dropped her gaze to the fisherman's son as he stared deep into the empty water.

Now that the fish had gone and he was surrounded by waiting light, he thought about what he had done, and how the wishes, if they made it, could not be taken back. He slowly stood up from his boat, hands perched above his head for a dive. It was then that the Moon surfaced from her reflection and spoke to the fisherman's son.

"My child, why do you doubt when you know what you must do?"

"Because if my wish comes true, my father will be alone."

The Moon turned towards the single, lit window of the hut, and the fisherman's son did the same.

"How can he be alone when he is always watching the tides?"

To this the fisherman's son gave no reply. Somewhere in his heart a fire began to glow, but he didn't know the reason why. Something was afoot, and the Moon was going to tell him more. The Moon told the fisherman's son to close his eyes, and he did. She placed her cool hands over them, and he saw. He saw his father carrying huge bundles of sweaty bamboo. He saw the hollow frames like turtle shells waiting for an owner. He saw himself sitting with his father, eyes closed, listening to the lapping of the water.

"Do you see now, my child, how he points you to the tides?"

The tides. Rhythmic and predictable as the sun, he had watched them breathe until he did not need to look to know where he belonged. The fisherman knew this, too. The fisherman's son turned to face the Moon, and it was his turn to ask a question.

"If I am the tides, and you are the Moon, does that mean that we are friends?"

The Moon smiled like waterfalls, and she nodded, yes, yes, my child, we are friends.

When I awoke the next morning, I had the strange sensation that I was pleasantly submerged. I had forgotten about this story. But when I went to the market, I saw that the fisherman's stall was filled with orange gold, and he was standing straighter than he had in many, many years. And the fisherman's son? The boy was nowhere to be found – his wish had come true.

Unending

Mabel G. Rytmeister

Odysseus and the winnowing oar –
A story beyond the story.
The infinitesimal inch toward the inevitable
The terror of The End.

Save my epilogue for the epitaph,
For I will outlive my own stories.
On an endless adventure.
Make youthful mistakes,
And make youthful mistakes,
And see how long it takes
For the dust to settle.

About the Authors

Memi Adams

I endeavour to share moments of inspiration and reflection through works of art. I explore the nature of humanity and the importance of human connection in my work. Writing poetry is a treasured form of expression in which I seek to convey a message of hope grounded in my Christian faith.

Tara E. Berg

I live and work on Wangal and Gadigal land (Sydney). I love playing netball, eating, reading and falling asleep on my super comfy couch. I have always loved writing (I used to make my own little books as a kid, with terrible illustrations and everything) and I am now undertaking a creative writing degree.

Shankari Chandran

I am an Australian Tamil lawyer and the author of the novels *Safe Haven* (2024), *Chai Time at Cinnamon Gardens* (2022,

Miles Franklin Literary Award 2023), *Song of the Sun God* (2022), *The Barrier* (2017) and *Unfinished Business* (2024, Audible). My work explores dispossession, erasure and the value of community. I am the deputy chair of Writing NSW and live in Sydney with my husband and four children.

Samantha Bowers

I am a writer, teacher, and former lawyer. I hold a Master of Creative Writing from the University of Sydney, and am currently a Creative Writing PhD candidate, also at the University of Sydney, where I am writing a novel exploring domestic abuse and female trauma through fiction. My writing has been published in a range of print and magazine publications including *The Sydney Morning Herald*, *Australia Financial Review*, *Hermes Journal*, *Newswrite Magazine* and *Australian Author Magazine*, and my poetry has been longlisted and Highly Commended in the Adrien Abbott Poetry Prize.

Sally Chik

I am a writer with experience in corporate and creative writing. My poems have been included in *Australian Love Poems*, *Cordite Poetry Review*, *FourW* and more. I have a Bachelor of Creative Arts (Hons) and Master of Information Studies, and I like to crochet.

Dunja Dudic

I am a second-year undergraduate Arts/Advanced Studies student majoring in English and History. I'm an aspiring writer interested in topics of time, cultural memory and generational trauma, storytelling traditions of myths and legends and the duality of ethnic-cultural identities.

Eeshita

I am a writer who is always on the lookout for stories around. Also an enthusiastic reader and I actually studied writing at the University of Sydney. So even if I struggle in life, I try to make sense of it on the page. That's why I write.

Tom Evans

I'm a recent graduate of the Master of Publishing degree at the University of Sydney. I currently work in book publishing and believe in the power of stories to educate and inspire.

Janika Fernando

I'm a passionate third-year law and arts student at the University of Sydney, majoring in English literature. With a keen interest in capturing the essence of important Sri Lankan cultural memories, I strive to weave diverse stories that reflect the richness of my heritage. My work has been published in the USYD anthology and esteemed journals like *Wattle*, *Avenue* (SASS), and *MOSAIC* (Law Society). Through storytelling,

I aim to foster empathy, understanding, and connection. I believe in the power of literature to explore themes of identity, heritage, and the human experience. Inspired by the untold stories of Sri Lanka, I aspire to share narratives that inspire and resonate with readers, celebrating the beauty and diversity of our collective voices.

Holly Ford

I completed my undergraduate – a Bachelor of Arts majoring in English and Ancient History – at the University of Sydney. I am currently completing a Masters of Publishing and am pursuing a career as a book editor.

Kelsey Goldsbro

I am a currently an undergrad Arts student at the University of Sydney who bares their heart as an example of female rage, as a romantic devoted to loving, and as a tired soul. Through referencing tarot cards, my pieces reflect hostilities found in escapism and delusion. Born from sea-foam and blood – how wondrous it is to love.

Komal Gupta

I'm studying a Bachelor of Arts, majoring in Music and English (Creative Writing).

Maxwell K. Han

I am an undergraduate student at the University of Sydney. I am studying to be an English and Latin teacher. I love to write, and I love to read, so I should probably do those things more.

Zara Hussain

I'm a reader of books, lover of language and literature, seeker of whimsy and wonder, and hoarder of niche knowledge – basically, the quintessential English/History student. You might previously have seen me in *PULP*, *AVENUE*, and the 2022 Anthology, *Moments in Between*.

Sharmila Jayasinghe

As someone who crossed a border out of her homeland and made a new home, I consider myself a writer with a hybrid identity – a part of a new species of writers, a person with a then and a now, a person with a here and a there, a person who thinks in one language and writes in another, a person with more than one culture. I am best represented by combining many labels into one. Essentially, I am a Sri Lankan-Australian, South Asian, diasporic – not to mention female – writer. I am one but also many, and there's no denying that the 'many' also feeds my writing. The Sri Lankanness, the Australianness, the South Asianness, the diasporic journey, and the femaleness all come together to provide me with a background of cultural richness. My writing reflects this hybridity.

I.C. Kaluza

I am a student at the University of Sydney who is currently pursuing a Bachelor of Science, majoring in Physics and English.

Gil Kerr

I am a 22-year-old student studying Environmental Science at the University of Sydney. While I have always enjoyed writing for school and university, I have only recently started writing for personal enjoyment. I enjoy writing because it allows me to better understand my experiences and use it as a tool to ground myself in the world around me. I continue to write for myself, friends and family through my blog and hope to expand this through undertaking a year in honours as I approach the end of my degree.

Michael Kowalczyk-Barker

I am an alumnus of the University of Sydney with a Bachelor of Science with First Class Honours, and a scientist, who, among other things, is passionate about creativity and the myriad of ways it can be expressed. I would like to thank my sister and current postgrad student Emilia Barker for her sharp editorial instincts when reviewing my story, and her continued support in my many life projects.

Kate Leckie

I am a Visual Arts student who has always struggled to choose between my loves of painting and writing. I write diversely across poetic and prosaic forms on themes of mythology, womanhood, and the body.

Harold Legaspi

I am an Australian writer. My first book is *Letters in Language* (Flying Islands Pocket Books of Poetry series, 2021).

Anna Liang

Living and working on Gadigal land, I am a postgraduate student studying Economic Analysis. My writing draws upon my love of food, my Chinese heritage and my desire to share stories that might otherwise be forgotten. I am always curious about how things work and enjoy exploring ways to describe the world around me – be it through writing or math. I am also an avid reader, an obsessive plant parent and a very guilty multitasker.

Josie Lu

I am a third-year English and Media Communications student who recently stumbled into writing as something to do for fun, and not just for university assignments. I have always been intrigued by all the stories around me, whether it belongs to the person walking across the street or on the bookshelf in my room, and I hope to start telling more of my own. "Tim" is inspired by my realisation of how writing (and art more generally) can be a way of navigating the world and getting through life – a delightful discovery that I plan on exploring further.

Alex Ma

Being an English student, I am an eternal lover of words. I'm often consumed by books or a story that I'm writing. I've been previously published in *AVENUE*, and *Moments in Between: University of Sydney Anthology 2022*. Apart from writing, I enjoy sewing, playing the piano, and poring over Rupert Brooke poems.

Gautam Mishra

I am a student at the University of Sydney. I write non-fiction: essays, opinion pieces, and editorials primarily, because I don't have the balls to write anything actually creative.

Zoe Morris

I am a writer from Sydney. I am currently in my third year at the University of Sydney, studying English and Politics. I love pretty things, and I love to write about them! I am also deeply inspired by the ecopoetics tradition. My poetry has previously been published in *Moments in Between: University of Sydney Anthology 2022, 1978*, and *AVENUE*.

Emma Murphy

I am currently completing my Masters of Publishing at the University of Sydney, while working in the book publishing industry as a marketing coordinator. In my free time I love to read and write poetry and prose.

Phil Nondum

I'm a third-year undergraduate student majoring in Mathematics and Philosophy. I have a keen interest in aesthetics and literature.

Matthew Platakos

I am a student and poet living on Gadigal and Wangal land (Sydney). My poems have been published in *Cordite Poetry Review*, *Jacaranda Journal* and *Otoliths Magazine*, among other places.

Jem Rice

I am a third-year arts student for whom poetry is a way of breathing. My writing has been published in *AVENUE*, *1978*, *PULP* and the University of Sydney Anthology. I love testing out my words at open mic nights, and write on the lands of the Eora Nation.

Katherine Rosonakis

I am a community worker and aspiring writer, living, loving and working on Gadigal land, with second homes in Mexico and Solomon Islands. I am studying a Masters of Creative Writing at the University of Sydney while searching for love, grieving and making sense of what I'd like to become next.

Mabel G. Rytmeister

I write poetry, essays and stories. I am studying a combined Bachelor of Laws and Bachelor of Arts (majoring in English) at the University of Sydney. When not working, I can be found obsessively searching through Depop or rewatching *The West Wing*.

Maysa Amy Sarkis

I am a Lebanese student double majoring in Film and English at the University of Sydney who has had a passion for reading and writing (specifically horror – thanks mum!) since I was a kid. My work has been shortlisted in the 2023 USU Creative Arts Awards and I have published my own poem anthology *Word Vomit*. To me, creating stories is a way to escape the dullness of reality whilst challenging our worldview. My poem does exactly that by considering life beyond the traditional inescapable end of death.

Jennifer Scarini

I completed my Masters in Special and Inclusive Ed at the University of Sydney in 2017. I currently teach students with learning and behavioural needs in Sydney's South West. I have always been interested in "creating stuff" and enjoy writing and painting as part of that inclination. I like to explore emotions with my work, delving into what makes people tick, unpacking all of the extraordinary beauty in what seem to be banal events.

Isla Scott

A Master of Publishing graduate, and former contributor to and editor of this anthology, I am now working full time at NewSouth Books. I am also a freelance proofreader and enjoy going down rabbit holes to fact check books.

Vanessa Vu

Since I was young, I have always been drawn to fiction and poetry, and reading was always a sure-fire way to escape the scruples of daily life in lands far, far away. I have dabbled in short stories and poems throughout my schooling and continue to play around with words during my time as a psychology student. I hope to connect people through my storytelling and share an appreciation of the little things that make us perfectly human.

Jannet Xie

I'm just a 24-year-old Australian-born-Chinese trying to heal from new and old diagnoses; trying to figure out what things actually mean and navigating what my own growth should look like. I'm a past primary teacher, a future registered nurse and will hopefully continue to do a lot of different things (too much at once, all at the same time)!

Ray Zhou

I am a PhD candidate in English at the University of Sydney. Coming through the untold sufferings of being a transgender man in China, I came to Sydney in January 2023 to restart my life. I wrote this memoir, my journey to both manhood and my first semester in Sydney. It is an epilogue to my past life and a prologue for my new life.

About the Editors

Sophie Bellotti

I'm a reader first and writer second, currently living and working on Wangal and Gadigal lands. Outside a day job in book marketing, I'm a freelance writer and editor, and I do my best to maintain a poetry practice of my own. I'm passionate about language and its power to shape worlds on and beyond the page, so it's been a privilege and a joy to play a part in bringing together the diverse voices of this anthology. Many of the works it contains engage with the idea of creativity as a means to reconfigure time and resituate ourselves within it, rejecting linearity as an oversimplification of experience. From inspirational personal triumphs to fresh, challenging perspectives to pure escapism, I'm confident there's something here that will touch every reader.

Aries Carlos

I was a banker with a decade of financial services training. But I have always been passionate about stories. I guess mine has taken quite a turn for the better. I am honoured to be a part of this year's anthology. I hope you can find your own beginnings and endings mirrored in these beautiful stories.

Eeshita

Stories have fascinated me my whole life. As a child, I loved listening to the folklore and mythological tales from my family (a plus point to growing up in India), and once I started reading, there was no going back. I have never been much of a planner, more like a wanderer. So, when people asked me what I wanted to be, I'd shrug and say: "Not sure, but whatever I become I'll make sure to write at least one book in my life." That single string of certainty amidst my tapestry of confusion is what drives me creatively. Every day that I spend writing, my mind wanders back to why I started. For me, it has always been about storytelling that defines, embraces and encapsulates life. As a part of this anthology, I got to work with many such wonderful storytellers, and it has truly been an honour.

Holly Ford

My story begins in the same way as many aspiring editors – I've been an avid reader since childhood and flew through series like Harry Potter and Percy Jackson at a young age. I worked in a bookstore during my undergraduate degree and I'm now working as a marketing assistant at NewSouth Books. Getting to care for authors and guide them through their publication journey is something that I had only ever dreamed about until becoming involved in this anthology. It has been such a privilege to take this first step towards living my dream and I am truly proud of the work and collaboration that has taken place to get this anthology into the hands of readers.

Michaela Gall

Ever since I was young, I have always been drawn towards stories, and to those who tell them. Fast-forward to 2023 and I am working towards my Masters of Publishing while working as a full-time editor at Scholastic Australia. Books have always been a creative place to escape, and I love reading fantasy and romance. Having worked on the 2022 Anthology, *Moments in Between*, I know just how special these anthologies are; the bringing together of unique voices on a united topic is an intricate thing and creates an incredible tapestry of voices. I hope all readers and writers enjoy these incredible pieces of writing!

Hanna Holford

For as long as I can remember, I have loved reading and writing. Language always fascinated me, especially when I learned a second language – Swedish – at age 9. I was intrigued by how grammar and sentence structure worked, and I often scrutinised the books I was reading to figure out how the authors had constructed their prose. Unsurprisingly, I am now studying publishing, in the hope of one day becoming an editor. I also work at a second-hand bookstore. I am surrounded by stories, and it is wonderful.

Jessamine Lobb

I like lemonade, thunderstorms, and enthusiasm. As one of the anthology editors, I've received a glimpse of the infinite perspectives out there, even just on campus. It's a privilege to peek into someone else's heart and mind. Because I would not make a very good neurosurgeon or cardiologist, I study English. The writers in this edition remind us that everyone exists within a painful but beautiful loop of beginnings and endings. I hope reading it makes you feel less alone.

Sumi Mahendran

After reading hundreds of books at the dinner table, over many long-haul flights, train rides and long queues, I started to delve deeper into the world of writing and publishing. Having almost two decades of a corporate career to pay for necessities, I spend the rest of my time in my real passion: literature and language. Speaking and reading in three languages has helped me cement my love of reading and kickstart my writing journey towards publishing my own work.

Linxiao Zhang

I have loved reading since I was a child. In my childhood home, I had eight bookshelves in my room filled with books I had bought. At that time, I would finish reading two to three books almost every week. So, I've always dreamed that in the future I could be involved in the publishing process of a book as an editor. I am very happy to have been a part of the birth of this anthology. Many thanks to everyone who contributed to this book! I hope you all will enjoy it!